MY SWEETEST AGONY

THE SWEETEST LIE DUET
BOOK 1

GWYN MCNAMEE

MY SWEETEST AGONY

© 2025 Gwyn McNamee

Cover Model: Jerrin; Photographer: Wander Aguiar

Cover Design: BlueSky Design

Editing: Stephie Walls at Wallflower Edits

To anyone who ever lost love but waded through the fog of grief to find it again...

TRIGGER WARNING

The Sweetest Lie duet contains many elements that may be triggering for some individuals (some of these elements will also be plot spoilers). Please visit my website to check the detailed trigger list here:
www.gwynmcnamee.com/thesweetestlieduet triggerwarnings

1

IVY

Most little girls dream about their wedding day.

The stunning white lacy dress.

The beautiful, fragrant flowers.

The poignant music.

The magical walk down the aisle.

To the perfect man standing at the altar.

The exchange of vows that mean love will last forever.

They certainly don't dream about saying "I do" to an anonymous driver in a uniform when he asks if you accept delivery of your fiancé's ashes.

They don't sign for and receive a cardboard box containing everything left of their soulmate with trembling hands.

Their tears aren't of soul-crushing agony.

Those little girls have a *dream*.

I am living a *nightmare*.

Lightning streaks across the pitch-black sky, splitting it open the same way my heart has been and casting a bright light across the dark patio where I stand frozen in place—just like I have been since Drew died.

The delivery driver turns and races back down the walkway to his truck through the driving rain that has continued all evening and has only seemed to increase since I opened the door. Almost as if the storm senses the tempest raging inside me and wants to match its ferocity.

Rolling thunder moves through me in a catastrophic wave, rattling my ribcage and drawing out the sob I managed to contain while that poor man stood here and handed Drew over to me, knowing what this box contains.

He *knew* what he was delivering. I could see it in his eyes—the apology, the pity, the *sorry* written all over the way he looked at me when I opened the door. But he couldn't understand the painful irony of delivering what I hold in my hands *today*.

Yesterday, I *might* have been able to handle it.

Tomorrow, it *could* have been bearable.

Literally *any* other day but *today*...

When I *should* be having my first dance with my husband at our reception right now, surrounded by our friends and family. When I *should* be the happiest I've ever been in my entire life at this exact moment, instead of lost in a black abyss of agony. When my entire future is supposed to be spread out before me and wide open to a thousand magical things with Drew as my partner and by my side. When he should be carrying me across *this* threshold as his wife...

Instead, I'm carrying this cardboard box that holds all my hopes and dreams and trying not to fall apart completely out here while the storm violently reminds me of the reasons I know I will.

Because there are too many unanswered questions.

So many things that don't make any sense.

I stare up at the seething sky—bright flashes, booming thunder, an angry deluge soaking the yard and street beyond it. To some, it might feel like a cleansing rain. It might wash away the surface layers of dirt, nourish the grass and flowers —and under normal circumstances, I would see it that way and relish it—but not tonight.

Tonight, all I see is my despair.

Each streak of lightning illuminates the billow of black clouds when all I want is some enlightenment about how it came to this.

How? How? How?

Another sob slips from my lips, this one swallowed by another crack of thunder, this one so close it shakes the ground and vibrates through my bare feet.

Why?

Why the hell did it have to be him?

I've asked the question so many times.

Begged for answers from whatever higher power might be out there.

And a month later, I have *none*.

No explanation for why Drew was even in that part of town that night.

Nothing that can tell me *why* he ran that stop sign.

He was the most conscientious person I had ever met. Always meticulous, focused, and thorough in how he did *everything*. From making love to treating his ER patients to driving...he never left anything to chance. And he was always the *best* at what he did.

So, lying to me. Being so distracted that he would run a stop sign and—

I shake my head, squeezing my eyes closed as the warm

summer rain splatters my skin and the box. Tears streak down my face, combining with the fat, driving drops until I can't tell what is from me and what comes from the sky anymore.

After four years, countless promises, and the dream I was so sure had become my reality, all I'm left with is *this.*

My hands tremble around the box, and I take one last look at the storm outside and kick the door closed. Water drops to the wood floor as I take unsteady steps across the living room to place the wet cardboard on the mantle before I do something stupid—like drop it.

Drop *him.*

Oh, God...

He's really in there.

Agony wraps around my chest like a vise, the familiar stranglehold that steals all the air from my lungs, the same way Drew and our future together were stolen from me.

I choke on a sob as I struggle to draw in a breath that only brings Drew's scent with it—spearmint from his natural shampoo and soap mixed with that crisp, lightly antiseptic smell that always clung to him even after he left the hospital and showered. My vision fades in and out as I stare at the box, seeing Drew's warm grin and crystal-blue eyes instead of what he is now...

My legs give out, and I collapse in front of the empty fireplace, where there isn't any heat from flames to reach the chill in my soul. Even if there were, their warmth couldn't fill the emptiness, the massive, gaping void I've felt in the center of my chest since I got the call that night that took everything from me.

For a second, I'm tempted to strike a match, light the stack of logs, and throw myself into them, to let myself become ashes like Drew is now, so we can be together again—

The shrill ring of my phone on the end table beside the couch drags me away from the very dark place my mind was traveling to, where I've spent so much time over the past four weeks.

It rings a second time, the sound so damn loud in the otherwise silent house. A house that used to be so full of music and laughter, that used to be so warm, instead of this cold, hollow place it's become. I can't even have any flowers in here—the first time in my entire life that my home doesn't hold any of that beautiful *life*. Because I can't bear to see it.

I don't want to move.

I don't want to have to heave myself up off this floor.

A third ring makes me wince.

If I don't answer it, she'll just keep calling.

For the past month, it's been the same routine. The same calls. And I learned that first week that if I don't pick up, Marlo will be at my front door within twenty minutes.

Using my hands braced against the brick fireplace, I stagger to my unsteady feet, swiping at the tears, as if she can somehow see them.

Thank God she can't.

If she could, she would be here in fifteen, and the thought of her racing across Philly, worried and distracted, makes panic twist my empty stomach.

Marlo's name flashes across the screen, and the fourth ring sounds.

Shit.

My hand trembles as I snatch the offensive device off the end table and swipe to accept the call. I release a long breath to try to steel my voice, at least making an *attempt* to get my lungs to cooperate enough that it isn't readily apparent I've been sitting on the floor sobbing. If I don't, she'll know. She *always* knows.

I bring my phone to my ear and lower myself onto the couch. "Hi..."

"Hey, girl!" Something rustles in the background, and she grunts slightly, muttering something unintelligible under her breath. Likely a completely inappropriate curse. Considering she's at work at the shop right now and any customer could overhear her, I should probably be more worried about it, but I can't bring myself to care. "Sorry, just trying to get some restocking done before we close."

Which is where I should be.

Instead, I've abandoned the business Nonni and Mom spent so many years building into what it is today...and left it in Marlo's hands.

Acid that tastes an awful lot like guilt climbs my raw throat, and I swallow it back with a wince.

"Take as much time as you need..."

It doesn't matter how many times she says those words to me; I can't help but feel like I've failed Nonni, Mom, and their memories by not being able to get my shit together enough to go in.

Buds & Blooms has always been a second home to me. I took my first steps in the greenhouse with them watching, but putting together bridal bouquets and dealing with husbands stopping in to purchase flowers for their wives proved far too difficult when I *did* make the single attempt to return to work since Drew's death.

I inhale deeply, trying to fill the lungs that failed me earlier and prevent myself from sobbing again because I can't do company tonight, no matter how well-meaning

Marlo is. And if she hears my voice crack, if she thinks for one *instant* that I'm anywhere near crumbling, she'll be here in an instant.

"Was everything all right the rest of the day?"

Not that I think much has changed since we spoke a few hours ago, but things can get crazy this time of year, with people doing summer planting, throwing parties, plus all the weddings...

So many beautiful flowers for so many stunning brides.

My eyes drift to the box on the mantle—pale brown with darker spots where the rain outside hit it during the driver's race from the truck to the porch and into my hands. All while I stood frozen at the door, for who knows how long, watching the storm.

A boulder lodges squarely in my throat, and this isn't something I can so easily swallow down.

Not tonight.

Drew would have loved the flowers I chose for our ceremony...

White peonies—a symbol of new beginnings.

What we should have had...

Together.

Marlo makes some very unbecoming grunting noise, then sighs. "Of course. Trina and I have everything under control. I was just calling to see how *you* are doing."

What she's really asking is if the ashes came.

I keep staring at the box, trying *not* to think about what's in it.

It's just a cardboard box.

Just a box.

Just a box.

"I'm..." I squeeze my eyes closed, drawing in a ragged breath. "Not great."

Whatever Marlo was doing in the background stops, the other end of the line now dead silent. "What happened since the last time we talked?"

It's incredible how much can change in only a few hours.

One minute, I was in bed under Drew. Lost in his touch. His kiss. His absolute devotion. Blissfully happy. Falling into that ethereal haze that always surrounded me when we were together.

And three hours later, he was gone.

"I just signed for—"

A sob slips from my throat instead of the words I'm trying to find.

The box?

The ashes?

Drew?

What do I even call that thing *on my mantle?*

I slap my hand over my mouth, trying to contain the all-out breakdown threatening to come that I'm not sure I would be able to find a way out of. "Shit, I'm sorry—"

"Oh, God. No, Ivy. Do *not* apologize. I can be there in forty minutes if I stop to pick up wine and sushi. Thirty minutes if it's only the wine. Twenty if you don't need the alcohol."

Despite the anguish attempting to consume me, her offer brings a laugh bubbling up. "I already ate." *Lie.* "And I have a bottle in the fridge." *Though I've barely touched that, either.* "But I'm okay." I take a deep breath, willing it to be true even though I haven't been *okay* in a very long time. "I'm going to head to bed soon anyway. You don't need to come over."

"Are you sure?"

Am I?

Curling up on the couch to eat sushi and watch something funny and mindless with Marlo does have its appeal, but I just want to be alone tonight.

Well, not alone.

My eyes move to the mantle again, and I swallow through the emotion clogging my throat again. "I'm positive. I'll see you tomorrow."

Marlo releases a little sigh. "You don't need to come in. You can take more time off. I promise, we can hold down the fort."

If anyone else were trying to keep me away from Buds & Blooms, I might take offense, but Marlo means well and is only attempting to give me what she thinks I need. But more time won't change anything. It won't bring Drew back or fill this void in my chest that festers like an infected wound.

"...And since it sounds like I won't be able to convince you to let me come over tonight or to take another day or two, I guess I'll see you in the morning."

The morning.

A new dawn.

A new beginning.

One I eventually have to start taking advantage of.

Starting tomorrow...

"You *will*."

"Did you..."—she hesitates a moment, long enough to make me brace for whatever she's about to ask—"talk to Nancy?"

Instantly, that vicious vise tightens around my ribcage again, and the tremor in Drew's mother's voice plays in my ears as if I'm still talking to her now. "Yes. She called earlier to see how I was doing."

"How is *she* doing?"

Dropping my head against the back of the couch, I stare

at the beams across the living room ceiling. "I guess as well as can be expected." I wipe away tears that slide down my temples. "She said she wanted to make sure I knew that she would always consider me a daughter even though the wedding didn't happen."

"Oh, hon..."

Nancy should have been my mother-in-law by now. She should be out on that dance floor with Drew in the beautiful silver gown she bought for the wedding, enjoying watching one of her sons get married. She shouldn't be mourning his loss the same way I am, shouldn't be grieving and asking questions that have no answers.

That sense of utter disbelief overwhelms me again, as it has every single day since Drew drove away and never came back.

Because none of it makes any sense.

He shouldn't have been there.

He said he was going to the hospital, that they needed his help on a shift...

Marlo inhales deeply, the sound breaking the silence lingering on the line, and when she speaks, the raw emotion in her voice tells me she's near tears even though she would *never* admit that to me. "I'm so happy you have her."

I sniffle, wiping the snot from my nose. "I am, too."

Nancy's words earlier today bolstered what I've always felt since the moment I met the woman. That pure, unadulterated acceptance and love. The same her son always gave me. I may have lost him, but Nancy will never disappear from my life.

At least I can be grateful for that when everything else seems too pointless and bleak.

The sound of the speaker system at the greenhouse cuts through the line, announcing closing time.

Marlo jostles the phone again and says something to someone I can't make out. "Hey, Ivy, I have to run. We're closing, and I need to wrangle a few stragglers from the aisles."

"Okay, goodnight."

"Goodnight. Call me if you need me." Her stern tone makes me smile, picturing that *look* she always gives anyone when she means business. "*Really.*"

I end the call, knowing I won't pick up my phone again even if she does call. Not because I don't appreciate her efforts; I just need to be alone with him. I've spent the four weeks since Andrew's death trying to hold myself together. Attempting to be strong. Moving through each day and night with this emptiness threatening to consume me—a black hole that devours all light, all happiness, everything good and pure I once had.

Tonight, now that he's home, I'm going to let it.

I need to allow myself to mourn what I was supposed to have. What today was supposed to be. Who *I* was supposed to be when I came back to this house—Mrs. Doctor Andrew Usher. Instead of what I am. Not even a widow, just...*alone.*

Thunder rumbles the house, close enough that the metal frame holding the photo of Drew and me that sits on the end table beside me actually vibrates against the wood slightly.

I reach out and take it with a trembling hand, brushing my fingers across my favorite picture of us—on the shore, with the sun shining down on us, the waves crashing in the background, and Drew lifting me and spinning me around.

The joy of that moment when I said, "yes," radiates from the snapshot.

His dark hair disheveled in the wind. Bright-blue eyes

filled with so much warmth and affection as he looks at me. A smile so wide the photo can barely capture all of it.

"Fuck..." I battle another sob. "Why the hell did you leave me?"

I'm never going to see his face again.

I'll never experience the same happiness I had in his arms.

"Shit. Shit. *Shit!*"

I slide the picture face down onto the end table, then drop my head into my hands, rubbing the heels of my palms into my wet, swollen, painful eyes.

Thunder rolls again, and a shiver slides down my spine.

The storm hanging over the city doesn't want to seem to let up, almost as if God Himself is mourning with me.

Maybe that should be a comfort, but I can't find comfort in anything right now.

Still, I push to my bare feet and pad across the hardwood floors to the front door. Going outside to stand in the warm summer rain might help wash away some of this despair— even if only for a few moments.

And I need it.

Something.

Anything that might help.

My body vibrates as I unlock the deadbolt and turn the handle, like it can feel the energy of what's waiting outside. For the briefest split second, I hesitate before tugging the door open.

Storms like this can be dangerous. But the potential threat waiting for me doesn't stop me from pulling the door toward me. It can't overpower the need to seek any way to temper the agony.

I stare out at the unlit porch, under the burned-out bulb Drew never got around to replacing.

Someone stands at the edge of the poured concrete slab in the rain.

Back to me.

About to step off and onto the path that leads down to the sidewalk.

Leaving without ever knocking or ringing the bell.

A tall man.

All I can make out is broad shoulders covered with a black leather jacket.

Thick, dark hair, soaked from the rain that still pours down.

The sound of the door opening makes him freeze.

Slowly, the man turns toward me.

Lightning flashes, illuminating his face, and my breath catches.

Goosebumps break out across my skin, and my body trembles as inky darkness encroaches around the edges of my vision, blurring out the face I never thought I'd see again. "Drew?"

2

CAM

F*uck.*

3

IVY

The scent of fresh summer rain, wet leather, and something clean and citrusy like lemon soap invades my breath, and I inhale it deeply, tugging the fluffy blanket tighter around me to stay in the perfect dream I've been floating in so magically.

One where Drew is *here*.

Where I can see his face again...

A warm, gentle hand cups my cheek, turning my face to the side. Calloused fingers brush across my temple. "Ivy?"

"Hmm?"

I lean into the touch, the familiar warmth and comfort of it enough to make a little sigh slip from my lips. The same electric buzz that always comes from his soft caress makes me want to luxuriate in it forever.

Drew always knows what I need...

"Ivy?" His voice sounds rough tonight. Off. A little unsteady. Like he's upset about something. Maybe a bad night in the ER. "Can you open your eyes?"

Were they closed?

The thick, gray fog clouding my brain starts to clear slowly, but I try to cling to it. Try desperately to make it stay so *he* will stay.

A crack of thunder rattles the house, and I groan and roll toward the only touch that has ever lit me on fire.

"Drew...mmm...was sleeping..."

Those fingers at my temple still. "Ivy, I need you to open your eyes for me."

Ugh...

So demanding.

That isn't like Drew.

He's so patient. So kind. Always putting everyone else's needs first. Taking care of me the way only he can. Like now...

"Ivy, *please*."

That strain in his normally smooth voice finally shatters the last vestiges of sleep, and I force my lids open.

Shadows engulf the room, the lights I swore were on in the kitchen and living room now off. Only the occasional flash of lightning through the front window illuminates the space.

Drew squats in front of me, where I lie on the couch, cocooned in the thick, fuzzy blanket I remember being draped across the back. His normally bright-blue eyes seem darker tonight as he examines me, hand still pressed to one cheek, keeping my face tilted toward him. "Are you feeling okay?"

Huh?

Why wouldn't I be?

He always worries so much.

It's so hard for him to take off his "doctor" hat, even when he's not at the hospital and there's no reason to worry.

I push myself up slowly, his hand falling away with my movement, and he shifts back slightly and rises to his feet.

It takes a second for my eyes to adjust to the darkness to be able to see anything.

The pale wood floors.

Booted feet.

Black motorcycle boots.

Dark jeans.

A black T-shirt pulled taut over a sculpted chest.

Tattoos swirling up his left arm...

What?

I blink a few times, trying to clear the remaining fog I've been floating in.

Lightning flashes again, followed by another rumble of thunder.

The man standing in front of me retreats a step, then another, until he can lower himself into one of the chairs across from the sofa.

But something is wrong.

Very wrong.

My heart lurches into my throat.

That isn't Drew.

Tears pool in my eyes as they sweep up to the mantle—where the cardboard box sits. Exactly where I left it—*him*—when I answered the call from Marlo.

An inked arm reaches up and switches on the lamp in the corner behind his chair, bathing the room in a warm glow and enough light to see that the man sitting in the leather chair most definitely *isn't* Drew—even though he has the same face.

God, I've missed seeing him...

But it isn't quite right.

Longer hair that, in its current wet state, curls haphazardly over his forehead and around his face. Small silver hoops hang in his nose and ears. Slightly broader, more muscular shoulders and arms fill the chair. Tattoos over his exposed skin when Drew refused to ink his. And the eyes—though they're the same vibrant blue—seem haunted. Somehow shadowed more than the ones I've stared into for the past four years.

It takes a second for my brain to fully get on board with what it's seeing. For it all to finally *click.*

I suck in a sharp breath. "Camden?"

He clears his throat, shifting forward to rest his elbows on his knees. The movement shifts the collar on his T-shirt, showing a glint of a silver necklace. "I'm sorry about how I just...showed up like this. I should have called to warn you I was coming..."

"What?"

Shaking my head, I try to clear away the remaining cobwebs, try to make sense of what's happening.

His uneasy gaze darts to the front door, then back to me quickly. "You...called me Drew and passed out on the porch. I caught you and brought you inside to the couch."

I did what?

Cam swallows thickly, his Adam's apple bobbing under tanned skin. "I can't imagine what that must have been like... opening the door and seeing me..." He shoves a trembling hand through his wet hair, shifting it away from his face, only to have it fall right back. "I should have thought about what a shock it would be and called first."

My mind spins.

Flashes of memory return.

Wanting to go out in the warm summer rain.

Opening the door.

Someone standing there.

A flash of lightning.

Drew...

I squeeze my eyes closed against the wave of despair that washes over me. It threatens to drown me under its catastrophic power, twisting me violently, heaving me toward the truth I managed to forget for a few blissful moments.

My fingers curl around the soft fabric of the blanket Cam must have covered me with when he brought me to the couch.

Cam!

That wasn't Drew.

This *isn't Drew.*

No matter how many times I repeat it to myself, when I reopen my eyes, the man sitting across from me still *looks* like Drew. My heart still stutters seeing his face again. I've missed it—missed *him*—so damn much.

I never thought I'd see him again anywhere except in old photographs.

But it's like he's here with me even when he isn't.

Cam rubs his hand across a lightly stubbled cheek, his gaze drifting to the box on the mantle like he can somehow tell what's inside it even when it doesn't have any visible labeling.

My stomach pitches, the tears burning in my eyes threatening to fall. Because the longer I stare at him and see the differences, I also see all the similarities. Every little feature that matches. "I just didn't expect you to...look so much like him."

He gives me a grim half-smile that doesn't reach his eyes,

which I now see have dark rings under them, as if he's as exhausted as I am. "That's the thing with identical twins. Someone else always has your face."

Until they don't...

Anger flashes hot through my veins, my hands fisting in the blanket.

Because Drew is gone now.

But his brother is *here.*

"What are you doing here, Cam?"

He shifts restlessly at my question, clenching his hands together in front of him.

"I thought you were still in London."

Settling back in the chair, he nods slowly, his intense gaze locked on me, like he's trying to memorize *my* face when I'm the one who is struggling, seeing his. "I was. And now I'm not. I wanted to let you know I was back in town, so it wasn't a surprise if you saw me somewhere." He releases a little sardonic laugh. "Not that it could have gone much worse than that did."

What the hell did he expect?

Given his absence from Drew's life during our entire relationship, and even after his death, him simply appearing on my doorstep on my wedding day couldn't have been on my bingo card.

"Why now?" That bubbling anger shifts to something even hotter. "You didn't even come back for the funeral. So, why *now*?"

His lips press together into a firm line.

A muscle in his tense jaw tics.

Camden doesn't like me calling him out, but he deserves it—the anger, the scrutiny, the discomfort at having to face his actions.

Nothing should have kept him from coming to his brother's funeral.

Nothing.

Yet, *I* was the one there holding his mom while she sobbed during the service. I was the one accepting condolences from friends and strangers. I was the one helping Nancy make all the difficult decisions when all she wanted was her other *son* here.

When he *should* have been here.

He dips his head to avert his gaze, and his hair flops forward again, hiding his eyes—either because he *can't* or *won't* look at me. "I know you're angry about that, and you have every right to be. My relationship with Drew was..."— he releases a heavy sigh filled with so many emotions they seem to fill up the room as much as Cam's presence does, and when he lifts his head again, the pain filling his gaze matches my own, maybe exceeds it, which I didn't think was even possible—"complicated."

"Complicated?" My voice cracks on the word, emotion getting the better of me. "That's all you're going to say about it? That it was *complicated?*" I lean toward Cam as my anger rises. "He was your *brother.* You shared a damn womb. You share the same face. And you weren't here for your mom when she lost him. Does she even know that you're here now?"

The look he gives me answers before he does. Pure guilt floods his darkened gaze as his hands tense on the armrests. "No..." He shakes his head, and the steely set of his shoulders grows, until he looks like he's about to snap. "She doesn't know, and I know I have no right to ask this of you, but please, don't tell her."

"What?" I shift forward on the couch, mouth gaping as my entire body trembles. "You-you can't be serious."

Cam shoves to his feet and grabs a wet leather jacket off the back of the other chair, shoving his arms through the sleeves. It settles over him like it was cut for his body, perfectly molding to his shoulders and chest as he zips it. "Coming here was a mistake. Again, I'm sorry..."

He starts to make his way toward the front door but pauses beside the end table next to the couch, flipping the photograph I laid down up. His gaze rakes over the image, the corner of his lips turning up ever so slightly, but it doesn't take away any of the pain in his eyes. "He really loved you."

My breath catches, a sob crawling up my throat.

His hand trembles as he sets the frame back down, the photo facing me. Showing me what will now be the happiest moment of my life. When I thought I was going to spend the rest of my life with Drew. When I had *everything* in my grasp and was clinging to it so tightly that I thought I'd never lose it.

But somehow, it slipped through my fingers...

Sure strides bring Cam to the door before I can even get myself untangled from the blanket and to my feet.

I waver slightly when I finally manage it. "You're leaving?"

His hand pauses on the knob. With his back still to me, he inhales deeply, his shoulders rising then falling as he releases it slowly. "I'm sorry I came, Ivy. I thought I was doing the right thing, but—" He shakes his head, still refusing to look at me. "It doesn't matter. Nothing I do is ever the right thing."

With those words, he yanks open the door and steps out into the storm still blustering outside.

Another sharp flash of lightning illuminates his tense features as he turns and takes one last look at me before pulling the door closed behind him in time with the crack of thunder that shakes the house.

My head spins.

What the hell just happened?

I rush after him on wobbly legs, turning the knob and tugging the door open as he reaches the end of the walkway, where a motorcycle sits parked at the curb.

He isn't going to ride that in this weather...

Only someone with a death wish would.

Yet, he must have ridden it here.

Through the driving rain.

Coming here to tell me he was back was so important to him that he risked that and will again to leave.

He tugs on a helmet and throws his leg over the Harley Davidson without looking my way. Wind whips the rain almost sideways, more lightning cracking the sky as he fires it up and pulls away from the curb onto the soaked street, disappearing into the deluge and leaving me reeling.

Why did he come?

After four years of not speaking with Drew. After never meeting me or showing *any* inclination of ever *wanting* to. After staying in London and using it as an excuse to never come home. After missing birthdays. After missing his brother's funeral. After failing to be here for his mother during such a horrible, traumatic time...he just shows up at my doorstep one month later.

Why?

The storm swallows the sound of the motorcycle's engine quickly as he flees.

He's gone.

I stagger back a step, then close the door against the riot outside, turning to rest my shoulders to the smooth wood. My heart thuds wildly beneath my ribs. My hands won't stop shaking. Even my knees seem weak from the encounter with the *other* Usher twin.

Something made him return to Philadelphia now.

And something brought him to my doorstep tonight.

But I don't have the faintest clue what it could be.

I slide down the door until my butt hits the wet floor, but I don't care that my jeans are now damp.

Whatever reason Cam has for coming home, it's *his*.

It doesn't affect me.

I can't let it.

Not when I can barely contain the chaotic, soul-crushing emotions that swamp me every waking moment and the memories and nightmares that plague me when I try to sleep.

But not telling Nancy that he's back when she's grieving and needs her son, that's something else entirely.

A debate wages inside my head, between calling her immediately and telling her Cam is here or honoring his request. More of a plea, really. The way he looked when he asked me not to tell her, the pain in his gaze—it's enough to give me pause in grabbing my phone.

What is going on with you, Camden Usher?

Something tells me finding out the truth will be almost as hard as figuring out what to do with *that*.

My eyes land on the box, and I push myself to my feet

and slowly make my way over to it. I trail my fingers across the damp cardboard, my throat tightening.

"What should I do?"

Drew was always my sounding board.

No matter what was bothering me—issues at the shop with employees or stock, bridezillas who made my days so much harder, even my occasional spats with Marlo over trivial things.

He was the only person who ever got *all* of me.

I sink back to my knees in front of the fireplace where I was before Marlo called and Cam showed up. It's the closest I can get to him without pulling the urn from that box, and I don't have it in me to do that right now.

Not when I just saw his ghost.

4

CAM

Heavy thumping bass vibrates the old, worn wooden planks under my bare feet.

Radiates up my legs.

Through my stomach.

Across my chest.

Down my arms.

My fingers twitch.

I tighten them around the brush in my hand.

The music flooding the studio throbs in my ears, pulsates through my blood, the deep melodic chords urging me to concentrate on *it* and what I'm doing, rather than the demons plaguing me tonight. Old ones that threaten to drag me back where I've fought so hard to get away from.

Tilting my head, I examine the massive blank canvas laid out on the floor in front of me.

Flawless.

Pristine.

Too. Damn. Perfect.

The image materializes in my mind.
A quick flash of exactly what it's *meant* to be.
I thrust the brush into the black paint...
And give in to what it demands.

5

IVY

ONE WEEK LATER

Sweat trickles down my temple, and I swipe it away with my forearm, trying not to smear soil across my face in the process. Though, that's not an unusual look for me most days, since I'd rather spend them here than in the main store area behind the counter.

Working in the greenhouse this time of year can be stifling, but with certain plants—like this orchid—it's a necessary evil. And I'll happily suffer in here rather than do it alone at home like I have been for weeks.

Marlo seems unbothered by the heat and humidity, sitting in the plastic chair with her booted feet kicked up on the planting table, popping Cool Ranch Doritos into her mouth as she watches me work on repotting.

I cast a pointed look in her direction. "You could help, you know?"

She scowls at me and crunches on another chip. "I could, but you're the one who said you needed to come into work this week. That you needed the distraction and to get things back to normal. I'm also on my *break*, which I am legally entitled to."

One of her blond brows rises haughtily at me.

Goddamn her for actually listening to me.

And for being right about the break.

I point a dirty-gloved finger at her. "You're right. I *did* say that, but that was not an invitation for you to slack off and do zero work now that I'm back. Remember that."

She smirks victoriously and returns to her snack, rocking on the rear feet of the chair as she scans the greenhouse and the few customers milling around the front portion where we keep the plants and flowers for sale.

I roll my eyes and get back to working on loosening the roots. Hopefully, Gladys will do better in this larger pot. The thought of potentially losing Mom's last orchid is too much to even *consider* right now.

No more death.

Even *if* Gladys is only a plant.

At almost fifteen years old, she's reaching the end of her lifespan. I don't think Nonni or Mom ever got one to last longer than this, and even almost a decade after Nonni passed and five years since Mom did, this last tangible piece of their lives and their passion for this place has come to mean more to me than it probably should.

If it finally dies, I don't think I could handle it.

As it is, I'm barely getting out of bed. Barely getting dressed. Barely making it in to the shop. And I've mostly kept myself tucked away in the greenhouse or back rooms of the store, avoiding having to deal with customers because I *can't* yet.

The tears seem to come whenever they want to. Often, when I'm not even thinking about Drew. I'll just find a wet drop on my hand and realize I'm crying again. And I do *not* want to do that in front of a customer.

Bad for business.

Many have been coming here for all their gardening needs for decades, and over the years, they have grown accustomed to Nonni and Mom's bright, sunny dispositions.

The way *mine* used to be.

Before.

Back when I enjoyed this. Enjoyed work. Enjoyed laughter and food and good wine. Enjoyed life.

None of it feels right anymore.

Like I shouldn't be living every day while Drew just... isn't.

When I know I'm going to return home to that empty house where his big, vibrant personality used to take up so much space.

Even now, the sound of customers chatting outside on the main sales floor and wandering between the aisles in the greenhouse makes me shift restlessly on my feet.

Crawling back under the covers and hiding away from the world that seems to want to hurt me so badly still feels like a *really* good alternative. Even though I've forced myself to be here, to try to take baby steps forward since that night.

Something about Cam's sudden arrival and abrupt departure left me reeling in a way that left me two choices— either I was going to allow myself to fully tip over that edge into the bottomless black abyss, or I was going to start working my way toward more stable ground.

I hope I made the right choice...

Marlo starts rocking back and forth, still on the rear two legs of the chair, completely unbothered by the noise and chaos that is Buds & Blooms in the early summer.

She *is* on her break, so I guess I can't give her too much shit, even though I want to—*badly*. Because being around Marlo helps. At least, temporarily. Her sharp tongue and good humor are about the only things that haven't sent me into tears over the last several weeks. For a few brief seconds when I'm with her, I can almost forget how much has changed, how my life crumbled without explanation.

The way this soil is falling away from the roots as I clean them and get them ready for the new, bigger home that will hopefully help Gladys live happily for many years to come.

Marlo's rocking stills, and all four legs of the chair drop with a *thunk* against the concrete floor. Her hazel eyes widen at something behind me, and her jaw slides open. "Hooooooly *shit*."

"What?"

She glances at me, then back to whatever waits at the front of the greenhouse.

I quickly peek over my shoulder, expecting to find an unruly customer or someone trying to steal, but all the air rushes from my lungs.

My spine stiffens, my entire body seizing up completely.

Camden stands just inside the door of the greenhouse. Another black T-shirt pulls taut across his heavily muscled chest and biceps, showing off an intricate tattoo of one dark and one light snake entwined on his left arm that I never got a good look at last week. The same gray jeans hang perfectly from his trim hips as he saunters closer in black biker boots. Each step he takes echoes off the glass walls and ceiling, seeming to fill the space the same way his energy does. He swings his leather jacket over his shoulder and hooks it on his right thumb, making his bicep bulge as he approaches, his piercing gaze locked squarely on me.

"Jesus, Ivy..." Marlo gapes. "You told me he looked like Drew, but not that he looked like Drew if he went to prison instead of medical school."

I whip my head toward her. "Oh, my God. Will you shut up?"

She smirks, never taking her eyes off him as he approaches—and looking like she wants to devour every inch of him. "No, I won't. He's fucking scary *hot*."

"*Marlo!*" I hiss at her as quietly as I can. "*Stop. It.*"

Shrugging, she leans back in her chair again. "What? He is. What's he doing here?"

Messing with my ability to think.

My brain spins wildly, the same way it did that night he appeared on my doorstep.

Why is he here?

That all-too-familiar vise tightens around my chest, and I try to breathe through it, clenching my gloved hands tightly at my sides and squeezing my eyes closed.

Remember the differences.

The hair.

The nose ring.

The earrings.

The tattoos.

The *eyes*.

Don't think about how much he looks like him or how much you begged God to see Drew just one *more time.*

It never occurred to me what seeing Drew's face—again—might actually do to me after asking for it every day through strangled sobs. I never imagined being granted that gift would become such a source of agony.

Which is what it has been for the past week.

Worrying that he'd show up on my doorstep again.

Thinking about calling Nancy to let her know he's back.

Questioning why he's in Philadelphia at all when he has no intention of letting his mother know about his return.

Picturing his face and those tortured eyes.

Wondering what made them that way when Drew's were always so bright and filled with love for me and life.

After how awkward and tense our conversation was that night and the way it left me feeling so off-kilter, I had figured —and deep down *hoped*—Cam would go about his life and avoid me altogether.

Guess I was wrong.

"Ivy?" Marlo's voice finally makes me shake my head and tug off my gloves, wiping my sweaty palms on my apron.

"I don't know why he's here. I haven't seen him or heard from him since he left my house the other night."

And part of me wishes he wasn't approaching me now.

There are too many questions.

Too many things left unsaid, unexplained.

Given how he acted when he was sitting across from me, he doesn't seem inclined to offer me anything but more turmoil and frustration. But I can't exactly run and hide at this point, even if literally burying my head in the dirt in front of me doesn't seem like such a bad idea.

Cam's heavy steps stop behind me, and I can't avoid him any longer—no matter how much I may want to.

I cautiously turn to face him and find only a few feet separating us.

He offers me a tight smile, his gaze wary as it sweeps over my face. "Hey..."

"Um, hi. What are you doing here?"

He scans all the flowers in the greenhouse, before returning his gaze to mine. "Flower shopping?"

The corners of my lips twitch up, despite my unease at seeing him again and how uncomfortable it seems to be for him, too.

What happened the other night was so *damn* awkward.

I wasn't sure how to handle it—handle *him*—not with all the questions Drew created for me about him, or the ones Cam brought the second he walked through my door. Not to mention the way my heart and body seem to react to seeing him, seeing Drew *in* him, even when I know they're two different people.

And with him standing in front of me in bright daylight, it seems even worse.

He really does look exactly like Drew...

If Drew had gone to prison instead of medical school.

As annoyed as I am with Marlo's description, she isn't exactly *wrong.*

Drew's hair was always slicked back and perfectly in place, along with his ever-present, easygoing smile. But the man in front of me is disheveled. Thick, black locks falling across his forehead, his eyes still holding that haunting darkness they did when he sat across from me in my house the other night.

Even the daylight can't fix that.

He locks that troubled gaze with mine. "I wanted to apologize for what happened..."

His eyes dart away, and he shifts his weight, clearly uncomfortable with this—maybe as much as I am. He seems to be struggling to find what he wants to say.

I swallow through a suddenly dry throat, trying not to let myself feel bad for *him* when there are so many reasons for me to be angry. "You've already done that."

Cam nods and reaches back to rub at his neck with his

left hand, making his bicep flex. Marlo makes a strangled sound behind me, and I glare at her over my shoulder as she continues to ogle him.

Either he doesn't hear her or chooses to ignore the completely inappropriate noise.

"I wanted to. *Again*." His deep voice wavers slightly with the emphasis he places on the word. "I realize what sort of a position that put you in, and"—he shakes his head, letting his arm fall—"it wasn't fair to you, so, I'm sorry."

The sincerity in his tone melts away some of the unease I felt at his arrival, and some of that anger that heated me so thoroughly the other night. But the way he's watching me now, the way his gaze seems to rake over every inch of me and see every minute detail, sends another type of warmth spreading through me.

I have to look away—at anything but him.

Gladys still sits on the table, waiting to be repotted, and for the first time, I really *see* her—probably because I don't want to examine my reaction to Cam or the tangle of emotions twisting inside my stomach right now.

And how ironic it is.

She's survived almost fifteen years, but her world has been literally turned upside down—and dumped onto the old wooden table—like mine was. But she'll have a nice, new home soon. Somewhere she can hopefully flourish and grow. As for me...I'm just adrift. Alone.

"There was another reason I came by..."

Cam's admission draws my gaze back to his.

"What's that?"

To rattle me?

To crush my already shattered heart into a fine powder by having to stare at your face again?

Because the more I look at him, the harder it becomes.

To see Drew but also *not*.

To see the differences yet so much the same.

I want him to be Drew so badly that I can't even breathe.

Tears start to well in my eyes, but I refuse to let them fall. I've already made a fool of myself in front of this man once. I don't intend to do it again.

Camden isn't Andrew.

Camden isn't Andrew.

Cam isn't Drew!

No matter how many times I need to repeat it, I'll just keep telling myself that until my heart and mind get on board with it.

I bat my eyelashes a few times, trying to keep the tears from making an appearance while I wait for him to continue. "How did you even know how to find me?"

The corners of his lips twitch slightly, the same way they always did when Drew was fighting a grin. "Drew told me all about you."

"What?" I tilt my head slightly. "I thought you two weren't speaking."

For the past four years, as far as I know, they hadn't even said a word to each other. Partially because Camden has been in London the entire time, but also because of whatever falling out they had that Drew never wanted to discuss with me. Whatever drove them apart, it hurt him enough that going on with his life without his twin was a distinct *choice* he made, and I had no choice but to follow.

Cam shakes his head. "We weren't. He told me before..."

Before the mystery falling out.

That he always brushed off, saying it was a "family thing."

Isn't that what I was supposed to be? His family?

For a man who was always so open, who wore his heart on his sleeve, the fact that he never wanted to talk about what drove a wedge between him and his twin brother always bothered me. Even more so now, when I realize Drew had *other* secrets.

Like why he was in that area of town that night...

"Anyway"—he runs his hand through his hair—"my mom told me that you have all of Drew's things at your house. She said he came by her place and cleared out all of his stuff last year."

I nod hesitantly, unsure where he's going with this. "Yeah. So, your mom knows you're in town now?"

His shoulders tense, and he shakes his head, his jaw hardening. "No." He averts his gaze. "She just knows I'm searching for a few things that I think might be in those boxes. So, she gave me your number and said I should call and ask you, but I was hoping I could come by and look through them." His blue eyes cut back to mine. "Of course, I wouldn't take anything without letting you know what it was first, but—"

"No"—I hold up a hand—"I get it."

No matter what might have happened between them, they're brothers.

Things that were meaningful enough for Drew to keep are likely just as important to Cam.

I would never prevent him from taking something he wants, that holds good memories of his brother—even if their final years were spent in some sort of argument that broke their relationship so badly.

"There's a lot of stuff. His whole closet in his office is full of boxes, but you're welcome to come look through all of it, if you want to."

A bit of the tension slips away from Cam's body, and he inclines his head toward me, making that thick dark hair of his flop forward again. "Thanks. Hopefully, I can find what I'm looking for quickly and won't be in your way too much."

An embarrassing rush of air releases from my lungs.

That would be for the best—if he can find what he needs and be on his way. So we can avoid more of whatever this is.

"I'm off tomorrow. If you want to come by anytime, I'll be home."

One of his brows rises slowly, and he looks so much like Drew with that move that I have to fight back a sob. "You're sure?"

I nod.

He offers a tight smile. "Okay. I guess I'll see you tomorrow, then."

The *thunk* of the chair hitting the ground again comes from behind me. "You're not going to introduce me?"

I glance over my shoulder at Marlo, who still eyes Cam up like he's something to eat—thoroughly. "Sorry. Marlo, this is Drew's brother, Camden. Cam, this is my best friend, Marlo, who's also my store manager and who should have returned to work"—I glance at my watch—"five minutes ago, instead of sitting here, eavesdropping."

Marlo smirks. "But eavesdropping is one of my favorite pastimes. Along with *other* things." She winks at Camden in a way that makes it very clear what she's referring to. "It was nice to meet you."

He gives her a half-smile that suggests he finds her as amusing as she finds herself. "You too."

Sliding his jacket back over his shoulders, he turns and walks away through the greenhouse, weaving around several customers. Several of whom openly watch him with appreciation.

Marlo issues another little groan in her throat and smacks my arm. "*Giiirl!*"

I turn back toward her, ignoring the instinct to glance over my shoulder to see if he's gone yet. "What?"

"Camden is, *woooooooo.*" She starts fanning herself. It has nothing to do with the heat and humidity in the greenhouse, and everything to do with the man walking out of it.

It would be impossible not to notice how hot he is.

It's why I was attracted to Drew in the first place.

The way he just *fills up* a space. Consuming the oxygen and somehow enthralling everyone he smiles at. From the moment he approached me at the hospital nurses' station in his slick white doctor's coat with a smooth smile, I was a goner.

And Camden, despite his rougher appearance and darker nature, has that same magnetism his brother did.

But Marlo is also right about something else.

Camden is dangerous.

Drew told me as much, many times, over the years, when I tried to broach the subject of their rocky relationship.

Which means, I need to be careful with him.

6

IVY

I thought I had prepared myself this time.

Last night, after I finally got home from work, I spent hours looking at photos of Drew and me together, reminding myself of all those minute details about him that make him so different from Cam.

Even through the tears and sobbing, I could *see* them.

The way the corners of Drew's eyes crinkled because of his ever-present smile. The fact that his lopsided grin was slightly *more* crooked than the one Cam gave Marlo in the greenhouse. The pains Drew took to ensure his hair was always slicked back and perfectly professional looking, while Cam's seems so wild and unruly. And most importantly, their eyes.

In dozens of pictures taken over the past four years, Drew *never* looked at the camera—or at me—with the barely repressed darkness that seems to want to overtake Cam's gaze every time he looks at me.

Whatever torments Cam, it does so in a way Drew never experienced—at least, not when we were together.

So, no matter how much he may *look* or even *sound* like the man who was my everything, I can't let that affect me the way it has during our previous two encounters.

I won't.

He needs to work through Drew's death in his own way, which includes searching the boxes in the office to find whatever meaningful possessions and memories might be in there. Just like I need to handle it in mine, which mostly consists of lying in bed alone, clutching his pillow and wondering if it will ever lose his scent, or sitting on the couch staring at the unopened cardboard box that sits on the mantle and trying *not* to think about what's inside of it.

I did all this *work* so that when I opened the door this morning to his hesitant knock, I wouldn't end up flat on my face on the porch like I would have last time—if Cam hadn't stepped in and caught me.

Yet, here I am, left hand gripping the doorknob so tightly that my knuckles throb just to keep myself upright as I stare at the man waiting for me to invite him in.

My knees don't seem to remember all my mental preparations.

And my brain sure as hell doesn't either.

He isn't Drew. He isn't Drew. He isn't Drew.

I repeat the mantra incessantly, hoping that the more I hear it in my own head, the easier it might be to remember it's true. But my stomach flips, twisting violently like I'm stuck on a Tilt-A-Whirl at the county fair after gorging on fried foods. My heart stutters, as if it isn't sure whether to beat faster at the sight of him or stop altogether. Every nerve-ending in my body flares to life looking at him as he runs a hand through disheveled hair and offers me a sheepish smile that in no way matches his appearance.

He shifts nervously, glancing around the front yard that desperately needs to be mowed and over the bushes that have begun to grow out of control in Drew's absence. "Um... hi."

I somehow manage to swallow, despite my throat being as dry as the Sahara. "Hey..."

Cam's black brows draw low over his blue eyes, his unease as palpable as my own. "Is it...still okay if I'm here?"

Shit.

"Yes, of course. Come in."

I force a smile that I hope doesn't come across as such.

Cam doesn't know me, so maybe he won't notice how this entire situation has put me on a perilous edge. I was already walking a thin line between full-blown depression and something worse. And this man showing up so unexpectedly that night has created a new dangerous tightrope for me to balance on.

He takes a step toward me, close enough now that his scent hits me full force.

I retreat enough to give him room to enter, and his shoulder brushes against mine as he passes. He quickly issues me an apologetic half-smile and steps farther in, leaving me reeling as I clutch the doorknob.

Apparently all my preparations couldn't do *shit* for the way I react to seeing him. For the way it feels to have the other half of Drew in the home I shared with him...

Breathe.

But that's a very bad idea.

Because he's still close enough that when I do, his scent infiltrates my lungs—somehow soothing as it simultaneously wrenches my soul and twists it violently. My body somehow remembers waking to that scent the other night and how safe and warm I felt. How for a brief moment, things felt like they were *okay* again.

I hold my breath and squeeze my eyes closed, trying to give myself a minute to control the clashing emotions threatening to go into a full-on war right here, right now, with him standing in my entryway.

Because I don't know *how* I'm supposed to feel about Cam being here.

We never even *met* when Drew and I were together, never spoke a word to each other via phone, never exchanged Christmas or birthday cards. He was always this *person* who should have been the most important one in Drew's life but who had somehow become a pariah.

But it would have been impossible not to see how much it pained him when Nancy brought up Cam during our time spent with her. Or to ignore the times I found Drew sitting in the dim light in his office, staring at a photo he would surreptitiously slide into his drawer as soon as I entered the room—one of the two of them with their mom that couldn't have been taken long before he and I got together.

All this time, Cam has been an enigma.

The mysterious "other half" of the man I loved.

And now he's just *here*.

And Drew is *gone*.

"Ivy? Are you all right?"

Shit.

My lids fly open, and Cam stands only a few feet from me, his brow deeply furrowed as he assesses me with eyes now filled with concern in a way that reminds me so much of how Drew looked when he was in "doctor mode" that I have to swallow a sob.

"I'm fine."

Another forced smile.

A deep breath.

I give him my back as I shut the door, offering myself a few precious seconds to try to gather some semblance of control over my volatile emotions.

"If you want me to leave—"

"No." I whirl to face him so fast it makes my head spin—or maybe that's because I have barely been able to bring myself to eat anything since Drew's death. "Please. I'm just tired. It's fine."

Cam doesn't look fully convinced, his gaze roving over me in a way that feels somehow both clinical and profoundly invasive at the same time. "Are you sleeping?"

Of course not.

Eating. Sleeping. Breathing. It all feels so impossibly hard.

Every single day is utterly exhausting just *being* here without him.

If anyone *might* be able to understand my agony, it would be Cam, but this is the same man who didn't speak to his brother for four years, who couldn't even be bothered to come to his funeral, who is *lying* to his grieving mother about still being in London instead of here in Philly where he could offer her some comfort and support.

So, I bite back those truths that sit on the tip of my tongue.

The best thing to do is give him what he needs and let him get on with...whatever it is he does that keeps him so busy that he couldn't show for the service.

I push past him into the living room and lead him to the first closed door on the left in the small hallway that leads back to the bedrooms. He follows slowly, his eyes sweeping over the house now that he can see it in the daylight.

Each step he takes ratchets up my anxiety. Every booted footfall on the hardwood floors seems to echo in the tense silence between us. But it isn't merely about having a Drew look-alike in this house; it's about the fact that I haven't had the courage to open this door since the day Drew died.

This was his place.

Where he went to decompress after a bad shift or when he simply needed some time alone.

I do the same with the greenhouse.

Something about digging my hands into the dirt and the scent of all the flowers, the vibrancy of the life there, always seems to pull me out of whatever mood I might be in.

But I haven't been able to enter *Drew's* space. Haven't been able to bring myself to see that desk and know he'll never sit behind it again. To look at the couch he used to lie on with a book in his hand and a beer on the coffee table, relaxing on a day off, and have to accept it's going to remain empty.

My hand shakes as I turn the knob and push the door open. I hold my breath and step inside, my bare feet sinking into the carpet. Cam moves behind me, his heavy footsteps fading once he's left the wood floor in the hall.

I scan the room, afraid to breathe because Drew's scent *lives* in here.

Everything is permeated with it. Each piece of furniture. The sweatshirt slung over the back of his desk chair. Even the soft carpet under my feet will hold on to it the way I desperately cling to each memory.

Tears sting my eyes, threatening to fall, and my lungs

burn, begging for oxygen even as I fight the need for it. But it finally wins out, forcing me to suck in a long breath.

And just as I had anticipated, Drew's scent hits me so strongly that I stagger a step. But Cam moves closer, the shift of the air forcing in the smell of leather and citrus and the summer wind instead, helping bring me back from the verge of collapse.

"Th-this is Drew's office." *Was.* I swallow through the tightness in my throat. "The boxes are all in the closet." Motioning toward the closed door in the corner, I rapidly blink away the few tears that had coalesced. "I think there are like thirty of them, so I hope you can find what you're looking for."

When I turn to face him, he stands behind me, feet braced apart slightly, arms hanging at his sides, his eyes locked on me in a way that makes goosebumps pebble across my skin.

He sees me.

Sees that I'm about to fall apart.

His worried gaze sweeps over my face, his jaw tightening the longer he examines me. But this isn't some purely distant, objective assessment from a stranger checking to see if I'm okay. Like earlier when he arrived, this feels more like being stripped bare, like he can see straight through this wall of strength I try to put up so I won't break down every second of every fucking day.

It's too real.

Too intense.

Too much.

I wrap my arms around myself and rub at them, averting my gaze from his penetrating one, but all that does is make my eyes land on the wall behind Drew's desk. Where he has so many framed photos of us, along with random awards he received in college and medical school, and with his medical license—front and center.

He worked so hard for that.

Sacrificed so much so he could give back.

So he could *save* people.

But that didn't help save *him*.

Tears well, and I reach up and swipe them away before I turn back to Cam. I motion toward the couch and coffee table. "You can stay as long as you'd like. I'll be...around, if you need anything."

Hiding.

His dark, stubbled jaw works, like he's chewing on something he wants to say but can't decide if he wants to swallow it or spit it out. Finally, his Adam's apple bobs sluggishly, and he nods. "Thank you. I'm sure I'll be fine."

He smoothly walks over to the closet and tugs open the door, exposing boxes stacked three across and five high that go all the way back as deep as the small space allows. "You weren't kidding about the boxes."

A grin pulls at my lips, despite the way my heart aches. "You know how sentimental your brother was. He never threw anything away."

Cam's eyes drift over to me. "That's what I'm counting on."

His voice wavers slightly, enough that the hint of anger and animosity I've felt toward him and whatever reasons kept him away before slowly starts to melt away.

He grabs one of the top boxes, then turns and sets it on the coffee table before he strips off his jacket and tosses it on the corner of the couch. Lowering himself onto one of the cushions, he runs a hand through his hair. For a second, he just sits there, staring at the box, until he finally seems to realize I'm still standing here, watching him—like a total creeper.

One of his brows rises. "Did you want to join me?"

I immediately raise my hands, staggering back a step. "Oh, no." Shaking my head, I retreat toward the door. "I... uh...don't think I can do that."

Not right now.

Maybe not ever.

Drew had secrets.

The funny, affable man I fell in love with, who was always so open and giving in every aspect of his life, kept important things from me, and I can't bear the thought that more might be buried in those boxes.

Better Cam find them than me.

He offers me a sympathetic look and nods, then watches me until I slip out into the hallway to find something else to occupy my day.

I wander to the living room, plop down on the sofa, and flip on the television, but even after an hour of mindlessly scrolling through channels, my gaze keeps drifting to the mantle.

What other secrets were you keeping, Drew?

The thought of what could have made him go down to that area of town that night when he told me he got called into the hospital makes my stomach roil.

I try to concentrate on the TV, on the romantic comedy with the klutzy yet lovable heroine and the dashing hero who finds her charming and adorable rather than annoying the way she thinks she is to everyone around her.

It's exactly the type of movie I would have loved to watch with Marlo before. We would have laughed at the cheesy lines and swooned nonetheless. We would have talked about our love lives and her current flame, and it would have been *easy*.

But nothing is anymore.

I watch the movie almost in a trance. Barely seeing it while my own love story with Drew plays in my head.

The way he approached me at the nurses' station when I was stopping by to deliver flowers and got hopelessly lost, since it isn't usually something I do personally.

How his eyes sparkled as brilliantly as his smile as he introduced himself and asked if I needed help.

That slight curl of his lips as he shamelessly flirted and asked me out within five minutes of meeting me.

Despite the heaviness sitting on my chest, my lips pull into a smile.

Because that was what he always did to me.

Lifted me up.

Made me feel worshipped and worthy and wanted.

He completed me and my life in a way that I didn't know could happen.

And as the movie comes to an end, so does my ability to sit here, pretending like I'm not miserable.

All I want is to climb into bed and close myself off from the world as much as possible for as long as possible. But as I climb to my feet and make my way down the hallway, one glance through the open door of Drew's office stops me cold.

7

IVY

Camden sits exactly where I left him on the couch, and the light shining in from the window across from him makes the late afternoon sunlight fall on his face. A single tear trickles down his left cheek as he stares at a frame held in his hands. They tremble slightly. His jaw is locked, like he's trying to make them both stop but can't quite manage to get his body to obey him.

He looks so sad.

So lost.

I recognize it because it's exactly how I've felt since that night.

Exactly how it seems like I'll *always* feel.

But I should keep walking.

I should go to the bedroom, pull the covers up around me, snuggle Drew's pillow, and forget what I see.

I should let him work through his grief in his own way.

I should give him space.

All those things make sense in my head, but my chest

aches, seeing how devastated he looks, how tightly he grips that frame.

Another tiny chip of the anger I've felt toward him breaks off, and I allow it to melt away. I've spent weeks angry at Drew, angry at myself, angry at God and the world. Staying mad at Cam won't change anything or make me feel any better. It won't bring back what I've lost. All it will do is sour my soul even more and bring me more grief.

So, it's impossible to walk away.

Even if I *should*.

My bare feet carry me into the office instead of to the bedroom. "Are you all right?"

His head whips to the side at the sound of my voice, and he quickly reaches up and swipes away the tear before he clears his throat and offers me a sad smile. "Yeah. I..." He releases a pained sigh, then turns the frame toward me. "I had forgotten about this."

I slowly make my way over to the couch and lower myself onto the cushion next to him as he slides the frame into my hands.

The document encased under the glass bears a rainbow with a shooting star above it. And *Camden's* name. Not Drew's. And it certifies him as a "rising star."

I raise a brow at him. "Rising Star?"

Cam offers an almost sheepish half-grin, running a hand across the back of his head as he watches me read the rest of the certificate that contains the name of a school and a date thirty years ago. "I got that in kindergarten."

The corners of my lips start to curl up as I picture him and Drew, two little dark heads of hair, going off to the first day of school together, dressed identically. I've seen the photos at Nancy's home, but I never knew the other half of the matching smiles until now.

"Why'd you give it to him?"

He smirks. "Because I was being an asshole."

I laugh, but he shakes his head.

"No, I'm serious. I gave it to him as a high school graduation gift."

"*Why*?"

Cam thinks about it for a minute, his lips twisting slightly as he examines the certificate. "You know he was valedictorian, right?"

I nod and motion to one of the plaques hanging behind his desk. "He was proud of that."

Drew always worked so hard.

Took such pride in his achievements while never lording them over anyone.

He saw each one as a step in a process that would ultimately lead to him becoming a doctor. A way for him to help people. Save them.

Cam snorts. "Don't I know it. I got a little sick of him constantly bringing it up, considering I barely passed half my classes and almost didn't graduate. So, I wrapped this up and gave it to him. Told him that he may be valedictorian, but he will never be a rising star like I was."

I bark out a laugh that startles even me and press my hand over my mouth to try to hold in my laughter. But it keeps bubbling up out of me, the sound foreign, something I barely recognize. "Oh, my God, you *are* an asshole."

He snorts and nods. "I wasn't joking."

"Apparently not."

"But he kept it." He sighs wistfully and takes it back from my hand, brushing his fingers across it. More tears shimmer in his eyes, but he somehow keeps them at bay. The corners of his mouth tip up. "He kept it, but I noticed he didn't give it a spot of honor up there with his medical degree."

I snort-laugh and slap my hand over my mouth again. "I'm sorry. I guess I just haven't laughed in a really long time."

Five weeks.

It's been five weeks of stunningly empty silence.

Devoid of joy.

Missing anything that could make me smile or feel anything but agonizing despair.

Until today.

I smile at him, the first *real* smile I think I've given *anyone* since Drew died. "I needed that."

He grins, and for the first time since I met him, his eyes warm to the same Caribbean blue I was so used to looking into with Drew. "Then you'll love this."

He sets the Rising Star Award off to the side on the coffee table, then reaches for a stack of pictures to the right of the box that it appears he's already gone through. He digs through them and pulls one out of the middle, flipping it over to me.

It takes me a second to process what I'm seeing. "Oh, my God."

"Yeah. Now...compare to this one."

Cam hands me another, and the laughter bubbles up out of me again.

"What *are* these?"

He sighs and taps the first one. "This was our first day of high school."

"You two went dressed the same? I can't imagine..."

Not looking at Cam now.

But in this photo, they're both in the same navy polo shirt and khaki pants, both with their hair slicked back and perfectly in place.

They are identical.

Truly.

The torment that seems to dwell in Cam's eyes isn't there in this photo. If it were, I could tell them apart.

The corners of his lips twitch. "Kind of hard to believe I ever looked like that, huh?"

"What? No. That's not why..."

He pats my arm, a little buzz jolting between us at the contact, and quickly yanks his hand away. "I know. Let's just say I was trying to appease our mother, but it didn't last very long. That one is about three months into the same school year."

I flip the other picture.

It's the two of them next to each other. Camden's hair now disheveled and unruly like it is today. Instead of a smile, an annoyed scowl twists his lips while Drew beams from next to him, his arm thrown around his brother. And it's there, though not as pronounced as it is now. But there, deep in his gaze, a hint of it. That unsettled darkness.

Glancing over at him now, I see it's firmly back in place. Dampening whatever lightness telling that story about the Rising Star Award may have brought him.

He watches me for a moment, holding my gaze before his dips to the photo, reminding me I have to respond or things will get even more awkward than they already are now.

"Wow." I tear my gaze from his to stare at the photos side by side. "Quite the change."

Cam looks at them, too, his focus locked on Drew rather

than himself. "I guess you could say I found myself in high school. Or, if you ask my mother, lost myself."

I cringe on his behalf.

Something changed.

Something that made Camden go down a completely different path than Drew. Maybe one that led to their fractured relationship.

Most of what I know about Cam came from Nancy or the little Drew told me prior to completely shutting down any conversation. Bits and pieces. Small stories and memories. And even though it wasn't a lot, it was clear Cam was always a bit rebellious, a little rougher around the edges. Less worried about school and social norms, as most artists tend to be.

But seeing him now, I think it was more than that.

Cam was broken by something.

Maybe not even *one* thing.

He takes the photos from me. "Drew spent most of his time studying, making sure he had the highest grade in every class."

"What'd you spend your time doing?"

He snorts and pulls out another picture from the stack—of him with a bong.

I gape at him.

"Yeah." One corner of his mouth quirks up. "While he was doing extra work in the chemistry lab, I was experimenting behind the gym with *other* things."

It's so hard to believe that they're so different yet can look so much alike.

I flip back to the first picture. "Did you two ever try to trade places?"

His spine stiffens for a moment, and his gaze stays locked

on the photos as he nods. "When we were younger. Mostly elementary school and middle school. He enjoyed math and science. I always loved English class and art..."

"So, you switched and took each other's classes?"

The corners of his lips tilt into a devious grin that further confirms my belief that this man is dangerous. Mischief dances across his gaze. "We did get caught. Turns out there was a very easy way to get to tell us apart prior to *this*."

He holds up his arm, showing off his tattoo.

"Yeah." I raise a brow. "What's that?"

Because looking at the earlier photo of them together, I wouldn't have the slightest idea how to even begin trying to guess who was who.

Cam runs his thumb across his bottom lip. "Get us to open our mouths."

I snort.

"Drew loved school and was always brown nosing the teachers, sucking up to them, wanting to be head of the class. I just didn't give a shit. I wanted to take a sketchbook and go sit behind the gym and smoke weed. And I guess that came out *very* distinctly in the way we talked to the teachers. Even when we were young."

"Did you get in trouble?"

He nods. "Yep. Mom said it was the only time she wished our dad was here to punish us because he would've made us see God."

"She didn't miss him otherwise?"

His shoulders tense, his gaze dropping away from mine again. He clasps his hands in front of him, suddenly shifting on the couch, his thigh brushing against mine. "We were barely six when he died, and I don't think she ever let herself miss him, to be honest. She just had to suck it up, be a single mom, and figure it the fuck out. But she didn't know what to do with us when we hit the teen years, especially me."

"I bet."

Mom always told me I wasn't particularly easy during that time, but at least she had Nonni to help her. Nancy was all alone with two little boys who missed their father. While I never had one at all.

It couldn't have been easy—for any of them.

I return the pictures to him, and he sets them back in the stack that appears to mostly be photos of the two of them together.

That pang in my chest returns.

No matter what happened, Cam still loved Drew—that much is clear.

I know I shouldn't ask.

I know I shouldn't pry.

But the question sits on the tip of my tongue, burning like acid, until I finally have to spit it out. "What happened between you and Drew?"

His entire body goes rigid, his eyes burning as they cut over to me. He locks his gaze with mine. The intensity of it makes me hold my breath for a moment. Another. So long that my lungs burn, and I'm confident he isn't going to answer me.

The column of his throat works hard. "I told you. It's complicated..."

Complicated?

That single word holds a thousand meanings and seems to weigh a thousand pounds as it settles into the air between us.

I let all the air rush from my lungs, not even bothering to attempt to hide my frustration at his response.

After all this time, he has *some* of the answers.

He can clear up *some* of that uncertainty.

I chew on my bottom lip. "Can you uncomplicate it? I mean, when he and I first started dating, he talked about you all the time. It sounded like you two were on the phone to each other almost daily."

Cam nods slowly, confirming those first few weeks when Drew and I were still getting to know each other.

"And then all of a sudden, poof." I throw up my hands. "It was like you were persona non-grata and a topic we weren't allowed to discuss." I lock my gaze with his. "And he wouldn't tell me what happened."

Cam's throat works on his response. "It's better that he didn't."

"Why is that?"

He pushes to his feet, snagging the jacket from the corner of the couch.

Shit, I scared him away.

He tugs it on, glancing at the window. "Because some things are better left buried." Shoving a hand roughly through his hair, he glances at the window again. "I have to go." He scans the various stacks of things on the coffee table and the three or four boxes around it. "I didn't get very far today."

I rise to my feet and clear my throat, trying to dispel the lump in it as well as some of the tension now permeating the air. "Well, you're welcome to come back, but I'm at the greenhouse most days from like 6:00 in the morning until 5:00 or 6:00 at night. Sometimes later if someone calls in sick, I'm closing, or if we have a big wedding coming up."

He nods, rubbing a hand across his stubbled cheek and avoiding looking at me again as he stalks toward the door.

Watching him walk away.

Not knowing if I'll ever see him again tugs at something anchored in my chest.

"Why don't I give you a key?"

His head jerks toward me, his eyes wide as they scan my face. "Are you serious?"

I nod and push up from the couch, leading him out of the office and to the kitchen. His heavy footsteps follow me. Along with his tense silence.

You idiot.

You shouldn't have pushed him.

He was actually talking, telling me things I never knew about their relationship or about him. And hearing him talk about Drew, the love in his voice, the joy in the stories, even in his sorrow, it made me feel something other than pain for the first time in over a month.

I tug open the drawer beside the sink and pull out the spare key, then turn and extend my hand toward him with it resting in my palm.

He reaches forward cautiously, like it might jump up and bite him. His calloused fingers brush across my skin as he takes it, sending a little shiver through me. "You're just going to give me a key to your house?"

Am I?

I lean back against the counter to put more space between us and assess him.

Everything about the man standing in front of me screams dangerous, from his tattoos, to his haunted eyes, motorcycle jacket, and the secrets he keeps.

But I can't *not* see Drew standing in front of me, too.

This is his brother, a man raised by Nancy just like Drew

was. And I can't imagine, for one second, that she would've raised a son I couldn't trust with a key to my house.

"You're Drew's brother. We would've been family if things had been"—I suck in a long, deep breath to keep myself from releasing a sob—"if things had been different. I trust you. Feel free to come by whenever you want."

His dark brows draw low over stormy eyes. "You're sure?"

Am I?

Even questioning if it's the right decision, I nod gently, and he slips the key into the pocket of his jeans and clears his throat, retreating a step.

"Thank you for this. I guess maybe I'll see you next time I stop over."

I give him a tight smile. "I'd like that."

And as much as I hate to admit it to myself, I would.

Talking to him, hearing his stories, made me feel for one brief second like somebody else understands my pain. There is somebody else on this planet who loved Drew the way I did and is suffering just as badly. Someone who understands he also had secrets, which I can't ever bring up to Nancy.

My eyes start to fill with tears, and Camden's retreating steps stop.

He watches me carefully. "If me being here is too much for you, I won't come back, Ivy. I don't want to make this any harder on you than it already is."

"No." I swipe away the tears from under my eyes. "Today was good. Really." I offer a half-smile. "That's the first time I've laughed in weeks."

He gives me a tight smile that doesn't quite reach his eyes. "Good. You need that, to laugh, to *sleep*." His emphasis on that final word makes it clear I'm doing a shitty job covering my exhaustion. "And to *eat*." That penetrating gaze sweeps over me again. "You look like you've lost weight."

"What?"

I glance down at myself, even though I know he's right.

At least ten pounds since Drew died.

My appetite seems to have vanished along with my fiancé.

"Just take care of yourself." He swallows stiffly. "Drew wouldn't want to see you like this."

With that, he turns and stalks from the house.

The click of the door closing makes my eyelids drop, and I stand frozen in place in the kitchen, gripping the counter behind me as I consider what just happened.

I so badly wanted to be angry at him, wanted to hold it against him for whatever shattered their relationship.

But he's grieving, too.

I lost my other half, but so did Camden.

And maybe the only way to find ourselves again is not to forget that we lost the same person.

8

IVY
THE NEXT DAY

He's been here.

    I know it the moment I step into the house.

    That leather, citrusy, summer breeze scent permeates the air, hitting me the moment I nudge the door closed behind me. And for some reason, I inhale it deeply, taking it in and holding it in my lungs. My body relaxes, all the tension of the day melting away. Because the house seems less empty, less lifeless—the way it has felt since Drew died.

I pause for a moment and listen for any signs that he might *still* be here, holding my breath for one heartbeat. Two. But his bike isn't parked out front. And there isn't any sound or light coming from the open office door.

The air I've been holding in rushes from my lungs as my shoulders deflate with the realization that I'm alone again.

Deep down—in a place I'm not ready to examine—I had hoped he would be here today. Hoped I wouldn't come home to this quiet loneliness. Hoped that maybe Cam would give me some more stories, open up about their rift, and help me understand what really went down.

So much for wishful thinking...

I set my purse on the counter and find a note, written in almost the same scratchy scrawl his brother had resting in the center of the granite.

I replaced your porch light. I also left something for you in the office.
And in the fridge.
Please eat.

Please eat?

His words from yesterday come back.

"You need that, to laugh, to sleep. And to eat."

The worry in his voice then still echoes through me now, sending a little shiver across my skin.

Because it's all true.

I forgot what it felt like to laugh. I forgot what it felt like to have a good night's sleep and wake up content. And I haven't enjoyed a meal since that final night I ate with Drew...

"Just take care of yourself."

As if it's that easy...

I definitely haven't been. It's hard enough to get out of bed, to breathe, to keep going when everything I lost sits on the mantle, reminding me daily of what *should* have been.

Nancy and Marlo have both expressed their concern, the same way Cam did, but he's the first complete stranger who saw it and seemed to understand. The only one who offered any form of relief simply by being here and telling me a few stories.

"Drew wouldn't want to see you like this."

He's right about that.

And apparently, he tried to do something about it.

I move toward the fridge and tug it open. Takeout containers sit piled on one of the shelves, and I reach in and remove them, checking to see what's inside.

"Oh, my God. Dante & Luigi's? How did he—"

My eyes dart around the kitchen for anything that may have alerted him to my favorite restaurant and usual order, which I'm currently staring down at—eggplant parmesan, with a side of baked rigatoni.

But there isn't a menu clipped to the fridge with a magnet.

No leftovers he could have seen since I haven't been able to bring myself to order anything I knew I wouldn't eat the past month.

Not an old note to Drew asking him to grab it for me on his way home from a shift at the hospital.

Nothing.

So, how did he know?

There's likely some simple explanation. Perhaps Nancy mentioned it to him during a phone call over the past several years. Or maybe Drew and Cam were speaking and just keeping it a secret for some unknown reason and the topic somehow came up.

Regardless of how he learned the information, I'm glad he did because my mouth waters looking at it.

The first time in forever that I've actually felt *hungry*.

Because of Camden.

Another tiny piece of that wall of anger I put up between us chips off, slowly melting away to join the one that disappeared yesterday when we sat on that couch together and he told me those stories.

When I *saw* how much he loved Drew, no matter what I might think about how he's handled his passing and the situation with Nancy.

As much as I want to dig into the very thoughtful meal he's left for me, curiosity makes me push the food back into the fridge and head into the office to see what he found today.

Hoping, praying, there's something in these boxes that might be able to do what Cam did for me yesterday...

I flip on the light and find several more boxes stacked in front of the coffee table. Another note sits next to a few items laid out across the smooth, polished wooden surface.

In here, Cam's scent mingles heavily with Drew's, somehow tempering the overwhelming sadness that hit me when we came in yesterday. I inhale them both, squeezing my eyes closed as I do it, taking several long, deep breaths, trying to steady myself.

To remind myself that today at work was good.

It was a good day.

It was a good day.

The best you've had.

Better than things have been any other time I've been at Buds & Blooms.

I actually made it through the day without any tears, but now that I'm home to *this*, I don't think that's going to last very long.

It's impossible when everywhere I look, I see Drew and relive our memories built here together.

When I imagine the ones we would have made if he hadn't left me here alone. If he hadn't had so many secrets...

But if I concentrate on that, I absolutely *will* end up in tears again tonight, and I so desperately need another break from that. Just one full day and night of happiness rather than gut-wrenching pain and sadness.

I slowly peel my eyes open and examine Cam's note.

I thought you might enjoy these. I explained each on the back.

Because he knew I would want to know.

Because his stories made me *laugh* yesterday and he wanted to give me more.

Another little shard of that wall falls.

I set down his note and reach for the stack of photos to my left.

The first one draws a grin across my lips—likely taken by Nancy, it's of the two of them dressed as Mario and Luigi on what must have been Halloween, both beaming at the camera. Though she's shown me a few photo albums over the years, I know I never saw this one.

This, I would have remembered.

I flip it over and find a Post-it stuck to the back with more of Cam's writing.

Halloween. Third grade. He was Mario, of course, because he's older and got to choose. I was stuck being Luigi.

My smile widens picturing the argument that must have

ensued over who got to be the "better" of the fictional brothers. And they no doubt had disagreements over things like
that throughout their entire childhoods. But they must have
gotten over it quickly, given the pure joy that radiates from
their little faces.

I set that photo aside and move to the next one,
narrowing my eyes on the striking image of one of them in a
baseball uniform standing against a chain-link fence,
looking out at a field.

Is this Cam or Drew?

The fact that I can't tell them apart at all in most of these
photos makes me feel a little less like an asshole for passing
out when I saw Cam that first night.

They really are carbon copies of each other, yet their
personalities are so different.

This twin looks worried. His brow furrowed as a game is
played in front of him. His fingers twined in the links of the
fence, face pressed in tightly.

I flip it over.

*Drew, the year his little league team made it to the
state finals. I never played. Zero hand/eye coor-
dination.*

For some reason, that makes me chuckle.

I guess it makes sense, though.

Sort of.

Drew was always so good with his hands.

It was part of what made him such a fantastic doctor.

Yet, Cam's an artist...

I would have thought he wouldn't have had any problems with that, either.

But I guess I don't really know much about him or his art.

Nancy always said she was so proud of him for pursuing his passion and going to art school in London instead of a more standard tertiary education route, but other than a few pieces he drew or painted in high school that she kept, neither she nor Drew ever showed me anything he's created.

Just more secrets to add to the pile that surrounds Camden Usher.

Whatever he's been doing at the gallery he runs in London, it apparently kept him busy enough to keep him away for the past four years, or at least that's the way he wanted everyone to believe it was. But after how he reacted to my question that first night about telling Nancy he was home and yesterday when I pressed him about what happened with Drew, I'm confident there's more to it.

He stayed away because he didn't want to put his mother in the middle of their argument.

So now that Drew is gone, why keep Nancy in the dark?

That question rattles around my brain as I stare at the photo, and now that I *know* it's Drew, I can see all the little tells.

Always so immensely focused, like this little boy.

Always so concerned with coming out on top—whether it be valedictorian or—apparently—on a little league field.

He wears that same furrowed brow. That same ardent concentration Drew needed to succeed in the fast-paced ER on a daily basis, handling trauma.

And I have no doubt this boy already had his massive heart, too.

I know part of that concern on his face is for his team-mates. For how they worked to get to that championship game. For the devastation they would all feel if they lost. And I'm positive he would have been the first one to offer hugs and kind words to them or the other team after.

Because that was who Drew always was.

A tear slips down my cheek, and I allow it to fall, not wanting to put the photo down to try to wipe it away.

Why bother when more will just come anyway?

My phone rings out in the kitchen, still somewhere deep in my purse, and I reluctantly set down the photo and hustle back out to drag it from the confines of the bag.

Marlo's name flashes across the screen.

Why is she calling?

I answer it on the third ring. "Hey, what's up?"

"Oh, good. Are you home yet?"

"Yeah. Why?" I rest my elbows on the counter, eyeing Cam's note. "What's up?"

"I just got a call from Kari Webber. She wants to change the wedding flowers."

I wince as dread floods my veins that had been warmed so much by the photos Cam left for me. "You're shitting me."

She lets loose a low grumble. "I wish I were."

"Does she realize that her wedding is in five days?"

Marlo offers an incredulous snort. "*Apparently*, she thinks that's *plenty* of time for us to make the switch."

"Jesus Christ." I close my eyes and pinch the bridge of my nose, annoyance already starting to form a headache right behind my eyes. "What does she want?"

"You're not going to like it."

"I'm sure I won't."

At this point, there isn't *anything* I want to do besides get through my first wedding back at work quickly, quietly, and with as little drama as possible.

Unfortunately, this is the wrong bride for that dream.

"She wants to go back to the roses."

I cringe. "Of course she does." Letting out a long, slow breath, I try to tamp down my annoyance. "Did she say why?"

The woman has changed her mind four times in the past year that we've been helping her plan the ceremony, so it shouldn't be a surprise that she's waffled again, but this close to the big day, it could create a big problem for us.

"Said she realized it's just what she's always pictured in her head."

I should be mad about that, but an image of my own ceremony, what it was supposed to be, flashes through my mind instead.

The white and red peonies I had planned to fill the church with, the beautiful corsages and bouquets we had already designed well in advance because I knew precisely what they looked like because they'd appeared in my dreams for years and years and years.

It was always easy for me, maybe because I was raised around flowers, but for Bridezilla, it's likely harder.

"Okay...did you talk to the distributor we had ordered the lilies from and see if they can get us enough roses?"

Marlo huffs. "You're not gonna try to talk her out of it?"

I drop my face into my free hand. "There isn't any point. Let's just give her what she wants."

She releases an aggravated sigh that is filled with as much annoyance as I feel right now, but I can't actually be *mad* at a bride wanting her day to be perfect.

Not when I wanted mine to be, and instead I got a nightmare.

"What are we gonna do with all the lilies we already ordered that are coming in?"

"We'll figure it out, Marlo. Stop worrying."

"Okay." She reluctantly acquiesces. "And yes, I did talk to the distributor, and they said they can get the additional roses here, but not until Friday."

"Shit." I stand and turn to glance at the calendar hanging on the side of the fridge. "So, we'll have to do it all Friday afternoon and evening."

"Yep."

I groan. "Well, I guess it's not like I do anything else on Friday nights."

Marlo snorts. "Well, *some* of us do, so I'll be expecting overtime."

"Shut up."

She laughs. "Or at the very least, you owe me dinner. We'll order in while we work."

"Speaking of which..." My eyes drift to the fridge. "He was here again today."

"Who?"

I make my way back to the office. "Who do you think?"

Marlo gasps. "Cam?"

"Yep. And get this, he replaced my burnt-out porch light and left me dinner."

"He cooked?"

I laugh as I settle onto the couch. "No. He left me Dante & Luigi's."

"Really?"

"Yep. Eggplant parm."

Another exaggerated gasp floats through the line. "With the side of baked rigatoni?"

"Yep."

"How did he know?"

I release a flustered sigh, dropping my head back on the couch to stare at the ceiling. "I'm not sure. Maybe Drew told him, but..."

"Did you two go to Dante & Luigi's before they had their big fight or whatever? When they were still talking?"

"I don't know. I've been trying to remember that since I walked in the door and saw it, but I really can't remember. And somehow, he *knew*."

"Well..." Marlo's voice softens. "That's actually really sweet of him."

"It is." And it shows he isn't the heartless monster Drew made him out to be whenever I tried to bring up the topic. "He also left me a stack of photos and a few other things I'm still going through with little Post-its explaining what they are. Pictures of Drew, him..." I lift my head and scan the coffee table, snagging a plaque. "This one looks like some sort of award Drew won for a science fair in eighth grade."

Marlo laughs. "That sounds like Drew."

I smile, the tears starting to well in my eyes. "It does."

"And that's also very sweet of him to do that for you. To give you those memories."

"It really is."

Because I'm not sure when, or even *if*, I would ever have had the courage to go through these boxes by myself, or even with Nancy.

I couldn't even set foot in here, let alone consider looking at all his prized possessions, stuffed into boxes the way he is on my mantle.

A tear rolls down my cheek.

"So, maybe the brother isn't such a bad guy?"

I stare at the spot where Cam sat next to me yesterday. "I'm still not sure how to feel about it. I told you he clammed up and basically ran out of here when I tried to press him about their fight, and he still hasn't told Nancy he's here, so he's put me in a shitty position, but, yeah, maybe he's not such a bad guy."

"Did he say anything about when he's going to be back?"

I shake my head. "No. At least, I haven't found any notes about it. Honestly, I think I scared him off with my questions yesterday. I'm a little surprised he came today."

"He wants something out of those boxes, maybe the same thing you do. A connection to Drew, reminders of the good times. Of a life they shared that's now gone."

More tears fall.

But they aren't all sad ones.

Cam has already helped in a way no one else has been able to. He got me to open this door. He forced me to come in and face the memories in these boxes. And he gave me *new* ones to clutch tightly in my heart that I never had before about the man I thought I'd be *making* new ones with.

"You should tell him thank you…"

"I would, but I don't have his number, and it's not like I can call Nancy and ask for it without raising a lot of suspicion."

"Have you spoken to her recently?"

I toy with the hem of my shirt, twisting my fingers around it. "Not since the night he showed up on my doorstep."

"What are you gonna tell her when you do?"

"I don't know. I don't wanna lie to her, but there might be

a very good reason Cam doesn't want her to know he's here. So, I don't feel right outing him, either."

Marlo sighs, making a little *tsking* sound. "He did put you in a shitty position."

Nodding, I snag the stack of photos he left again, flipping through them. "He did, but I'm going to give him the benefit of the doubt until he gives me a reason not to."

It's the least I can do for the man who brought the first hints of laughter and joy back to my life.

9

IVY

FRIDAY NIGHT

arlo comes in carrying the rest of the vases for the centerpieces and sets them on the corner table, examining the arrangements I'm putting together. "I still can't believe she went back to roses."

I release an annoyed sigh. "I know. They're beautiful but..."

She tilts her head. "I really wish people would realize there are far more interesting and unique flowers to use for your wedding."

Like peonies...

A sad smile pulls at my lips as I jab another red rose into the center of the white bundles, exactly as the bride requested. Pretty. Elegant. But pretty much the same as ninety-nine percent of wedding arrangements I do these days. "I agree, but it's her day. If this is what'll make her happy, then we have to do it."

Marlo sighs and comes over to start helping me. "I know." She plasters on a saccharine-sweet smile. "This is me. Doing my job happily."

I chuckle and jab another red rose in, adjusting the surrounding blooms to ensure it's perfectly balanced.

She glances at me out of the corner of her eye. "What's gotten into you today?"

Shit.

Here I thought I was doing a pretty decent job at hiding my frustration all day. Maybe the fact that I've been here since dawn and only ran out briefly to grab us dinner—and stop by my house for *reasons*—is finally getting to me. Or maybe it's what I found when I stepped through that door.

Either way, I am not in the mood to have Marlo grill me about it tonight. Not when we still have hours of work to do and have to get up early tomorrow to deliver everything to the church and reception venue.

I do my best to appear relaxed as I offer a smile. "Nothing."

"Really?" One of her blond brows rises. "Because you seem a little off; you have been all week."

I press my lips together to keep from unloading on her because I know what she's going to say, and I really don't want to hear it. *Again.*

But the longer we work, only the sound of the music being piped over the speakers filling the silence between us since the shop is closed, the harder it becomes for me to keep it in.

Because it *is* bothering me.

Eating away at me like pests do these flowers.

A growing annoyance, and if I'm honest with myself, hurt, too.

It's kept me awake at night all week, more than the fact that Drew's side of the bed is empty. This simmering *need* to understand what happened between them. A hammering desire to understand Cam and maybe get some answers to the secrets both he and Drew were keeping.

It might give me some closure on this whole thing.

And I might not lie awake in bed at night, wondering why Drew lied. Why he died instead of staying there with me, where he should have been...

"Okay, fine." An annoyed sigh slips from my mouth. "He was there again today."

Marlo's hand freezes, and she slowly sets down the bundle of roses and turns to face me. "That's every day this week?"

I bite my lip and nod.

Every single day since he came to see me at the shop on Saturday.

Marlo's eyes widen, the little flecks of gold in her hazel irises glittering under the lights with her curiosity and interest. "What did he leave you this time?"

My cheeks heat for some reason under her scrutiny, even though they shouldn't.

He's never left anything inappropriate.

Never overstayed his welcome or overstepped in any way.

The photos, trinkets, and stories he has left for me over this week have given me so much insight into him, Drew, and their relationship when they were growing up.

But they've also left so many *more* questions.

"More notes...and pad thai from Baan Thai."

Her jaw drops. "He nailed it. *Again!*"

I nod and wipe my hands on my apron as I go over to the corner of our workspace where the lockers are, pull out my purse, and dig around, then bring the stack over to show her. I don't even know *why* I brought them with me to the shop tonight.

Maybe because I knew I'd eventually break down and talk to Marlo about it...

"Four days in a row and four of your favorite meals from your favorite restaurants..." She continues gaping. "Do you think it's the twin-telepathy thing? Do you think he knew *every time* Drew ordered you dinner?"

I slap at her shoulder as I hand her the photos. "Stop it."

Her brows rise incredulously. "I'm serious."

"So am I." I shake my head. "There's no such thing as twin telepathy."

"That's not what I've been reading."

I release an annoyed sigh. "Why have you been reading up on twin telepathy?"

She raises a shoulder and lets it fall nonchalantly, but I don't miss the slight curve of her lips. "Call me curious."

"Does your curiosity have anything to do with Cam showing back up here?"

"Hmm." She shrugs again. "Maybe."

"Don't, Marlo."

Her mouth falls open. "Don't what?"

"Don't involve yourself in anything having to do with me and him."

"*Is* there a 'you and him?'"

Fuck.

I squeeze my eyes closed and shake my head. "Jesus, that's not what I meant."

Marlo snorts. "Because if there was, that could get a little *complicated.*"

I growl low at her to shut her up, but when I open my eyes again, she's just smirking at me.

She starts flipping through the photos, glancing at the back of each one to read the notes written on Post-its, humor playing on her lips. "He certainly has a way with words, doesn't he?"

I can't help my answering grin. "He does."

It's been one of the best parts about the notes he's left me this week—the way even his short explanations of each photograph or keepsake so easily convey the emotions connected to it. As if I can see him sitting right next to me, telling me the story the same way he did the Rising Star Award.

And it makes it feel like Drew is there, too, enjoying reminiscing with his other half.

She clears her throat, examining one particular story on the back of a photo of one of the young boys—who I learned was Drew—sitting with his arms crossed over his chest, looking pissed. "Ahem. *The time Drew locked me in the basement for so long that I pissed my pants and my mom grounded him for a week, yet* he *was the one mad.*"

Her laughter fills the air as she examines the photo again. "Do you really think Drew did that to him?"

I shake my head. "I'm not sure. You know—" I clear my throat—"*knew* Drew. I never saw him lose his temper or be mean to anyone, so it does sound a little out of character. But they're brothers and couldn't have been more than maybe eight when that photo was taken. It wouldn't surprise me if there were some pranks that went too far when tempers flared."

"But I thought they had a good relationship prior to whatever happened."

I return to work as she keeps flipping through the pictures. "They did, as far as I know. Drew only really talked about him for those first couple weeks we dated, and then it was like..." I shrug. "I don't know; he pretended he didn't exist. The only time I ever heard his name was when we were with Nancy, and I could always tell Drew didn't want to talk about Cam with her."

She sets the photos on the table, eyeing me. "Have you called her?"

Guilt licks fire across my chest, making me squirm. "No."

Marlo's eyes widen slightly. "So, she still doesn't know Cam's back?"

I chew on my bottom lip. "I don't think so. I feel like she would have called me and mentioned it if she did know."

"Jesus." She shakes her head, resting her palms flat against the table as she leans toward me slightly. "He's been coming to your house every day, going through all these boxes of memories and things that were important to Drew, but he still hasn't told his *mother* he's here?"

I release a resigned sigh. "Apparently."

And her shock over it matches mine.

After everything that's happened, I would think Cam would *want* to be here for Nancy, yet he seemed so adamant about not wanting her to know he's in Philly.

There has to be a reason.

But I haven't been able to come up with a good one.

Just like I haven't been able to come up with a reason Drew lied that night and left our bed to drive to an area of town he would normally never travel to...

Unless he was cheating.

My stomach turns even thinking about it, yet it's the only thing that has made any sense. The sole explanation for why he was being so secretive.

That trait certainly seems to be embedded in the Usher brothers' DNA.

"Are you going to tell her?"

I grab a bundle of white roses and begin arranging them in the next vase. "I'm considering it. I don't like lying to her. And I've given him two weeks to do it..."

Marlo resumes working as well, snagging the red roses and handing a few to me to add to the arrangement. "How long are you going to give him?"

A very good question.

Even though I'm not technically *lying* to Nancy by not telling her, it certainly feels like that. And I've never liked having to lie to anyone about anything or been particularly good at it, either.

I shrug. "I'm not sure. Until I crack, I guess."

Marlo snorts and shoves another group of flowers into a vase. "So not long, then?"

"What the hell is that supposed to mean?"

She rolls her eyes. "Oh, come on, Ivy. You live by your emotions, and that's totally fine. It's one of the reasons I love you so much. You're not going to be able to keep that woman in the dark. You love her too much."

A resigned sigh falls from my lips. "You're right..."

It won't be long until I crack and rat out Cam, but I'd feel a lot better about doing it if I knew *why* he doesn't want her to know. If I understood even a *fraction* of what happened between him and Drew or why that prevented him from coming home when he died or being here now to support Nancy.

"I just wish I could ask him why...but by the time I get home every night, he's gone." I finger a thorn on the stem of one of the roses, gently pressing my fingertip into it. Not hard enough to draw blood. Just enough to start to feel the bite. "I think he's avoiding me."

"Why would he do that?"

I shrug, remembering the look in his eyes before he left that day. How quickly the entire mood in the office shifted because of what I asked him, because I *pressed* when maybe I shouldn't have. "I don't know. Things are just weird and tense between us. The situation is awkward, at best."

"So..." She gives me a pointed look. "*Do* something about it."

"What do you mean?"

"Go home early every day until you find him there and *talk*. Clear the air."

"I don't know if that's possible."

She rests her hip against the table. "Why not?"

"Because I think I overstepped." I shake my head, shoving the rose in my hand into the vase with the rest far too aggressively. "I've been wanting answers for so long that I pushed him for them, and I shouldn't have."

"You have every right to want to know what went down between him and Drew."

"Do I, though?"

Drew is gone.

Does it matter why he was fighting with his brother?

Does it matter why Cam wasn't here for the funeral?

Does it matter why Cam doesn't want Nancy to know he's home?

Is any of it my business?

"I'm not an Usher, Marlo. I never—"

A sob works its way up my throat and cuts off my ability to speak. She closes the distance between us and pulls me into her embrace. Her arms wrap around me, holding me tightly, and she shakes me gently.

"You *are* an Usher in every way that matters. Nancy told you she will always consider you a daughter and part of her family. That makes Cam your brother-in-law, I guess. And you *should* want to know something that affects that family."

I sniffle, swiping away the tears that have started to fall. "You think so?"

She nods, a few strands of her blond hair falling from her ponytail. "Absolutely. What harm could it possibly cause to go talk to him? I feel like you two have just been dancing around each other for weeks and need to confront it head-on."

Confront it head-on.

It sounds so easy when she says it like that. As if *demanding* he tell me what happened and asking if he knows why Drew was lying to me will somehow make him spill all the information he seems so intent on keeping close to the chest while we do this *dance*.

"We kind of have been."

Marlo squeezes my shoulders, locking her gaze with mine. "So, *stop* dancing."

10

IVY
THREE DAYS LATER

C am's bike remains parked at the curb.

In *exactly* the same spot it has been occupying for almost two hours...

Untouched other than by the last fading rays of the summer sun that is gradually disappearing behind the buildings and casting shadows over the city.

A dark, lonely sentinel that reminds me so much of its owner.

There isn't any sign of *him*, though.

I scan the surrounding street, examining each and every building, for what feels like the hundredth time since I followed him from my house, but I still can't figure out where he might have gone after he climbed off that thing.

It's quiet this time of night.

Not much foot traffic.

Only a few cars driving by.

And *no* sign of the man who barreled into my life and has somehow twisted me up enough that I have to know what happened between him and Drew and what he's hiding. Enough that I literally *followed* him when I turned onto my street and saw him leaving before I could catch him to talk.

Clenching my jaw, I glance down at my phone again to check how long it's been since I last stared at the screen to see how much time had passed.

Ten minutes.

But the longer I stand here, tucked between these two buildings in the alley, leaning against the brick and peeking around the corner at his bike, the more obvious it becomes that I have lost my mind.

This is stalking.

Full-blown.

Flat-out.

Criminally convictable.

Stalking.

I knew it when I followed him here. Logically, I *knew* I should have let him drive away from the house like he does every night and disappear until he decides to come back... only to repeat the cycle.

It shouldn't matter what he does when he leaves.

It shouldn't matter *why* he always leaves before I come home.

It's none of my damn business.

Stop dancing.

But somehow, Marlo's words keep repeating in my head.

It does feel like some strange, cosmic dance.

Cam waltzed into my life so unexpectedly. Appeared on my doorstep like a ghost the day that I was supposed to marry Drew, when I had just brought what was left of him home. And he has swept me away in a storm of questions when I didn't think I could possibly have more than I did the night Drew died.

Yet, he possesses the ability to give me something no one else can—answers.

That doesn't mean you should have followed him...

My conscience knocks violently against my skull, trying to convince me to walk back to where I parked my car a block away and go home. To do this the *right* way—like maybe leaving him a note at the house asking him to call me or to stay late one night so we could talk.

That would have been the right course of action...

Not standing here, staring at his bike, waiting for him to reappear.

I release a ragged breath, giving the Harley one more longing look. Like the man who rides it, it's somehow dangerous looking. Something you *want* to climb on because it will feel incredible but also maybe kill you in the process.

There was a reason Drew never went *near* a motorcycle. After all the injuries and deaths he saw in the ER because of them, it would have taken an act of God to get him on one.

Yet Cam shows no fear taking off on one in the middle of the driving rain.

And taking off is exactly what I need to do.

I release a frustrated sigh, letting all the anticipation and frustration that's been building up in me since I saw him pulling away from my house out with it.

Eventually, we'll talk.

Forcing anything right now would only make the situation more fraught with tension that I'm quite sure neither of us needs at the moment—

"Did you follow me here?"

"Shit!" I whirl toward the voice behind me and find Cam,

leaning against the old, rough brick of one of the buildings we stand between, lighting up a cigarette that dangles from his lips.

Pressing my hand over my thundering heart, I try to steady my breathing and come up with any excuse—anything *at all*—that might explain why I would be here.

Aside from being a complete and total stalker.

"No, I—"

One of his black brows rises to meet the hair falling across his forehead. Accusation darkens his blue gaze the longer he holds mine. "Just happened to be hanging out in this alley for fun on a Monday night?"

He takes a long drag from his cigarette as he waits for me to respond, looking so casually sexy and dangerous in his leather jacket, dark jeans, and T-shirt reclined against the wall with one knee up, booted foot pressed flat to the brick.

The man has caught me red-handed—or red-cheeked as I feel the heat creeping over them.

My throat tightens, strangling my ability to come up with any response when I know there isn't one that would make any sense.

"Um..."

Shit.

Shit.

Shit.

There isn't any way out of this that will allow me to walk away with my pride intact. It left the moment I decided to follow this man.

"Okay, so maybe I was following you."

A long stream of smoke floats from between his lips, and he raises both brows slowly. "Because?"

I let out a heavy sigh, my cheeks heating so badly that I *know* they are candy apple red by now. Averting my gaze, I concentrate on the grainy, uneven texture of the brick on the wall immediately next to him instead of having to keep looking at him while we have this conversation. "Christ, this is embarrassing..."

He doesn't say anything.

A second passes.

Another.

Sounds of cars passing on the streets and the smell of the smoke float over me, but Cam remains absolutely still and silent until I finally force myself to look at him again.

The corner of his mouth twitches before he shoves the cigarette back there, still watching with that consuming gaze that seems to see straight through me.

Be honest, Ivy.

It's really the sole option. Even if I were a good liar, I don't *want* to lie to Cam. That would only continue this *dance*, and we need to get *off* that floor and somewhere that I'm not spinning and spinning endlessly.

There are already too many secrets.

Too many unspoken truths.

Between Cam and Drew. Between Drew and me. And now, between Cam and me.

"I haven't seen you in over a week, yet you've been at my house every day."

His shoulders tense slightly, but he releases another puff of smoke casually, as if my statement didn't somehow rattle him. Anyone else might not have caught that tiny muscle movement, the shift in his stance against the brick, but in so many ways, he's so much like his brother that it seems I can read him just as well.

It *was* intentional—him being gone by the time I got home each night.

He didn't want to see me.

That knowledge somehow makes acid burn in my throat, because this entire week, even if he hadn't been single-handedly ensuring I've been fed and leaving me those little glimpses into Drew's and his past, I would still *know* he's been there.

I can *feel* it—his presence in the house.

Not to mention the fact that his scent seems to permeate the air long after he's left.

I've come to *expect* it to be there the last week, and the thought of walking in one day and it not being there makes my eyes burn with tears I don't understand.

He watches me, as if he's expecting me to expand upon my observation. When I don't, he takes another long drag from his cigarette, then languidly releases it. "Do you not want me to come anymore?"

My gut tightens painfully, and I press my trembling hand over it. "No, it's not that. I just...thought maybe you were avoiding me."

His eyes never leave me as he inhales more smoke and lets it go in a round plume like the damn Cheshire Cat. Slowly. Deliberately. As if he's *trying* to drag out my agony and leave me standing here longer looking like a complete and total *idiot.* "I haven't been avoiding you, Ivy."

Something tells me that isn't completely true.

The slight downward turn of his lips and the steely set of his jaw. The way his shoulders tensed when I brought it up in the first place. The tightening of his fingers around his cigarette...

"What have you been doing then?" I glance at his bike

behind me on the street and scan the area, still completely clueless what he would be doing in this area of town since he had already parked his bike and disappeared by the time I got through the stoplight that delayed me and found where he ultimately parked. "What are you doing *here*?"

The corners of his mouth twitch, the tiniest hint of humor dancing across his blue eyes. "If I told you *that*, it would kind of defeat the entire purpose..."

"Defeat the purpose? What the hell are you—"

Oh, shit.

Oh, shit, shit, shit, shit.

I squeeze my eyes closed and bury my face in my hands. "Shit. I am *such* an asshole."

Cam clears his throat, the sound as rough as the brick fencing us in on two sides. "You have never been, nor could you *ever* be an asshole, Ivy."

Letting my hands fall, I force myself to open my eyes and look at him again. *Really* look at him and that torment in his gaze. And think about all the little comments he made that day at my house about high school and how he spent his time. And the things Drew alluded to at times, about Cam being dangerous whenever I tried to bring him up. "You were at a meeting."

He nods cautiously. "NA. I've been clean and sober for a year."

Oh, God...

"Do you go...every day?"

It would explain why he's been leaving before I get home every day. He would *have* to in order to get here in time for it to start.

Glancing away to the other end of the alley, he places the cigarette between his lips and inhales deeply. Like he needs a moment and the nicotine to come up with his response. A few seconds later, he releases the smoke, still watching something on the street opposite me. "Lately, yes."

Lately.

"Since Drew died?"

He swallows painfully and nods as he returns his attention to me.

Fuck.

And I've been *annoyed* with him for always leaving before I came home.

I thought he was trying *not* to see *me* for some reason. That I had done or said something wrong. I made it about *me* when it was about *him* and what he's been going through. "I'm sorry..."

He snorts a laugh and sucks on the cigarette that's burning precariously close to his fingertips now. "For what?"

"For being here. It's none of my business." I shove my hands through my hair, embarrassment and guilt mixing into a volatile concoction in my bloodstream. My legs tremble, begging me to bolt, to make a mad dash for my car to escape the sheer mortification I'm feeling under his scrutiny. "I shouldn't have followed you. I shouldn't have...inserted myself into your life when you clearly don't want me in it."

Cam's back stiffens, and he drops the butt and his foot from the wall, grinding the toe of his boot into it.

He turns and steps closer, until the smell of his jacket, citrus, the wind, and the light smoke clinging to him floods each breath I take. "*You* don't want to be anywhere *near* me or my life, Ivy. Trust me."

Tension vibrates through him, and Cam tips his head back and stares up at the thin strip of appearing night sky visible between the tall buildings on either side of us.

A minute passes.

Another.

Finally, his voice cuts through the night air, bearing an edge to it that's razor sharp. "I've done a lot of really horrible things in my life, Ivy. Drank myself to blackout. And when that stopped working, put just about every drug known to man into my body. Cocaine, heroin... I injected literal poison into my veins to escape my life." His eyes dart over to mine, what plagues him making them almost black tonight. "And that isn't even the worst of it because what I've done to other people is ten times worse. So, believe me when I say you should walk away now."

Those words and the absolute unwavering conviction with which he says them sting more than they should.

More than I should let them.

I'd love to believe it's because I'm looking at an almost carbon copy of Drew, and the thought of never seeing him— never seeing Drew—again is unfathomable, but Camden *isn't* Drew. And I've always known that.

At first glance, they may appear identical, but Cam's eyes hold that pain Drew's never did. A weight and heaviness that seems to settle onto his shoulders, too. He has been beaten down by something, broken by life or experiences in a way that Drew somehow escaped.

He isn't anything like the man I loved.

And the reason what he said stung has nothing to do with their shared face and everything to do with this connection I've felt with him since I woke in the house to find him kneeling in front of me in that damn storm.

Because no matter how many times I try to push it away, attempt to deny what I've been feeling the past two weeks, it's impossible to deny that I need him in my life. I need someone else who understands my pain, who is experiencing the same agony, in order to keep living through it.

"Isn't that my decision to make, not yours?"

He sucks in a sharp breath, then retreats a step, shoving his hands through his thick, dark hair.

Then he finally glances back at me. "I need to eat, and since you're here, I assume you haven't yet, and what I left for you is still sitting in your fridge."

"What did you leave for me?"

"Sweet and sour pork and sesame noodles from Emei."

My stomach growls, and my mouth waters imagining the meal waiting for me. More of my favorites. "How did you—"

He walks past me toward the street where he parked his bike. "You want to ride with me or meet me?"

Huh?

"Um, where are we going?"

His blue eyes meet mine over his shoulder as he pauses on the curb. "Max's. I'm dying for a cheesesteak."

11

IVY

Sitting across from Cam in the booth at Eagle Bar, I can't help but scan the massive wall of alcohol only a few feet from us and focus on the neon sign advertising "The Biggest Drink in Philly."

The smell of the two foot-long cheesesteaks spread out in front of us on pieces of unrolled paper mingles with that of stale beer and whiskey that always seems to cling to places like this.

Cam lifts half of his sandwich and takes a bite, groaning in a way that is wholly indecent as he chews and wipes the side of his mouth with a napkin. "God, this is exactly what I needed."

I clear my throat, staring at my untouched sandwich, unable to even *think* about eating it when my stomach churns with unease. "Um, should we *be* here?"

It's the question I've been internally asking since the moment he walked in here after ordering our dinner and slid into the booth.

Cam looks around us at the patrons sitting on stools at

the bar and in the few other booths, swallowing the second bite he just took. "Why shouldn't we be here?"

Leaning forward slightly, I drop my voice low so no one else hears our conversation. "It's a *bar*..."

His brows rise. "Yeah..."

Shit.

I shift awkwardly on the leather seat, the sound of the movement suddenly very loud despite the noise surrounding us. "Well, you just left a *meeting*, so coming to a *bar* seems a little...inappropriate."

Cam watches me for a second, sandwich held in one hand, the other resting on the table, so still that my breath catches.

Crap.

I definitely shouldn't have said anything.

It isn't my place.

All I've done tonight is step all over things that are none of my fucking business when it comes to Camden Usher.

My cheeks heat under his continued assessment, then the corners of his lips lift slightly.

"You worried about me, Ivy?"

Shit.

"I'm sorry. I know I shouldn't have—"

Cam chuckles low, shaking his head gently. "I appreciate the concern. Really. I do. But I'm fine eating a cheesesteak in a bar."

Maybe that's true.

And I might believe it.

If it weren't for the *other* thing.

My eyes drift to the draft beer sitting in front of him that had me practically biting off my tongue as he ordered it. "And what about *that*?"

His gaze follows mine, dipping to the table, to the untouched frosty glass with condensation dripping down the side of it. "I don't plan on drinking it, Ivy."

The conviction in his statement should settle me, but it doesn't make any sense why he would leave a meeting and order a beer half an hour later...

"So...you ordered a beer to what?" I raise a brow. "Test yourself?"

He drums his fingers on the table, staring at the light-amber liquid for a few moments before he looks back up at me. That haunted look that always seems to overtake his gaze returns, making my chest tighten. "Something like that."

Well, that sounds like a truly horrible *idea...*

I've never been to a meeting for any sort of addiction, but something tells me *ordering* a beer and eating dinner in a bar, surrounded by alcohol and people drinking, is a recipe for disaster when it comes to sobriety.

But it's none of your business.

That's what I have to keep telling myself.

I force my lips to stay plastered together rather than try to push the subject, which he clearly seems to think is closed, given the way he dives right back into his cheesesteak.

My eyes dip to mine, but the sloshing in my stomach—a mix of embarrassment for what a fool I acted like tonight, concern over the man across from me, and fear of why I care so much—prevents me from picking it up.

Cam watches me intently. "You need to eat, Ivy."

All the meals he's left for me over the past week flicker through my head. I've only managed to eat small portions of them each night, but I *did* eat. Far more than I had been. So, if that was his plan, he succeeded—at least, partially.

I nod. "I know…"

And it shouldn't have taken Cam ordering me dinner every night to make me do it.

I'm perfectly capable of getting my own food—either delivered or cooking it myself. I made dinner almost every night in that house after we moved in since Drew never particularly liked eating out and said it was healthier to prepare our own meals.

Which is part of the problem.

Everywhere I look in that house, I see him.

I *feel* him.

I remember his touch, his words, that playful grin that always danced across his lips. Every inch of that house is steeped in memories that are both comforting and agonizing in a way I didn't know something intangible could be.

But Cam was right about what he said the other night.

Drew would be pissed about how I've been living since he died.

Not sleeping. Not eating. Not taking care of myself at all.

It's almost like he sent Cam to ensure I would.

My gaze drifts up to meet his across the table, and he simply raises a brow in challenge. Almost like he *wants* me to attempt to get out of eating so he can *force* me to do it.

Something about the hard set of his shoulders and the tension in his stubbled jaw tells me he would do just that.

There's still a very good chance he's been avoiding me— despite having a legitimate reason for leaving the house before I come home every night. But he does care. Maybe in the only way he's capable of.

I reach out and grab an untouched half of my sandwich,

then take a tentative bite. The juicy, delicious meat and creamy cheese melt in my mouth, and a little groan slips out as I chew. Flavors dance across my tongue. So simple yet so fucking perfect.

Cam looks smug. "I told you. Max's is the perfect food."

Right now, I can't argue with him.

God, this is good...

I finish chewing and swallow, staring down at the cheesesteak in my hand. "This is pretty good. My mom always preferred Dalessandro's."

Cam practically chokes on his next bite, his eyes going icy cold. "Stop that blasphemy in here."

A grin pulls at my lips. "Wow, I didn't realize those were fighting words."

He leans forward slightly, resting his elbows on the table. "They are in the Usher house. My dad used to bring Drew and me here whenever he was home. He said it was the single best thing to eat in the entire city of Philadelphia."

I chuckle, examining the sandwich in my hands and rolling the flavor over my tongue. "That's a pretty bold statement."

His lips quirk. "He was a pretty bold man."

That matches what Drew always told me about their father.

I guess you *have* to be bold to be an Army Ranger. To go headlong into that kind of conflict and violence. To spend so much time away from your wife and children in order to protect freedom on a level I can't even fathom.

"Is that why you still lived here instead of D.C. when he was stationed there?" I wiggle my sandwich. "Because he couldn't give these up?"

Cam smirks. "Probably. Well, that and my mom told him

she'd never leave Philly when they got married. He knew they'd have to spend a lot of time apart, but he wanted her to be somewhere she was comfortable and happy." He shrugs. "So, she stayed here with us, and he would come home as often as he could."

The hint of sadness in his voice matches the one I always heard in Drew's when he spoke of their father. Losing him at such a young age profoundly affected him.

He lost his hero.

It had to be the same for Cam.

He plays with the edge of the sandwich paper spread on the table, his lips tilting slightly. "As soon as he got home, the first thing he would do is throw the two of us in the car and drive over here. We'd sit out on the curb and eat—"

"Drew sat on a *curb*?"

Camden barks out a laugh, bobbing his head. "Hard to imagine, right?"

I scan the bustling street beyond the massive windows to my right. "I literally can't."

Drew was always so *cautious.*

I think the doctor in him couldn't overlook risks everywhere he looked. So, him as a small child sitting on a curb, eating on a busy corner in North Philly, definitely wasn't anything I ever would have pictured.

A sad smile pulls at Cam's lips. "He wasn't always like that, you know?"

"Like what?"

"So cautious."

His choice of words and willingness to talk about Drew creates a mix of longing and fear I'm not sure how to process. Longing for the man who is gone and never coming back, and fear that Cam might stop giving me these insights into him, and I'll never learn all these things only he knows.

"What happened?"

Cam sighs, rubbing his jaw with his palm. "I mean, he was always the more responsible one. Always telling me we shouldn't be doing this or that. Worried we would get in trouble, but when our mom got sick, a switch kind of flipped in him."

"You were what? Fourteen?"

He nods slowly. "Freshman year. She got her diagnosis a few months into the school year."

The photo of them that he showed me the other day flickers through my head—that *drastic* change in his appearance and the darkness clouding his eyes even then.

It changed him, too, whether he wants to admit it or not.

Cam's throat works hard, the muscles straining with his thick swallow. "When she started chemo and radiation, Drew took on that meticulous caregiver role so naturally." His lips pull into a sad smile. "I think that was the moment he decided to become a doctor."

"He was a really good one."

Emotion clogs my throat, and I have to clear it with a rough-sounding cough before I take another bite of the sandwich rather than fall into tears in front of Cam and somewhere so public.

I swallow, forcing down the food that *is* delicious, but I suddenly don't want to eat.

He stares at me as if he can see right through my attempt to cover my almost breakdown. That crystal-blue gaze, possessing so many mysterious corners that hold so many secrets, locks on mine, saying so much before he even speaks another word. "He really loved you..."

His voice breaks along with my already shattered heart.

The sob I've been fighting slips out, and I slap my hand over my mouth to keep from completely losing it in the middle of the bar.

Squeezing my eyes closed against the onslaught of tears, I shake my head, trying to heave in a breath without releasing another strangled sound of anguish.

When I open my eyes again, Cam is still watching me, his brows drawn deep over the tempest swirling in his gaze.

He really believes that.

But he doesn't know.

He doesn't understand.

"I'm-I'm not so sure that's true."

Cam's back stiffens, his shoulders tensing along with his jaw. "Why?"

"Because..."

The truth sits on the tip of my tongue. The accusation that's rattled around my head but I've only ever voiced to Marlo. The weight that's been crushing me since the night he died.

I shouldn't say it.

I shouldn't speak the poison that's been seeping into my heart since I got that call that he was dead.

Especially not to Camden.

But I can't seem to stop myself now that the question is hanging out there.

"Because I think he was...he was cheating on me."

Cam recoils, his jaw locking so tightly and eyes flashing with so much rage that heat seems to lick across the blue.

He leans forward across the table, close enough to make me tremble. "Listen to me very carefully, Ivy, because I need to make sure you hear me. Drew *loved* you. More than *anything* in this world. You lit up his life and were the center of it. He *never* would have considered even *looking* at another woman, let alone *touching* one like that. Drew *never* would have cheated on you. *Never.*"

My bottom lip quivers, another sob threatening to spill out. "But, he *lied* to me that night. He told me he was going to the hospital, but he was on the other side of town. He was—"

He reaches out and pulls my hands into his, his touch warm and strong as he clasps them tightly. Rough callouses brush across my skin, sending a little shiver through me. "He was *not* cheating on you."

The sob slips out, and Cam refuses to let go so I can try to cover my mouth again and prevent the rest of the people in the bar from becoming unwitting spectators to my breakdown.

Strong hands squeeze my fingers, and Cam keeps his gaze locked with mine, though it's now blurry with tears. "Do you hear me, Ivy?"

I nod, sniffling.

"Do you *believe* me?"

Do I?

I so badly want to say that I do.

I so badly wish I could believe that there's some innocent explanation for why Drew left me in bed alone in the middle of the night, lied about where he was going, and drove across town to an area he had no business being in *other* than another woman.

But I haven't been able to come up with *one* in the weeks since he died.

Not a single one.

I shake my head. "I-I can't. And you don't know. You

weren't here. You weren't even speaking with him when it happened."

A muscle in his clenched jaw tics, his eyes hardening as he leans even closer, so close that his warm breath flutters across my lips. "I *do* know because he told me. He told me he was in love with you the day you *met*. He knew *then*, Ivy. He *knew*. He called me and said, 'I just met the woman I'm going to marry.' And from that moment on, you were *it* for him."

His words stoke a flame that had dwindled to ashes, the one that always burned so brightly when I was with Drew. The warmth of his love and that feeling of safety and contentment that always wrapped around me when I was in his arms.

Cam reaches up with one hand and brushes away my tears, a sad smile turning up his lips. "Don't ever forget that, Ivy. Don't ever question it again. Okay?"

This time, I nod.

This time, I don't question it.

Because Cam has just settled that restless demon that has chased me since Drew's death.

12

CAM

The music pulsates.
　　　　My body thrums.
　　　　Images flash through my head.
Vibrant.
Beautiful.
Horrible.
Stunning.
Those familiar demons crawl over my skin, making it too tight. Making it itch. Making me want to tear it off so it will finally stop.
But I learned long ago that won't help.
Nothing does.
Nothing except *this*.
A brush in my hand.
Paint on canvas.
Swirls of agony and ecstasy.
Of shared pain and constant anguish.
Misery and sorrow played out in each stroke of bristle

and splash of darkness that matches that which threatens to overpower me tonight.

Truth laid bare.

13

IVY
TWO DAYS LATER

The sound of Cam's motorcycle pulling up outside rumbles through the front window, and I drag my attention from the television and glance at the clock.

Nearly ten p.m.

What the hell is he doing here?

In the past few days, since our trip to Max's, we've fallen back into the same routine—him coming during the day while I'm at work and leaving to go to his meeting before I get home.

Which means I haven't seen him.

And that's probably for the best.

Because Camden Usher is so much more than he appears.

The man should be dangerous for a dozen different reasons.

Should be kept at arm's length.

He's hiding secrets.

He warned me away from him.

Yet, he's also the one who has somehow made me laugh again with simple stories and memories, who has ensured I'm eating by leaving me my favorite dinners every night, who brought me back from the brink of that abyss when he told me those words that Drew said.

When he *insisted* I believe them.

I glance at the still unopened box on the mantle, still hearing Cam's assertion replay over and over in my head.

"You were it for him."

That statement quieted one beast but left another roaring.

Then why did he lie?

I'll probably never know.

This gaping hole in my chest will never fill.

But at least Cam was able to give me *that* one little piece of comfort.

And maybe that's why he's here tonight—because he needs some.

I pad over to the window and peek between the blinds. Cam sits on the unlit porch with his back to the door, a cigarette dangling from his lips, the orange glow floating in front of his face.

He hasn't knocked. Hasn't made any move to come to the door and let me know he's here. Exactly like that first night.

If I don't go out, will he just leave?

I watch him for a few moments, taking a long drag off his cigarette and letting the smoke float out into the night air, but he doesn't seem inclined to move from that spot.

Almost like he's waiting for me.

Unsteady steps bring me to the door. I unlock it and open it, but he doesn't even turn to look at me as I pull it closed behind me and settle down on the step next to him in nothing but my sleep shorts and a loose tank-top.

"I wasn't sure you'd be up." His voice comes rough, uneasy, like he's carefully choosing his words, and that's somehow difficult for him in this moment. "I hope I didn't wake you."

"I don't sleep much, as you know."

Cam finally glances over at me, and there's a hesitant look in his eyes that sends a little shiver through me. Whatever reason he has for coming here at this time of night, he isn't sure I'm going to like it.

"What's wrong?"

He shakes his head. "Why does something have to be wrong for me to be here?"

I snort and rest my elbows on my knees, letting my hands dangle between them as I stare out at the empty street lit only by a few streetlamps farther down the road, leaving us plunged in almost total darkness. "Because you're usually long gone by now, and I haven't seen you in days."

He nods and takes a long drag off his cigarette.

Some of the tension eases from his body as he slowly exhales the smoke into the night air.

"Those things will kill you, you know."

A little snort accompanies his sad smile as he looks at it between his fingers. "This is the least of my vices." His eyes cut over to mine again. "I smoke so I don't put worse things in my body."

I cringe at his statement, suddenly imagining any number of horrible things he might have done when he was still using. "Your brother would tell you to quit."

He takes a long pull from the cigarette and releases the

smoke in a long, steady stream. "He told me a lot of things. Doesn't mean I always took his advice."

"Is that why you two weren't talking?"

Those brilliant blue eyes, darkened by the night and the demons Cam seems to carry with him, lock on me. "Drew and I had a lot of differences of opinion about how I lived my life."

It's the closest thing I've received to an answer about their rift. An opening in Cam's steel walls where his relationship with Drew is concerned. And I don't know when I'll ever get another one. If I don't press him now, I may never get what I need.

"Did he know you were using?"

He swallows uncomfortably and takes another drag off the cigarette, blowing the smoke away from me. "I'm sure he suspected."

Drew would have noticed something like that. Even with Cam living in London and them not seeing each other frequently, Drew would have known. He would have picked up on the little things Cam wasn't saying. Changes no one else might have picked up would have been glaringly obvious to his brother, especially with his medical training.

His warning that his brother was dangerous makes much more sense if he knew what was happening and understood that Cam was out of control.

And Drew wouldn't have let it just go on.

It wasn't in his nature to let someone struggle on their own.

He would have bent over backward to try to get through to Cam and get him help. And *that* certainly could have caused a massive rift if Cam wasn't ready and willing to accept it.

"Is that what you fought about?"

Cam glances over at me again, his clenched jaw ticcing wildly. "You're really not going to let this go, are you?"

I shake my head. "Should I? You were the most important people in each other's lives, and that got broken somehow. I'm just trying to understand it. Understand *him* better. Understand *you* better."

The hurricane spiraling in his eyes intensifies, the center focused squarely on me. "You don't want to know me, Ivy. It's better that you don't."

His warning hangs in the air between us, permeating it and making it somehow harder to breathe. The warm night breeze raises goosebumps on my skin that only seem to tingle more the longer he holds my gaze.

That's three warnings I've received now. One from Drew before he died, and two from Cam in less than a week. Yet, the thought of letting him walk away without knowing more, without understanding this man sitting beside me, makes my gut twist violently.

But he's still here, still sitting beside me.

"Did you come here for a reason, Cam?"

He nods gently, barely moving his head. "I've been here almost every day."

"I know."

"And every day I see that unopened box sitting on your mantle..."

My back stiffens, my breath catching.

He takes another drag of his cigarette that has almost reached his fingers. "I know what's in there, Ivy. What I don't understand is why you haven't done anything with him yet."

With *him*...

It's impossible for me to think of it being Drew. To

acknowledge that an entire person with such a big personality and beautiful heart can somehow be burned down to
just one tiny little canister of ashes. But that's the reality of it
that I haven't wanted to face, even though weeks have passed
since I received that delivery and Cam came into my life
with it.

Tears start to pool in my eyes, and I swallow against that
sob that seems to want to crawl up my throat. "I'm not sure
what to do with it, to be honest."

His throat works, his Adam's apple bobbing as he gulps
in a way that suggests he's struggling the same way I am with
this topic. "Do you plan to keep him on your mantle
forever?"

I shake my head. "No. That's not what he wanted."

Cam nods. "I know."

"Do you?"

He bobs his head again. "He wanted the same thing I did.
For the people we love and leave behind to celebrate our
lives. Not make monuments to us or spend their days and
nights obsessively staring at an empty vessel that isn't us
anymore."

His words slice through me violently, like he's taken a
scalpel and flayed me open with it. Stripped me bare by
saying almost exactly the same thing Drew once did.

The tear starts to trickle down my cheek.

More smoke curls from his lips. "I want you to come
somewhere with me."

"Now?"

He nods.

"Where?

With his gaze locked on mine, he inclines his head
vaguely east. "To the shore."

"The shore?" An image of the beautiful sandy beach Drew and I spent so much time on flashes through my mind. The bright sun. Warm skin. Drew's arms around me. Drew down on one knee... "But it's closed. It's the middle of the night."

Cam nods deliberately. "Which is why I came now."

"I don't understand."

He takes another drag off his cigarette and then drops the butt and grinds the toe of his boot into it, resting his arms on his knees. "There's only one place in this world he'd want to spend eternity."

Oh.

"You want to go spread his ashes in the water."

He nods cautiously. "I think it's the perfect place, but I'm pretty sure it's also illegal. Hence..." He motions to the dark around us. "A night mission."

I watch for any signs of humor that would suggest he's joking. "You're serious."

But Cam just nods again.

"Wow, you really don't give a shit, do you?"

A single black brow rises. "About what?"

"The law?"

He smirks. "I thought that would have been obvious by now."

I release an agitated sigh and run my hands through my hair, squeezing my eyes closed as I consider his suggestion.

Silence hangs over us, broken by a few crickets singing in the grass and the gentle swaying of the branches and rustling of the leaves on the trees that line the street.

"The longer you let him sit there, the harder it's going to be to finally let go."

I open my eyes and look over at him.

See the tension in his body.

The unshed tears shimmering in his eyes.

"Ivy, I'm not saying it's time to move on, because that's impossible. But those ashes sitting up there in that box are *not* Drew." Cam places a hand over his chest. "He's *here*." He reaches over and presses it against mine, the warmth of his touch seeping through my shirt and warming me from the inside out. "He's *here.*"

And he's right.

About that box.

I haven't even been able to open it.

Without Cam pushing me, I might sit there forever and stare at it, thinking about what's inside, clinging to Drew in a way he never wanted.

Even if I don't do it for me, at the very least, I can do it for *him.*

"Let's go, Ivy." Cam keeps his hand flattened to my chest, as if he's afraid pulling it away will somehow make me say no. "Let's go put him to rest."

It's those words that finally break me.

The tears trickle down my cheeks, and I nod, unsure if I'll even be able to say the single word that tries to come. "O-okay."

Cam slowly pulls his hand away, and I immediately miss the feel of it pressed to me, the heat and comfort he offered in our moment of shared grief. He pushes to his feet, then steps in front of me and reaches out a hand.

I slide my palm into his, allowing him to pull me up, but he doesn't release his hold. His thumb skates over my skin, sending a tiny shudder through me before he finally steps back, letting his grip fall away.

He clears his throat. "Put on jeans, boots, and a heavy jacket."

"Why?"

A smile plays at his lips, and he inclines his head toward the street. "We're taking my motorcycle."

"What?" I shake my head, panic immediately seizing my chest. "No. I've never been on one."

He snorts. "I figured. The last thing Drew would ever do is climb on a Harley." His smirk fills his eyes with humor. "Far too dangerous."

I can't help but grin, despite the anxiety threatening to crush my ribcage at the thought of actually getting on that death machine. "We can't take my car?"

Cam shakes his head. "I think this is the perfect way to go. Let him ride on a motorcycle *one* time, just to know what it feels like."

My heart cracks wide open as I see the beauty in it.

No matter my fears or Drew's while he was alive, something tells me he would take Cam's offer for exactly what it is —one final thrill. One final thing they can share. That we *all* can.

I nod. "Okay..."

We're doing this.

Cam scans me over one more time, as if he's ensuring I'm not going to bolt instead of climb onto his bike. "Go get changed." His eyes flick up to the window of the living room. "I'll get him."

Good.

Because I don't think I can do it.

I don't think I can reach up and grab that box again.

I'm not strong enough.

Maybe I never would have been strong enough to do this without Cam...

I turn away from him and move back to the house with his heavy steps following. He nudges the door shut behind us, and I pause at the edge of the living room and watch him approach the mantle.

He stops in front of it, feet spread wide, arms hanging loosely at his sides. Tattoos hidden beneath his leather jacket. He tilts his head slightly, staring at the box as if he's having some kind of private conversation with it, and I slip away into the bedroom, giving him a moment he likely needs.

I change into a pair of jeans, knee-high riding boots, and snag my leather jacket that I typically only wear in the fall from my closet, slipping it on as I step back out into the hallway.

The house is silent, and I cautiously move into the living room.

Cam still stands in the same position, staring at the box, but when he hears my approach, he glances over at me. "You'll want to tie your hair back."

"Okay."

I grab a hair tie from my purse and twist it into a loose ponytail. Out of the corner of my eye, I watch Cam grab the box carefully with trembling hands, as if he's handling something priceless.

Because it is.

To both of us.

He stares down at it for a few seconds, swallowing thickly and then squeezing his eyes shut. A minute passes. Another. Time seems to drag on as he processes the thoughts in his head.

My chest tightens looking at Cam holding that box. The way his head is dipped. His knuckles white clutching the cardboard. The tremble of his body. How his lips part slightly, as if he wants to say something but can't or won't.

I've spent so much time wallowing in my own grief, in allowing myself to drown in it, that seeing his and how closely it matches mine jerks something loose deep inside me. A sense of feeling *seen* and being able to see something in him that no one else does.

He finally looks up at me, his eyes watery, but he manages to keep his tears at bay. "You ready?"

For what?

My first motorcycle ride?

My first crime?

Or to say goodbye to Drew?

Even though the word "no" burns on my tongue, Cam's firm grip on the box and the strength and confidence he exudes as he approaches me cautiously prevents me from saying it.

I nod. "I am."

He gives me a soft smile, as if he knows I was about to answer differently. Because he always seems to sense what I'm really feeling, even when I do my best to hide it.

Stepping behind me, he shifts the box to one hand and presses his palm against my lower back, urging me toward the door. Offering me his assurance that we're doing the right thing, even when I'm not as confident that I can survive it.

But that steady hand keeps me moving forward. It stays with me while I open the door and step out onto the porch. It remains when I turn to lock it behind us and slip the key into my jeans' pocket and as we walk down to the street where his bike is parked.

The crickets continue to chirp. The branches and leaves continue to sway in the summer breeze. And I'm frozen in place. Not sure what to do.

Cam's touch disappears, and he steps around me to open his saddlebag. He pulls out a helmet and hands it back to me before carefully placing the box inside and securing it.

When he turns to me, he holds out his hand, and I take a deep breath before sliding mine into it. Squeezing gently, encouraging me through the thoughts that threaten to derail our plans, he leads me around the bike.

On the other side, he takes the helmet from me and settles it on my head, securing the strap at my chin. The corners of his lips tip up.

"What?"

His grin deepens. "It looks good on you."

My cheeks heat at the compliment, and he turns and swings his leg over the bike, settling easily onto it, looking like it was made for him, or him for it.

I chew on my bottom lip as I look at the space on the seat behind him.

We're going to be close.

Very close.

With Drew at my side.

Something about that just feels right.

It allows me to push away the remaining reservations.

Cam extends a hand, and I accept it, allowing him to help me slide my leg across the seat and settle behind him. He keeps his eyes on me over his shoulder. "Wrap your arms around me and hold on tight. Lean into the turns, and you'll be fine."

Somehow, I believe him, despite *everything*.

There's so much confidence in the way he says it. In the strength of his body pressed to mine. His unwavering voice.

I nod my understanding and wrap my arms around his torso.

He fires up the bike, and the rumble of the engine below me makes me jerk. His low chuckle fills the night, blending with the sound of the bike as he revs it. "Ready?"

His firm chest and abdomen ripple beneath my palms, and I bury my face against his back and nod. And it's all the confirmation he needs. He pulls away from the curb with my heart in my throat and my life in his hands...and in his saddlebag.

14

IVY

Warm summer air whips around us as we shoot down the Atlantic City Expressway toward the coast.

With my arms wrapped tightly around Cam, the miles fall away too fast to process.

And it feels like we're flying.

Really.

Truly.

Flying.

The single most exhilarating rush I've ever experienced.

Despite pulling back my hair, loose strands get ripped from the low ponytail and float around my face like feathers caught in the wind, tickling my skin. And the farther we move away from Philly, the closer I find myself shifting toward Cam.

I lower my head to press my cheek between his shoulders.

Smooth, warm leather slides across my skin, and I inhale

the scent that's all him, somehow heightened by the swirling wind as we cut across New Jersey toward the ocean.

My eyes drift closed, and the engine rumbling beneath us, his solid presence in front of me, and this strange sensation of floating melt away the tension in my body, despite what we're on our way to do.

For a brief moment in time, grief doesn't overwhelm me.

It doesn't rear its ugly, snarling head, trying to snap at me and bring me to my knees.

It doesn't gut me and make me feel like I can't breathe.

It quiets.

It floats on the wind like we do.

Cam reaches down and slides his hand over mine, where they rest on his taut stomach, entwining our fingers and squeezing. That simple gesture sends warmth flooding through my body, and I press in even closer, until every breath I take is all air and speed and Cam.

Now I understand...

This.

Why he loves it so much.

Why he wanted to do this for Drew.

Because it feels like *freedom.*

Freedom from all the questions. Freedom from all the pain. Freedom from all those agonizing things that were keeping me pinned in place, unable to move an inch in any direction without crippling me. Freedom from the blistering reality of life without Drew.

Time and everything else weighing me down disappear the farther we pull from Philly. The more I concentrate on the *feeling* rather than what we're doing, the easier it becomes to just *be.*

But it can't last forever.

And far too soon, Cam pulls his hand away and slows the bike.

The road's almost entirely deserted, as the highway was for most of our trip, and by the time we pull up to Strathmere Beach and I lift my head to scan our surroundings, it's a ghost town. No one on the streets or sidewalks. No one on the sand. The rumbling of the engine as we pull into the tiny beach town seems to echo off all the concrete, combining with the rushing of the waves only steps away.

And it's stunning.

Clouds billow in the sky, threatening another summer storm, but the moon peeks out from behind them, doing its best to break through and illuminate the night.

Cam pulls to a stop near one of the beach entrances and kills the engine, knocking down the kickstand. The sudden change from flying to coming back to Earth makes my head spin momentarily. But the smell of the ocean and the peacefulness of the night settle over me quickly.

He tugs off his helmet and hangs it from the handlebar, then glances over his shoulder at me. "You good?"

I nod, releasing a long, steady breath. "Yeah, that was..."

The corner of his lips curls as he offers me his hand to assist me off the bike. I gladly accept it, and the second I get on my feet, I wobble. His other hand shoots out to grasp my hip, keeping me steady.

He smirks, amusement dancing across his eyes. "It can be a little hard on the legs the first time."

They feel like Jell-O underneath me, still vibrating from the feel of the engine between them and the thrill the ride gave me. "You're not kidding."

He grins as he climbs off while still managing to keep one hand on me to keep me from face-planting onto the pavement. "Just give yourself a minute. You'll be fine." His gaze flicks up to my helmet. "Let's get this off."

I reach back and grab the seat to keep myself steady as his fingers slide to the buckle under my chin and unstrap it.

He tugs it off my head and examines me, tucking a stray strand of hair behind my ear with so much tenderness that my chest aches. His scrutinizing gaze scans my face like he's looking for more than only if I physically survived my first ride. "You sure you're good?"

Am I?

My legs don't tremble as badly, and I slowly release my death grip on the seat to fully support my weight on them. But that isn't really what he's asking. I nod regardless, unwilling to give up the last vestiges of that flying feeling to have to focus on the task in front of us. "Yeah."

That was exhilarating.

A rush I never thought I would feel.

With how Drew always talked about motorcycles being absolute death traps, I probably never would have climbed on one if it weren't for Cam. Never would have gotten to experience *that.*

The way my heart seemed to beat in time with the motor and his under my hands, the way the wind whipped around us, blowing away all my thoughts and letting me just *be.*

Drew didn't know what he was missing...

But Cam managed to give it to me—and him.

A final farewell ride.

Cam retreats and hangs my helmet on the other handlebar, then opens the saddlebag and pulls out the box with shaking hands. All those magical feelings that overwhelmed me during our ride here vaporize the instant my eyes land on it.

Something lodges in my throat, making it difficult to swallow.

A vise tightens around my chest.

The legs I was so sure were stable now start to tremble again.

That strength I was so sure I had to follow through with what we're about to do vanishes as quickly as the tide washes away a grain of sand from the shore.

And I'm tumbling again.

Down.

Down.

Down.

To that dark place where nothing can reach me.

Black spots form at the edges of my vision as Cam reaches into his boot and pulls out a knife that he uses to cut the box open. He pauses for a second, staring down into it where it rests on the seat. His shoulders tense, his entire demeanor shifting as the air seems to cool around us.

Time ticks by slowly now.

With each second that passes, we seem to be more lost in our own thoughts and memories.

The last time I was here with Drew...

Bright sunshine and warm breezes.

Pale sand and crisp waters that we sank into together, wrapped in each other's arms.

Tears slide down my cheeks, and when Cam finally looks up, they glimmer in his eyes, too.

He returns the blade to his boot and lifts the box with shaking hands.

This was never going to be easy. We both knew that and

accepted it. But now that we're finally here, about to do it, it feels like being punched squarely in the gut.

I try to draw in a breath, but it catches on a swallowed sob. Still, I force my feet to move, to step forward and reach into the box to pull out the small metal urn that holds all that's left of Drew.

My eyes keep burning. The tears keep falling. And I want to blame it on the wind whipping into them during the drive, but it would be a lie.

This is it.

There isn't any turning back now.

This is what Drew wanted.

Not to sit on the mantle or a shelf somewhere.

This is where he belongs, and he deserves that.

I can't let my own grief hold me back from giving it to him.

Cam steps past me, over to a large garbage can, and tosses the box in. Then he shoves his hands through his hair as he returns to me, clamping his jaw tightly like he, too, is trying desperately to rein in his emotions.

Given the darkness overtaking his eyes and the way his entire body trembles, he isn't doing much better than I am...

He inclines his head toward the beach entrance but doesn't move toward it himself. Instead, he waits for me, watching as my gaze darts between him and the urn in my tight grip. "You ready?"

I shake my head, swallowing a knot of anguish stuck in my throat. "No."

How could I ever be ready to say goodbye to Drew?

He was my life.

My heart and soul.

My everything.

Which means *everything* is wrong now.

Nothing feels right anymore.

And maybe it never will again.

Cam offers me a sad half-smile that's filled with his own pain but somehow manages to ground me, too. It reminds me that he's suffering just as badly as I am. That I'm *not* alone in any of this. And that this is the right thing to do.

He holds out a hand.

It's the lifeline I need to move.

Shifting the urn into the crook of my right arm, I slide my palm against his. Rough callouses scrape across my skin, sending a little shiver and goosebumps pebbling over it. He squeezes gently, then starts walking, essentially forcing me to move, despite the fact that my legs don't seem to want to move.

A thousand things I want to say to Drew race around my head, but there aren't enough hours in my lifetime or words in the English language to truly encompass them all.

Our boots fall heavily on the wooden boardwalk, and Cam moves straight past the sign indicating the beach has been closed for hours, the emptiness of it swallowing us up the farther we walk until our boots move from wood to sand and sink in.

He leads me straight toward the water without hesitation, without any of the reservation trying to hold my heart back, and I let him. Because he's right. If I had left this urn sitting on that mantle, it would have controlled me. It would have run my life for as long as it was there. I would have stared at it day and night, thought about what was in it, tortured myself with what-if questions.

They'll still be there, but *he* won't.

It's time to let him go, even if parts of me aren't ready.

I draw in a fortifying breath as we reach the lapping waves, the tide pulling at the grains of sand, trying to drag them out into the ocean.

Cam pauses short of the water, mere inches away, some of the stronger waves overtaking the steel toes of his boots. He glances at me out of the corner of his eye but then returns his attention to the water, to the way the bright moon overhead, breaking through the clouds, reflects off the incoming swells.

They roll toward us effortlessly and crash at the shore, then lap up near our feet, the constant push and pull of the water starting to lull some of the anxiety tightening my chest.

"He always loved it here." Cam's voice fills the night air, weighed down with so much pain I can feel it throbbing in time with my own. "Our dad brought us here, too. Our grandmother lived a few miles north of here."

I nod slowly. "Drew told me. He said you spent most of your summers out here."

Cam continues watching the water, the corner of his lip tipping slightly. "We built sandcastles, buried each other up to our necks, tossed Frisbees and chased each other, threw each other into the water. It was...perfect."

"I think that's why he brought me here..."

My voice wavers slightly, and I swallow through the sob that threatens to slip out, remembering our first time walking onto this very beach. Cam squeezes my hand tightly, offering me his strength as the memory assaults me, so beautiful and painful at the same time.

"He told me how special it was to him. To both of you. We came whenever we could, but with his schedule, it wasn't enough."

Not nearly enough.

I needed more time with him.

If I had known how soon he would be gone, I would have done *anything* to spend every waking moment with him. I wouldn't have thought twice about selling Buds & Blooms to ensure nothing took a second of our time together and that each one was filled with telling him how much I loved him.

But now, it's too late...

Cam scans the sand around us. "He proposed here."

"Yeah, he did." My eyes automatically drift down the beach to the exact spot—the one captured in the photo framed on the end table in the living room that was snapped by one of Drew's friends who was in on the whole thing. I tear my gaze from down the beach and peer up at Cam. "Thank you."

His eyes cut over to mine. "For what?"

Releasing a heavy breath, I try to sort through the jumble of emotions threatening to consume me. "For bringing me here. You're right, I never would have done this on my own, and this is the only place that makes sense."

Cam's jaw locks, his lip trembling as if he's fighting the same way I am to keep himself together, and he gives me a simple nod. Maybe because he doesn't trust himself to actually say anything.

I'm not sure I do, either.

Because I have no idea *what* to say, what words could possibly be enough for a goodbye.

But I have to *try.*

I tug my hand from Cam's and step forward until the water touches my boots. The moon reflecting on the waves sends a column of light stretching from far offshore into the beach, almost like a cosmic highway calling me to step onto it, to *run* down it if I want to get to Drew.

And I'm tempted.

If Cam weren't with me, my feet might have moved farther into the water.

I might have let it lure me away from the safety of the shore.

But not with Camden here.

Not with his arm brushing against mine.

Not with the breeze bringing his citrusy, leathery scent into each breath.

He's a reminder that I'm *not* alone, no matter how much I may feel that way.

I inhale deeply, then let it out, squeezing my eyes closed, tightening my grip on the urn. Drew's face fills my mind, that lopsided smile he gave me that always made my blood heat and heart melt for him. The feel of his hands on me, his body sprawled across mine. His kiss and the way it always washed away the world around us and ensured my entire focus was him and the way he loved me.

Whatever secrets he had will probably always stay that way, but he never withheld his love from me, and I'll cling to that, use it as a life raft when it feels like I'm floating in the black, fathomless ocean of pain.

How do I say goodbye to him? How do I let go of everything we had and all the promises for the future?

Anguish rushes over me like a wave crashing onto the shore where we stand, but unlike those lapping at our feet, this one threatens to drown me. To drag me down into that dark void where I can unleash it all and let it consume me at the same time.

My knees start to buckle, but Cam slides his arm around

my waist. Holding me steady. Giving me his strength when all of mine is gone. Sharing my despair and reminding me that he's still right here. Right where I need him to be more than I'll ever want to admit.

I force myself to swallow through the sob lodged in my throat, to get out some words even if they're the wrong ones. "I love you, Drew, and I hope—"—I choke out a ragged breath—"I hope that wherever you are, you know that I always will."

It's all I can say before the tears and sobs completely take over.

Cam tugs at the lid of the urn and gets it free, but I can't look into it.

I can't see Drew that way. It would break me even more than I already have been. I have to keep seeing him the way he is in my head, how he looked that night before he left the house, smiling down at me in the bed as he made love to me and made me unravel in his arms.

Cam's hand shifts around the edge, sliding over one of mine, his warmth engulfing it and stopping the trembling. I open my eyes and peek over at him instead of what's in our hands, locking my gaze with his tormented, dark-blue one. His face bears the evidence of his tears, the lines they left on his cheeks reflecting the moonlight.

He gives me a simple nod, then we tilt the urn and release the ashes.

The light breeze immediately catches them, and despite my reservation about looking at the contents of the small container, I turn to watch them float into the water.

They disappear into the churning waves at the shoreline, and something inside me snaps.

That last little string that tethered me to the hope that

this was all some awful nightmare I might wake up from someday.

That delusion that he might walk back through that front door.

That fantasy that Drew wasn't gone.

It vanishes with the last of his ashes.

15

CAM

I stare at the water.

The dark waves crash against the shore as the ocean starts to surge with the incoming storm that threatens to steal all the moonlight with each passing cloud.

Ivy turns into me, burying her face to my chest as her sobs rend the night air.

Hot tears slide down my cheeks.

But I don't try to stop them.

I couldn't even if I wanted to.

He's truly gone now, ripped away and scattered by the tide, taken from the person he loved most in the world, who now trembles in my arms.

Red-hot anguish sears through me, threatening to consume me and burn me down to ashes like those we just scattered.

And I want to let it.

Goodbye, Drew.

16

IVY

Cam kills the engine, plunging my street into utter silence.

This early in the morning, nothing is stirring. No vehicles. No people. Even the summer crickets aren't chirping, quieted by the coming dawn, or our loud arrival scared them away.

I scan the neighborhood Drew and I loved so much.

The towering trees along each curb, the ones nearest the streetlights casting leafy shadows onto the pavement. The quiet homes lining each side of the street—all dark, their residents fast asleep in their beds. Husbands and wives snuggled together. Children tucked in with kisses and fairytales. All sweetly oblivious to the turmoil brewing inside me just outside their closed doors and windows.

It's so peaceful, so perfect.

Then my gaze lands on my house.

With the porch light off, it may appear like the rest of them—a place where a happy family slumbers undisturbed by the turbulence of the world outside—but it doesn't *feel* like they do.

Not to me.

Not when I know how *empty* it is inside.

Not when no one is waiting for me to crawl into bed with them.

No one is there waiting to hold me.

Nothing but cold sheets and another sleepless night without Drew waiting for me behind that door.

And the ride back from Strathmere has left me shaking in a way that has nothing to do with the thrill of being on Cam's bike.

It's a cataclysmic crash.

A full-blown collapse of my ability to remain strong or pretend that everything will be okay.

The tears at the beach were merely a fraction of what I've bottled up inside me, and as it vibrates under my skin, seeking release, I know that if I'm alone tonight, it will be with intrusive thoughts and suffocating grief.

And I'm not sure I'll survive it.

Not alone.

Cam glances over his shoulder at me, holding out his hand to help me off while he searches my face carefully, taking in every detail and cataloging it behind his darkened eyes. I slide my palm into his and swing my leg over until I'm standing on the pavement beside the bike on shaky legs.

He starts to pull his hand away, and all the air rushes from my lungs on a panicked exhale as I tighten my grip.

One of his brows rises. "Ivy?"

My bottom lip trembles, and I stay standing through sheer will alone on knees that want to buckle. I don't want to need this. I don't want to need *him.* I want to be strong enough to walk through that door myself and spend the night alone, the same way I have every night since Drew died.

But I don't have it in me tonight.

I just can't.

"Will you..." I swallow through my suddenly dry throat. "Will you stay...for a while?"

I hate how needy I sound.

How helpless.

Cam's entire body tenses, the leather of his jacket creaking as he rolls his broad shoulders, his hand still clasped tightly in mine. "Ivy—"

No!

I can see his reservation.

The hesitation in his gaze.

"Please. I just"—I shake my head, willing the tears to remain at bay—"don't want to be alone right now. I don't think I can be. I don't trust myself to be..."

Not after what we just did.

I don't say those final words, but I shouldn't have to.

Cam was there to watch me crumble on that beach.

He witnessed my devastation.

Held me through it.

Helped me remember how to breathe.

Assured me that things would get better when, in that moment, it felt like it never would.

So, he *knows* how I'm feeling.

He *understands* what I'm saying without voicing the words.

Cam watches me for a moment, his gaze locked with mine so long that I almost get lost in the murky-blue waters that swirl with reservation and uncertainty. "Okay..."

Despite the clear hesitation in his acceptance, relief rushes from me on a heavy breath.

I slowly release his hand—not fully trusting my legs—and step back, giving him room to climb off the bike as I brace my hand on the seat. He does it tentatively, his jaw tight, shoulders tense, and pulls his helmet from his head, shaking out his thick, dark hair.

He approaches cautiously, lifting his hands to release the strap on mine, carefully removing it. Then he tucks it into the saddlebag and turns to face me again.

Tension rolls off him, along with an uneasiness I haven't felt from him since the first night he showed up on my doorstep. When we were total strangers.

So much has changed between us since then.

We're...

Friends?

I'm not sure that word fits, but nothing else seems to, either.

With everything we've shared with each other, the harsh reality we're both living in with Drew's loss, we should be friends. Yet, he's still keeping secrets. Things that could help give me answers about those lingering questions that keep me awake at night.

But tonight, I don't need them.

I just need to *not* be alone.

To be with someone who can understand how I feel right now.

And he's the only person on the planet who does.

Cam follows me up to the house, and I dig the key from my pocket and unlock the door, pushing it open to the emptiness I knew I would find.

So different from how this space once felt.

It was our haven, where we planned our lives together, laughing and loving.

Tonight, it's quiet.

That spark *gone.*

All that love and joy sucked away the moment his heart stopped beating.

I used to walk in and feel mine swell.

Now, it's merely an empty void in my chest.

This is why I didn't want to be alone.

I *couldn't* be alone.

My eyes move to the now-empty mantle, and almost instantly, they burn with the threat of tears I thought I had completely cried out at the beach.

Cam closes the door behind him, shrugs off his jacket, and drapes it on the chair he sat in that first night he came. He runs his hands through his already disheveled hair, the thick locks falling over his forehead and curling at his temples as he slowly lowers himself onto the couch and spreads his arms across the back.

I peel off my jacket and lay it over his, trying to keep my gaze from drifting to the mantle. "You want something to drink?"

He shakes his head, his eyes going to exactly that spot. "I'm okay."

I am definitely *not.*

My knees tremble, and I grasp the armrest of the couch, using it to help me sit beside him.

His eyes lock on me, taking in every movement, assessing me in that piercing way he always does. As if he's trying to catalog each minute detail for later reference.

The scrutiny heats my skin, and I stare at the empty fireplace rather than at him. But it isn't long before my eyes drift up to the mantle where the box sat—its presence massive even though it was small enough to rest there unobtrusively.

It only occupied that spot for a few weeks, but its absence has hit me almost as hard as the news of Drew's death did that night I got the call from Nancy.

And the longer I look at it and see the empty spot, the harder the reality of what we just did hits me.

He's really gone now.

All of him.

My chest tightens, squeezing relentlessly until I can barely breathe, and a sob I didn't know I still had left in me falls from my lips, breaking the silence of the house I was so scared of.

"Shit, I'm sorry..." I bury my face in my hands, the tears flowing down my cheeks and dampening my palms. The hiccupped sobs rip from my chest, and I try to breathe through them. Try to rein it back in. "I-I thought it would be better."

What we did tonight was the right thing to do.

What Drew would have wanted.

So why does it feel so wrong?

Cam shifts beside me and settles his hand on my back, rubbing gently. "I'm sorry, Ivy." His voice sounds gravelly, as if he is struggling the same way I am, just doing a much better job at hiding it. "I honestly don't know if it ever will get better, but what we did tonight..."

I lift my head and meet his gaze. His blue eyes swim with concern and a dozen other emotions I can't distinguish.

"It had to be done. For *you* and for *him*."

For you and for him...

Those words batter against my skull, and I know he's

right. Deep down in my gut. But my heart doesn't seem to want to agree.

The memory of watching the ashes float away in the wind and disappear into that dark water clutches my chest so tightly I struggle to drag in air. "I just don't..." I fumble with my words, unsure how to explain the suffocating sense of uncertainty and loss overwhelming me. "I don't know what to do without him."

No answer has come in the weeks since he died.

And it feels like one will *never* come.

Hiccupped sobs overwhelm me, stealing my ability to speak any further. And there isn't anything left to say, anyway.

This agony won't ever dissipate.

This loneliness and hollowness are my new normal.

This is my new life, even though it doesn't feel like living at all.

Cam slides his hand from my back to around my shoulders and reaches over to drag me up onto his lap, wrapping his arms around me and allowing me to bury my face against his neck.

He holds me to him tightly.

Keeps me from shattering.

Offers me his strong body to give me something to cling to when it feels like I'm free-falling.

Leather and citrus fill my labored breaths, each one so painful that I want them to stop.

I want all of this to just *stop*.

Cam's warm breath flutters over me as he presses his lips into my hair, his arms securely gripping my trembling body. "You keep doing what you have been doing, Ivy. Making it through each second, each minute, each hour, each day. That's all you can do."

His voice doesn't waver.

His hold doesn't yield.

His confidence in his words as steady as the man who said them.

I pull my head back and look at him in the moonlight streaming in through the front window. His hooded eyes hold so much pain, and yet somehow, they ground me because they also possess an profound certainty that I wish I could share. "You say that like it's so easy."

Cam shakes his head, brushing hair away from my face and swiping away my tears with his thumb. "It's far from easy, but it's all you can do. It's all *I* can do."

He isn't just talking about losing Drew...

It's how he lives his life now in recovery.

Day in and day out, he has to face the agonizing pull of his addiction.

And now he's lost Drew.

It's precisely the kind of thing that could drag him back into that dark place he fought hard to get out of.

He truly does understand it.

All of it.

My grief.

The gut-wrenching sorrow I feel every day.

And the gaping hole in my chest where Drew once was.

He's the only one who *can*.

This buzzing need to experience anything but pain that I've felt for almost two months claws at my soul, twists in my gut, vibrates through every nerve in my body as I stare at the man who looks so much like Drew but is so fucking different.

Darker.

Harder.

Full of secrets.

Tortured and tormented in a way I may never fully comprehend.

But he's been here for me since the moment he arrived on my doorstep.

Worrying about me.

Taking care of me.

Giving me a shoulder to lean on, to cry on.

Offering me strength when I didn't think I had it, even when he's dealing with his own issues, his own struggles and pain that terrorize him so severely.

A tear trickles down his cheek, and I reach a shaky hand to wipe it away.

My fingers drift over his stubbled cheek and down along his strong jawline.

I brush my thumb over his lips, and he shudders under me.

His eyes stay locked with mine, his gaze hooded and filled with a thousand warring emotions I share.

"Cam..." My voice comes out uneven, as shaky and restless as my body feels. "I..."

I don't even know what I'm trying to say. Don't understand why I can't seem to look away from him. Why my body heats the longer he holds my gaze.

All I know is I don't *want* to look away.

I shift on his lap, sliding my thigh across his so I can face him fully.

So I can *really* look at him.

A dubious darkness crosses his eyes as he stares at me, but it does nothing to dim their vibrancy or striking beauty.

They churn like the waves on the beach tonight. Tumultuous. Dangerous. Yet they somehow draw me in, make me want to dive headlong into their depths even without knowing what truly may lurk there.

His jaw tightens beneath the stubble covering it, and he lifts one hand to settle it on my hip.

Heat seeps from his palm to my skin.

And a warning plays in my head.

Don't.

The way Cam looks at me is saying the same thing.

Yet, I can't deny this pull, this warmth that's spreading through my body the longer I stare into his fathomless blue eyes, the more I see his anguish that matches my own. It's like looking in a mirror, and all I want to do is shatter it. Destroy his pain. Obliterate my own.

Any way possible...

The *only* way I know how.

I lean in and feather my lips across his.

His entire body stiffens, his hand going tight at my hip, the other curling into the leather of the couch with a creak.

But he doesn't pull away.

Doesn't do anything but remain frozen in place, his gaze still locked on mine with that same searing intensity.

I kiss him again, harder this time, pressing my mouth fully against his with clear intention. Not tentatively but with enough reservation for both of us, giving him every opportunity to stop it.

Cam isn't the type of person to do anything he doesn't want to.

And if he doesn't want this, he will end it before it goes any further.

His chest rumbles with a groan, those fingers digging in

even farther on my waist, and my body thrums back to life, heating everywhere after only the barest of brushes of our lips and the heady reaction to my kiss.

"Ivy"—my name comes out as a mix of warning and plea against my lips—"you don't want this..."

The ragged waver in his voice matches the unsteadiness of my heartbeat.

I rest my forehead on his, closing my eyes and sliding my hands from his shoulders up his thick, corded neck and into his hair, holding him in place while my head spins in a thousand different directions.

He's probably right.

I probably don't *really* want this.

And it's probably a horrible idea.

But it's the most alive I've felt in months.

With my body pressed to his. His heart beating rapidly against my chest. My lips floating across his, and that taste...

God, he even tastes the way he smells.

Like something rich and sumptuous, yet somehow bright and fresh with promise, even as the darkness that always seems to envelop him coats my tongue as I glide it along his lips.

Cam groans, his body still locked up tight, but his cock stirs between my legs, and I shift along it, settling myself more fully onto his lap. His other hand lifts from the couch to tunnel into my hair, and for a second, my heart stops, thinking he's going to force me away and end this insanity before it really starts.

He holds me still and pulls back slightly, his eyes searching mine as uneven breaths fall from his parted lips. The heat I see blazing across his gaze matches that burning in my core and searing in my chest.

Another tear slips from my eye, and his gaze follows it down my cheek.

He lifts his hand from my hip to swipe it away.

He's going to stop this.

I can see it in the way his hand trembles and the uncertainty in the way he looks at me, but all I can think about in this moment is how alive I'll feel. How *good* it will feel. And how badly I want to just feel *anything* but this agony I've lived in for weeks, and weeks, and weeks.

This is what I need.

No matter how wrong it might be.

No matter how many reasons there are to stop.

So, before he can try to talk me out of it again—or I can talk *myself* out of it—I crush my mouth to his.

No hesitation this time.

The type of all-consuming kiss that tells him exactly what I want and how I feel in this moment so he can't possibly doubt it.

He issues another throaty groan, his grip on my hair tightening, and his other hand falls back to my waist, trying to hold me still, but I can't stop my hips from rolling over his hard length.

"Fuck..."

A single word muttered against my mouth is our undoing.

His lips move over mine. Our tongues clash. Souls collide in a way they only can when something so wrong feels so damn right. When two people come together with a shared, pulsating need that can't be stopped even by stark reality.

I move against him, hungry for that friction that sends

little spirals of heated pleasure spreading out through my limbs.

So.

Damn.

Good...

It's been so long since I've felt *anything* good.

And this is exquisite torture.

My body buzzes, swimming in the feeling, drowning in his lips devouring mine and his hard body beneath me. I thread my fingers through his hair, the thick strands so damn soft under my fingertips as I angle his head and adjust my position so that the head of his cock, encased in his jeans, rubs my clit with each grind of my hips.

A guttural groan rumbles in his chest, his hands tightening at my hips and around the tendrils of my hair clenched in his fist.

"Please..." The word tumbles from my parted lips, so needy and desperate I barely recognize the sound of my own voice. "Please, Cam."

His mouth presses to mine greedily, but he shakes his head, a battle waging inside him that he can't seem to quell. "Ivy, we can't." He gasps in a ragged breath. "We can't..."

"Please." I kiss him again, pushing all my anguish and need into the act. "Please. Please."

I don't stop my hips, and he doesn't stop kissing me, even after his half-hearted objection to the madness.

And this *is* madness.

The kind of powerful, thought-stealing attraction and need that eliminates any ability to think. All we can do is *feel.*

Those reasons this is so fucking wrong disappear in the cloud of lust now enveloping us.

It consumes our entire beings, each kiss more frantic.

Our clutching hands more frenzied. A feverish rush toward something we both need so desperately.

His hand shifts from my hip and glides forward to the waistband of my jeans. The brush of his calloused skin across my abdomen makes me twitch on his lap, grinding down even harder against his length, and he easily flips the button open and slides his hand inside.

Fuck...

The second his fingers find my slick core, I jolt at the contact, and he groans, so low, so deep it sounds almost painful. Rough fingertips glide up, brushing my arousal across my clit, and I buck in his hold, my hips moving faster, pinning his hand against his cock as I ride it.

Pleasure bursts through me with each of his expert ministrations.

He works me up.

Twisting me higher.

Coiling tighter.

And he slides a finger inside me as his thumb circles the apex of my thighs.

A gasp tumbles from my open mouth, and he captures it with another kiss, one that robs me of my breath and any semblance of control I may have maintained up until this moment.

My legs start shaking as he continues to devour me like I'm providing him with oxygen, giving and taking as I come apart completely. The orgasm slams into me so hard my vision goes dark before I see bright stars flashing across my lids.

My body jerks against his.

My hands tighten in his hair, tugging him closer as my mouth falls open on a strangled cry.

My pussy clenches his fingers as he continues to pump them up into me and circle and glide his thumb across my clit, dragging out my pleasure so long that my lungs start to burn from the lack of air getting to them.

Cam moves under me, his cock pinned beneath where his hand is shoved into my jeans. He groans, heavy and low, his hips jerking wildly, lips frantically seeking mine out to capture the last of my gasps, until I finally float down, and he sags back against the couch.

His hand still cups my core.

His fingers stay buried inside me.

He stills, and I collapse onto him.

A sob of relief falls from my lips but quickly morphs as something wrenches from deep in my chest.

Sorrow.

Anger.

I unleash it all along with the tears I didn't know I had left.

They coat his skin as I bury my face into his neck, and he pulls his hand free of my body and tugs me up against him fully, holding me to him as his tears join mine, and we both completely fall apart.

17

CAM

I'm sorry.

18

IVY

"Are you not hungry?" Nancy's voice pulls my focus from pushing my food around on my plate, and I jerk my head up and meet her concerned blue gaze that matches that of both her sons.

I force a smile, clearing my throat to relieve the tension there. "I'm sorry."

The same two words I found scrawled on the Post-it on the coffee table when I woke on the couch this morning. Covered in the same blanket Cam draped across me that first night. His scent still clinging to me and the taste of his kiss lingering on my lips and tongue.

Maybe that's why I can't eat anything.

Or maybe it's because the woman across the table from me has come to know me so well over the past several years, has become like a mother to me in the absence of my own, and I hate lying to her.

Not just about the fact that Cam is here in town, but about what happened with him last night.

If she knew...

God...

I cringe thinking about her reaction.

Even I can't fathom how or why it happened, and I was *there*. I was a very willing participant. And yet, I can't process it. I can't get my head around what I did. What *we* did.

I squirm under her assessment, as if she can somehow see the fact that I did something very wrong and very stupid with him less than twelve hours ago.

Very wrong.

Very stupid.

I swallow my nerves and force myself to take a bite of the chicken salad she prepared. Chewing slowly, I watch her watch me until I swallow and take a sip of my lemonade, but the citrusy scent only reminds me of Cam's, tightening my stomach uncomfortably. "It's good."

She smirks in a way that's so similar to her sons that I can see where they learned it. "You don't have to lie to me, Ivy. We've known each other long enough that I don't think you need to."

A tiny bit of tension releases from my shoulders and gut, and I offer her a real smile this time.

Because she's right.

I push my plate away and rest my hands on my lap so I don't fidget, something she would definitely notice, too, because I haven't been nervous around Nancy since the first time we met at her birthday party right here in this house. And one minute with this woman showed me exactly how Drew turned into such an incredible man—because he had a mother like *her*.

Kind.

Intelligent.

Strong.

Confident.

Dedicated.

Unrelenting in her focus to give her children a good life.

Between losing their father and fighting cancer, Nancy has had her share of hardships, but she's managed to weather each storm and come out stronger on the other side.

I'd love to know her secret.

Because right now, it feels like I'm failing.

And like she can see right through me the same way Cam seems to.

She takes a few more bites of her own meal and pushes her plate away, wrapping her hands around her glass. "I'm glad you could come join me for lunch today."

"Me, too."

I smile at her, but I can see the inky circles under her eyes, the lines around her mouth. She isn't sleeping, so maybe she isn't dealing with Drew's death as well as she makes out she is.

If she knew Cam was here...

My chest tightens, guilt slithering through me like a venomous snake releasing its poison. Because last night, after crying more tears than I knew possible, I passed out securely in Cam's arms, and got what was probably the most sleep I've managed in almost two months.

Don't think about why that might be...

I'd love to believe it's because I finally spread Drew's ashes, finally got *that* release as opposed to the one *Cam* gave me, but the way my body heats at the memory of his touch. How he played me like a goddamn guitar, his fingers moving over me expertly, working me up and making me explode with the kind of pleasure and escape from reality I so desperately needed in that moment...

Nancy narrows her eyes on me. "Are you feeling okay?"

Shit.

That heat spreads across my cheeks, and the poor woman probably thinks I'm about to pass out or something. I nod. "Yeah. I'm good. I promise."

She leans back in her chair, looking at me in a way that tells me she doesn't quite buy it. Those same assessing eyes Drew and Cam inherited roam over me. "You don't look like you've been eating or sleeping."

Or hiding it well, apparently.

I let out a shaky sigh, pushing my hands through my hair. "I have been, just not well."

Though definitely better since Camden's been leaving me meals, essentially forcing me to eat by bribing me with all the delicious foods I love and can't turn down, even when my stomach doesn't want it.

She offers me a tight smile. "If I'm being honest, I haven't been, either."

That admission from her takes me aback.

Nancy has always been such a rock for Drew and for me, so to hear those words from her brings a combination of relief that I'm not the only one struggling and concern for the woman I've come to love so much.

Tears start to well in my eyes.

I have to tell her what I did.

If I don't, I feel like I might burst.

"I, uh..." I bite my lip, trying to limit it to the necessary words and not everything that seems to want to spew out, including Camden's secret and my own new one. "I spread Drew's ashes yesterday."

Her back stiffens slightly, but she forces a smile and nods. "Good. Where did you do it?"

When he died, she made it very clear—despite my protests—that she wanted me to make that decision. To her, it didn't matter that the ceremony hadn't happened yet. For all intents and purposes, I was Drew's wife in her eyes, and it was up to me to determine where he spent the rest of eternity.

The only requests she made were that I didn't tell her when I was going to do it because she already said her good-byes to him and that I did it somewhere that meant something to him...and to me.

I think I succeeded in that.

"Strathmere Beach."

A single tear slips from the corner of her eye, and she bats it away and offers me a smile filled with so much affection it makes my own tears fall. "Good. That's how he would have wanted it. The perfect place."

I nod, fingering my lemonade glass even though the thought of drinking it makes my stomach churn slightly.

Will I ever stop smelling Cam's scent and remembering how intensely he kissed me last night? Or the way his body jerked and trembled beneath mine? Or how tightly he held me afterward as we both cried?

Wiping away my tears, I force myself to take another sip just to clear my throat. "He deserved to be there instead of in a box on my mantle."

Nancy gives me a sad smile and nods. "I'm glad you did it. I hope..." She draws in a deep breath. "I hope it gives you some sense of closure. Not on your love for him because that will last forever, but in terms of being able to move forward."

That's what *she* had to do with two young sons when her husband died.

She didn't have the luxury of falling apart and wallowing

in her misery the way I have been. Because she had Drew and Cam to take care of. She had to take on two roles and be everything for them. And she did it so damn well.

Her hand slides across the table and over mine. "If you ever need me for anything, now or ever, I'll be here. Always."

Drew said similar words to me so many times.

Promises that he would never leave me.

That he would *always* be there for me.

But he's gone...

And if Nancy knew what I'm keeping from her, it might change everything between us.

Just like what happened last night with Cam will with him...

I let my gaze drift over to the family photo of the three of them hanging in the living room off the kitchen. The same one I often caught Drew looking at in his office before he would try to hide it away from me, almost like he was embarrassed to be caught with it.

They look so happy.

Even Cam does, that anguish that lingers in his gaze now somehow abated in this picture.

I swallow my nerves, hoping I'm wrong in anticipating her answer to the question I'm about to ask. "Have you heard from Camden?"

She follows my gaze, and when I return it to her, she offers a tight smile. "He called a few days ago."

"Oh." I hold my breath, waiting for her to say that he admitted he's in town, that he explained his absence from the funeral, but instead, she releases a long sigh, pushes her chair back, and walks over to the counter to refill her lemonade from the pitcher. "Is he...okay?"

Nancy pauses with the carafe halfway raised, then sets it

down and turns around to face me, leaning against the counter, resting her hands behind her. "Honestly, I don't know. I never can tell with him. Drew was always so open and honest with his emotions, but Cam..." She shakes her head and releases an exasperated breath, staring out into the backyard where the boys played their whole lives. "It was always so hard to tell with him."

"Because he isn't emotional?"

Her head whips back, and she laughs slightly. "Sometimes I forget you don't know him." She offers a tight smile. "Cam is *far* more emotional than Drew and always has been."

"Really?"

I picture the man I know—or am getting to know—how quiet he is, reserved, shut off, always hiding and holding something back. Until he gives me these little bursts of insight, cracks in his armor where his emotions flood out so vividly they overwhelm him.

"Drew always wore his heart on his sleeve. He needed to talk things out. To have a hug and be comforted when he skinned a knee or was emotionally hurt. He thrived on human contact and relationships. That was why he was so good with patients. But Cam was more introspective. He was always in his own head and often got lost there for far too long."

Now *that* sounds like the Cam I know.

Always bottled up.

Struggling to control his demons.

Desperate to keep his secrets buried.

Nancy returns to pouring her drink and then retakes her seat, wrapping her hands around the glass as her eyes drift to another photo on the wall—of her with her late husband. "When their dad died, Cam completely shut everyone out."

"Even Drew?"

Her gaze cuts over to me. "Especially Drew." She offers a slight shrug. "Cam was a little copy-paste of his dad. Reserved. Introverted. Drew fell apart. He cried for a year straight, every night. But Cam..." She shakes her head, her eyes getting a faraway look as she delves into her memories. "He shut down, got quiet, turned in on himself in a way I didn't even know was possible for someone that young. And it only seemed to get worse as he got older, but I could always see it under the surface, you know? In his eyes."

I nod, because I *do* know.

I've seen it.

I've drowned in those eyes and was left gasping for air, my head spinning, not knowing what direction was up or down or what was right or wrong anymore.

She forces a swallow, tears shimmering in her eyes that look so much like theirs. "Cam could have done anything, been anything. I had them tested as kids, and his IQ was off the charts, even higher than Drew's." Her fingers glide over the side of the glass, wiping at the condensation absently. She shrugs. "But he just didn't care. His passion was all poured into his art rather than school." Her gaze lifts to meet mine, now shining with pride. "But Cam is an incredible artist. A true talent...I think because he feels more, cares more, loves harder than anyone I've ever met. He *sees* people and the world in a very different way that allows him to connect on a level even Drew couldn't." Her breath catches slightly as she fights the emotions trying to overwhelm her. "They were very different, but they loved each other deeply, maybe because of those differences. And that's why their falling out has been so hard for me to understand..."

It's the most she's *ever* said about Camden.

In all the years I was with Drew, the conversations were always led away from his brother. Fleeting mentions. Brief references. But this discussion is opening up a whole level of knowledge I never had about Cam. About how his mind works and why he carries so many secrets.

Because he always has.

Because he has always carried the weight of his emotions internally.

He has allowed them to eat away at him from the inside out—including whatever caused the rift with Drew.

"You don't know what happened between them?"

She glances up at me and gives me a tight smile. "I'm not entirely sure. Several months ago, Drew made an off-hand comment when I mentioned Cam that he was a 'selfish piece of shit.'"

I recoil slightly.

That doesn't sound like Drew.

He may not have been happy with his brother, but I never heard him speak about *anyone* that way during our entire time together. Drew was forgiving of just about anything with anyone, always looking for the best in people and situations. Yet, with his own brother, he was unwilling to bend. And apparently, he was relentless in his belief that he was righteous in his anger toward him.

Maybe he had a good reason.

Cam *is* lying to his mother even now, when she needs him the most. And prior to Drew's death, Cam didn't come home *once* in the entire time we were together. Four long years of never setting foot in his mother's home for a birthday or a holiday.

It's easy to write it off as being selfish, but knowing Cam the way I do, I think there's more to the story. He's been so selfless and giving with me that I can't imagine he would intentionally keep his mother at arm's length unless there was a very good reason.

Like his addiction issues...

He didn't want her to know.

The answer slaps me in the face, and I don't know why it never occurred to me before that he was keeping it from her —and probably from Drew as well. He already told me Drew suspected he was using, and if he had come home, Drew likely would have seen the evidence and been able to read his brother like an open book.

Coming home would have meant *admitting* he had a problem to the two people he loved most in this world.

My heart shatters for him.

For having to bear that burden all alone.

But Nancy has no idea.

If she did, she would have mentioned something—to Drew, to me. I would have *known* she knew.

"Do you think their rift had anything to do with the fact that he rarely came back from London?"

She gives me a soft smile. "Maybe, but I understood. Cam's studio, his business...when he's working, when he gets in that headspace, he kind of..."—she lifts one shoulder and lets it fall—"shuts down and blocks everything else out, including people, and anything else he cares about. It all takes second seat behind whatever he's working on."

"Isn't that kind of what all artists do?"

She laughs lightly and nods, pushing out of her chair

and motioning for me to follow her into the living room. "That's why it never really bothered me. Of course, I would have loved to see him more, loved for him to call more, but I also understood it. He has a life there. A business, friends..."

Something ugly twists in my gut.

Something that feels an awful lot like jealousy I shouldn't be feeling.

I trail after her, pressing my hand over my churning stomach. "Does he have a girlfriend?"

Her brow furrows as she stops in front of several black-and-white sketches Cam did in high school that Nancy framed and hung along with some of their family photos—the only time I've ever seen any of his artwork. "You know, I don't actually know the answer to that." She shrugs. "Maybe. Cam never had any problems in that department."

That doesn't surprise me at all, really.

There's something about Cam that just draws you in, makes you want to be close when he gives you every reason to move away.

I got caught in that trap far too easily.

Nancy stares at the stunning portrait of Cam's grandmother he did in charcoal and the landscape beside it showing the small house just miles from Strathmere Beach where they spent so much time with the woman.

Drew always said it was like a second home for them growing up.

But this is Cam's *real* home.

The place he belongs, even though he insists on staying away.

I swallow through my suddenly dry throat, glancing toward Nancy. "Do you think Cam will ever come home?"

She offers me the saddest smile I may have ever seen

from her and shrugs. "I hope so. I've prayed that he will, but I think losing his brother may have been too much for him."

"What do you mean?"

"I don't know." She places her hand over her heart, tapping it lightly on that spot. "Mother's intuition, I guess. I just have this bad feeling, that there was a reason he didn't come back. Something he didn't want me to know, didn't want me to see."

She doesn't know how right she is.

And I desperately want to tell her so she can help him, so she can reach out and maybe get him to open up to her about everything.

I want this chasm between them to close.

"Well, I hope he does come back soon."

For her sake.

It has nothing to do with the fact that I don't know what I'll do if he doesn't show back up at the house again. If I don't open the door after work and smell that leather and citrus scent permeating the air. If I don't find the little Post-it notes left all over. If I have to feel like that house is empty again without his huge presence. Because I can't want those things.

I can't want Camden Usher.

19

IVY

THREE DAYS LATER

I secure the cellophane wrap around the bouquet of stargazers and hand it off to the gentleman on the other side of the counter with the same smile I've been forcing for days. "There you go. I hope your wife enjoys them. Happy anniversary."

He grins, and the joy reflecting in his eyes as he thinks about going home to her with the flowers makes my heart stutter and my eyes well with tears I thought I had finally managed to control. "I'm sure she will, thank you again."

My gaze follows him as he weaves around several customers and exits the shop, but even after the door closes behind him, I keep staring at it.

Watching those little bells hanging above it.

Wanting them to ring.

Willing someone else to walk through it.

A *specific* someone.

The same person I've been waiting for the last several days, who has not made an appearance here or at the house, despite my stupid hope that he would.

But there hasn't been any sign of Cam.

That apology written on a Post-it note is apparently all he has to say about what happened between us. I wish I could so easily push it away and go on with my life as if nothing has changed, but the massive upheaval of the last couple of months has left me desperate for *something* that I thought—just maybe—I might have felt that night.

Which leaves me standing here, just as lost and alone, if not more so, than I was before we drove to the shore and said goodbye to Drew.

A throat clears behind me, and I whirl with my hands on my chest, heart thundering against my ribcage.

When did she sneak up on me?

Trina leans against the counter, her gray eyes locked on me, scanning me from head to toe with the kind of look only a woman who has lived seven decades can give someone. "What's up with you today, kiddo?"

Shit. How long was I staring at the door?

I swallow thickly, returning to the stack of orders in front of me to have somewhere else to look and something to do with my hands. "Nothing, why?"

"Because you seem distracted."

"Nope." I smile at her, doing my best to appear completely unaffected, like I've struggled to do for days. "I'm good."

Let it go.

Please.

But she won't.

The old woman has always seen too much.

Even when I was a little girl, running around here while Nonni and Mom operated the shop, Trina was always poking her nose where it didn't belong, interjecting her opinions and offering advice no one asked for. And she's had her eyes on me all day. Observing everything. Gearing up for this exact moment.

I knew the inquisition was coming; I just had hoped to have avoided it like I have been Marlo for the last several days.

Scheduling myself when I knew she'd be off.

Ensuring I'm busy with orders or customers whenever she tries to hunt me down.

That girl knows something's up as well as Trina does.

Marlo eyes me now from across the shop and motions to Trina to keep going, giving her a look that assures me they're colluding.

They're in on it together.

I should have known.

My shitty lying skills, combined with the way my mind has been seriously preoccupied the last couple of days, mean I *know* I haven't been myself. And they've both been watching me like a hawk since I came back to work. Always checking to ensure I'm doing okay.

They wouldn't have missed my wandering mind.

And boy has it been wandering...

To the way Cam kissed me.

To the feel of his touch.

To the taste of him on my tongue.

To the ecstasy and agony that combined that night to combust into something beautiful and oh so wrong.

But I am not about to have *that* conversation with my mother's best friend—or mine, for that matter.

Not yet.

Not when I still don't know how I feel about it. Not when my lunch with Nancy only brought more questions that I can't seem to wrap my head around, even days later. Not when I don't even know how *I* feel about the situation.

Instead of spilling all my dirty secrets, I force a smile. "Really, Trina, I'm fine."

"Mmhmm." She purses her lips, crossing her arms over her chest, giving me almost the exact same look Mom used to when I was trying to hide something from her. "Then how come you're staring wistfully at all the men who come in here buying flowers and keep watching the door like you expect Prince Charming to walk through it and sweep you off your feet?"

I gape at her. "I am *not* doing that."

She raises her white eyebrows behind her thick, black-rimmed glasses. "You *are*. This have anything to do with your almost-brother-in-law showing up?"

My back stiffens, and I do my best not to have a knee-jerk reaction and lash out at her. Because *that* would be a dead giveaway that something happened and that my current behavior is tied completely to the man in question. "What? No." I shake my head a little too vehemently. "Did Marlo tell you that?"

Her lips curl up into a knowing grin. "She didn't have to, sweetheart. You just did."

Dammit.

I walked right into that one.

Why can't I be a better liar?

Because this is something I can't lie to myself about.

Not anymore.

I never thought anything would occupy my head or heart

as much as how much I miss Drew, but somehow, what happened with Cam has taken up residence in both places. The two men have become twisted together, inexplicably entwined so tightly that I don't know that they'll ever come apart.

The irony of that isn't lost on me.

Nor is the absolute absurdity of thinking this could ever end well with Cam.

What we did...

It can't happen again.

It can't be what I think about at night, lying alone in my bed.

My body can't heat each time I remember how charged and frenetic it became or how wholly mind-bending my release was—

"Your cheeks are pink, girl."

Shit.

I turn away from Trina, willing away the evidence that I —yet again—fell down the rabbit hole of memories. "Did Marlo send you over here to talk to me?"

Trina huffs. "Why would she have to do that? She's your best friend. You would talk to *her* if you had something to say, *right*?"

The accusatory tone in her voice makes me bristle.

But her point has been well made.

Which she *knows*, given the smug half-grin on her face.

I give her a pointed look. "True, so...off you go."

She laughs as she walks away, back toward a cluster of customers she *should* have been assisting instead of giving me the third degree, which has left me more rattled than I care to admit.

My hands shake as I sort through the order slips, the names and details blurring together so badly that I can't even process them anymore.

Hell.

For all my intent to keep what happened between Cam and me a secret, it's eating me alive not being able to talk to someone about it. And when it comes down to it, no matter how much of a smartass or over-stepper she can be, Marlo has always been my sounding board where major life decisions are concerned.

And how I choose to address the Camden issue *is* a major life decision.

That man was supposed to be my brother-in-law. He was supposed to be *family*. If I fucked that up, if I fucked it up with Nancy by giving in to...whatever it was that made me kiss him that night. I don't think I could live with that.

That means I can't ignore Marlo—or *it*—anymore.

Swallowing my pride, I stalk across the store, headed directly toward Marlo, where she leans against the wall, apparently waiting for me.

With her arms crossed over her chest, she eyes me from my hair piled in a bun high on my head over my face, my smock, and down to my Chuck Taylors on my feet. "Finally going to acknowledge I'm here, huh?"

"Will you knock it off?" I cast a quick peek over my shoulder at Trina, who is busy with customers. "Enlisting that old woman to help you..."

Marlo cracks a smile and chuckles. "Trina is not some innocent bystander who got roped into a secret mission. She was perfectly willing to try to find out why you've been avoiding me."

"I haven't been."

She snorts. "Bullshit. You've barely said two words to me in three days, and while I'm used to you being quiet and sometimes short with me lately, this is something *else*, so spill."

Spill.

That's what I did that night at the beach.

I poured out Drew's ashes into the ocean and then dumped a tsunami of pain and grief squarely on Cam's lap. It overtook me so hard and so fast that it was impossible to stop it, and I let it drag me somewhere I had no business going. No matter how *good* it felt.

Grabbing Marlo's elbow, I lead her toward the back of the greenhouse, well away from prying eyes and ears.

She waggles her eyebrows. "Oooh, privacy! This must be juicy."

I scowl at her, and when we finally make it to our workspace, I release her arm, lean against the table, and heave out an annoyed sigh. "I need you to promise me no judgment."

"Oh." Her eyes widen, and she grins. "This *is* juicy."

She has no *idea.*

This is the kind of thing that ruins relationships and splits apart families, and I let it happen. I *pushed* for it when Cam was clearly torn and trying to do the right thing by stopping it.

If Nancy knew...

My stomach turns at the thought that I might lose her from my life when I need her in it so desperately.

And I don't even know *where* to start explaining everything that went down to Marlo without it sounding as awful and wrong as it actually was. Maybe there isn't any way to temper it. Maybe blurting out the ugly truth is the only way to move past this massive boulder of guilt and dread that seems to have blocked my path forward.

"You know that I went and spread Drew's ashes."

She nods. "Yeah."

That's *all* she knows.

I intentionally kept the details to a minimum and only told her I drove out to the beach where he proposed and spread the ashes because it was *time.*

Telling her anything else would have opened the door to questions I wasn't prepared to even think about, let alone answer.

Ones I'm not prepared to answer even now.

But keeping all this turmoil welled up inside will eventually do more harm than good. Deep down, I know that. It's just a matter of convincing myself that accepting Marlo's reaction and potential reproach might be worth it to get the release of what's festering inside me.

I chew on my bottom lip, pushing off the table and pacing as I twist my hands in front of me, trying to get the feel of Cam's thick hair off them, to get them to stop tingling, wanting to delve into it again. "Well, I didn't go alone."

"Nancy?" Her eyes widen when I shake my head. "Cam?"

Nodding, I tug out my ponytail and run my hands through my hair. My entire body vibrates with an anxiety built of a volatile concoction of regret, confusion, and need I still feel even days later. "We drove to the shore on his motorcycle."

"You *what*?"

I pressed my body against his for hours, held his hand, cried in his arms...

And that was only the beginning.

Yet, I find it more difficult to get those words out than I

had imagined it would be. Talking to Marlo has always been a way to unwind and get things off my chest. This is different, though.

The guilt over what we did weighs ten times as much as anything else I've ever experienced. So heavy that it's a constant weight crushing me. Making it impossible to take another step. Impossible to move forward, day after day, pretending it didn't happen.

"I wasn't exactly sure how to tell you..."

Without completely breaking down.

She gapes at me. "What do you mean? *Exactly* like you just did. When did you two do this?"

A vision of the dark, deserted beach, the moon peeking through the billowing clouds overhead, and the waves lapping at the shore flashes through my head, along with the feel of Cam's hand clasped tightly in mine.

"In the middle of the night so that nobody would catch us."

"Jesus, girl."

I cringe. "I know."

"And...?"

Stopping my pacing, I face her and find her watching me intently like a child waiting for the magician to finally pull off the big reveal. "And it was good. It..." My throat tightens on the words, not wanting to say them even though they're true. "It needed to be done. Staring at that thing was driving me crazy."

"I noticed."

And every time she came over, her eyes drifted there, too, like she couldn't look away from the unopened box. It held too much power over me. She and Cam both knew it well before I was ready to admit it and do something about it.

"I'm glad you did it, Ivy, but I don't understand why you didn't just tell me."

I chew on my lip again and return to my pacing. "Well, because..." *Shit.* "Um..."

"Whoa, you're kind of freaking me out."

"Sorry..." I shake my head, pressing my palms into my temples as the intrusive thoughts that have been bombarding me for days come back full force. "I don't mean to, it's just..." I glance around to ensure no one's close by, but all the customers are lingering at the front of the greenhouse or inside the main store and we're alone in this corner. The perfect place for me to spill my dirty secret. "Well, when we got back, I didn't want to go in alone, so I asked Cam to stay with me for a while."

"Okay..."

She watches me expectantly.

"And...I fell apart. I was sobbing and a real fucking mess."

Marlo nods, her gaze softening. "Understandable, given what a big step that was."

It was.

I can forgive myself for that part, for not being able to hold it together once I stepped back into the house where I built my life with Drew, but what happened *after* is eating away at me like a cancer to my heart and soul.

"And he pulled me onto his lap to hold me..."

Her blond brows pop up. "He *what*?"

Squeezing my eyes closed, remembering the feel of his arms around me, his chest pressed to mine, his strong body beneath me, his cock settled between my aching legs.

Shit.

I clench my thighs together against that dull throb that

always reappears each time I let my mind drift to that night. "And one thing led to another and—"

"Holy shit!"

My eyes snap open to find Marlo gaping at me.

"You two didn't..."

"God no. *No.*" I hold up my hands and shake my head. "No, we didn't, but we did kiss. And—"

"There's an *and*?" Marlo practically screeches, then slaps her hand over her mouth and scans the greenhouse before leaning closer and lowering her voice. "Ivy, what did you *do*?"

I wince, unable to look at her as I make the confession.

It feels like something I need a priest for. Like I should be on my knees, begging for absolution. Though I don't know if it exists for me, for what I've done.

"I may have...climbed him like a tree, gotten off on his hand, and made him come in his jeans."

"Are you fucking kidding me?"

This time, her screech carries through the greenhouse, and I quickly whirl to check on the customers. Several sets of eyes below raised brows land on us in the corner.

I plaster on a smile and wave. "Do you need help with anything?" They quickly return to whatever they were looking at, and I whirl to face Marlo again. "Will you keep it *down*?"

She places a hand over her chest, like she's trying to regain control of her breathing. "I'm sorry. I'm just a little shocked here. I mean, whoa." Her wide-eyed gaze locks on mine. "I. Mean. *Whoa!*"

"I know."

Whoa.

It's somehow the right word and the wrong one at the same time.

Because it was *so* much more than just *whoa*.

It was somehow the single moment in my life when something felt completely right and completely wrong equally.

Marlo rolls her hand in front of her, urging me to keep going. "So, what happened after?"

I cringe again, because the *after* was sheer agony. "We both cried, and I ended up falling asleep on him on the couch."

Her shoulders slump. "Well...that's depressing."

A resigned sigh falls from my lips. "No shit."

"What about when you woke up?"

Lifting my head from the throw pillow to find myself alone in the house and that note on the table isn't an experience I ever want to repeat. It felt like that gaping hole in my chest was ripped wider, like I had lost something *else*, even though it was never really mine to begin with. Something I never should have craved or touched.

"He was gone." I reach into my apron pocket and pull out the tiny piece of paper. "But he left a note."

She snatches it from my hands and examines it. "You've been carrying this around with you?"

I nod and try not to look at the two words scrawled across it.

I'm sorry.

But I don't need to be looking at it now to see it in my head.

It's seared into my mind, embedded so deeply that I won't ever forget it.

"Wow." Marlo leans against one of the counters, waving

the note back and forth in her hand. "This is heavy, Ivy. Like, *heavy* heavy."

"I know." I tug at my loose hair, practically ripping it out at the root with the need to feel *something* right now besides this spiraling confusion. "I don't know what to do..."

"Has he been back since then?"

I shake my head. "No, but there's been a food delivery at six thirty on the dot every night."

"He's still sending you dinner?" She practically swoons, pressing the note over her heart. "My God, Ivy. What have you gotten yourself into?"

"It's bad, right?"

Marlo tries to offer what I think is supposed to be a reassuring smile but comes across as more of a wince. "I wouldn't say *bad* but...complicated?"

Complicated.

"That seems like an understatement."

She snorts. "Do you...like him?"

This is why I put off talking to Marlo about this. Because I knew she would ask the hard questions. And this is the hardest of all of them.

One I've been asking myself for days, but sorting through my feelings for Camden Usher is almost as difficult as finding lilacs in the dead of winter.

Basically impossible.

"I don't know." I rest my ass on the edge of the table and close my eyes, trying to gain control over my conflicting emotions. "Everything with him is so wrapped up in Drew, and...I don't know how to separate my feelings for them. Or how to process what happened. Or how to know if any of it was real or just both of us feeling the same anguish and needing the connection with someone who understood it."

Marlo reaches over and squeezes my hand in hers. "Then, you need to talk to him about it."

"What?" My eyes fly open to meet hers. "No. I can't do that."

She snorts. "But you can let him stick his hand down your pants?"

Oh, Jesus...

I scowl at her, but she snorts a laugh and clamps down on my hand even harder, like she's *really* trying to make a point.

"Well, here's what I know, Ivy. We've been friends for what? Twenty years?"

"Yeah."

"And in two decades, I've only ever seen you this twisted up about *one* guy—Drew. And Cam and Nancy are all you have left of him besides your memories, so of course, you're going to feel a connection to Cam. I mean, he looks like him, he sounds like him. Even if he doesn't act like him, it would be impossible for you *not* to feel something there. But whether that's *real* or not, and whether it's a good idea or not, are very different and difficult questions."

I release a frustrated growl, tugging my hand from hers. "You think I don't know that?"

She slips the note back into my apron, giving me a knowing look. "This is going to drive you crazy until you talk to him."

As much as I'd love to stick my head in the sand and ignore what we did that night, the last few days have proven that's an impossible task. One I am apparently not at all equipped to handle.

Maybe talking to him would help.

Maybe I could figure out a way to deal with all these feelings if I sat down face-to-face with the man causing them and laid everything on the table.

"But he hasn't been over." I shake my head, exasperated by the entire situation. "I don't even have his phone number or any way to get in touch with him."

Marlo grins. "That never stopped you before."

20

IVY
ONE WEEK LATER

The old brick warehouse towers over me, mostly unlit and slightly foreboding from where I sit in my car at the curb, watching the door I saw Cam enter almost an hour ago now.

My knee bounces wildly under the steering wheel, and I chew on my lip until it hurts, continuing the debate that's been relentlessly echoing in my head as the minutes have slowly ticked by since I followed him here after his meeting.

Stalked him, really.

Again...

I shouldn't have done it.

If I were acting even remotely rationally, I would have just given him space and allowed him to come talk to me when he felt it was appropriate. But it's been almost two weeks since we spread the ashes, since he touched me like *that* and splintered me apart in the best and worst way. And Marlo's insistence over the last several days that I need to talk to him or I'll keep obsessing over it and torturing myself has proven true.

I can't take another sleepless night.

So, even though it's wrong, I still found myself driving down to where I found his bike parked for his meeting that first time, hoping it would be in the same spot.

I still waited until he appeared again, sticking a cigarette into his mouth and lighting it up as he stalked back to his ride.

I still sat mesmerized as he smoked it slowly, leaning against the seat, looking absolutely destroyed with his hair disheveled and his hand shaking until he smashed the butt on the sidewalk and rode away.

I still followed him through evening traffic to Frankford and watched him park his bike on the side of this building and go inside.

I did it *all,* knowing it was wrong.

Just like I knew it was wrong to kiss him the other night, to push him to act when I needed him to be something for me that he shouldn't have been.

He may have left me that note, but I'm the one who should be apologizing...for all of it.

For relying on him so heavily to get me through this when he's struggling himself, which I could clearly see tonight.

His eyes were dark when he came out of that meeting. His shoulders were tight under his leather jacket. His entire body seemed to vibrate with a barely restrained tension that he needed to release.

But whatever he's doing in this building, he hasn't come out.

And I haven't mustered up the courage to go in after him.

Night has fully fallen now, that last thin streak of light

dipping behind the horizon, casting an eerie, unnerving darkness onto the street and the buildings that line it.

I can't sit out here in my car anymore.

This might be my only chance to talk to Cam. My sole opportunity to make any sense of the madness that happened the other night and to apologize for my role in it.

And I can't pass it up.

My hand trembles as I pop open the car door, and I step out onto the street, staring up at the building. No one else has gone in or exited since Cam arrived, the windows all unlit, save for some on the top floor.

I cross to that side of the street and stare at the entrance. Flaked-off lettering on the glass door announces it as a textile manufacturer, but given the state of the building and the signage, I don't think that's accurate any longer.

So many properties in this area have been abandoned, left to rot away rather than anyone taking on the task of trying to save them until more recently. This building appears to have survived the worst that time attempted to do to it.

It stands straight and tall.

Worn.

A little rough around the edges.

But strong.

There's something almost charming about it, and I reach forward and try the door, which tugs open easily. Either Cam left it unlocked, or it never had a working one to begin with.

Goosebumps pebble across my skin as I step inside, instantly scanning the small vestibule for any evidence of where Cam might have gone and why.

Several hand-written signs taped to the wall and arrows pointing down a hallway indicate that the first floor is occupied by a ballet studio. The list of class times below it shows there will be a late class in about an hour—likely why the door was left open. The second floor appears to be occupied by a tech company that would be closed this time of night, if its hours of operation below the name are correct.

Which means Cam likely went to the top floor.

Music floats down the massive metal staircase to my left, and I take the treads up on shaky legs. The higher I climb, the louder the thumping notes and strong vocals become until I reach the third-floor landing.

Heavy steel doors stand slightly ajar in front of me, allowing the deep bass of the song playing from within to slip out to where I stand.

There isn't any signage to indicate what lies behind them or why Cam might be here, why *this* is where he fled to after his meeting, when he appeared so shaken and out of sorts.

Holding my breath, I inch toward the opening and peek inside.

Camden stands with his back to me, halfway across a vast loft space—shirtless, barefoot, his dark jeans hanging low on his hips as he stares down at something on the floor in front of him.

His shoulders and body are rigid as he tilts his head.

All the air rushes from my lungs at seeing him so tense, so intent on whatever his task may be.

Oh, God...

Whatever he's doing here, I shouldn't be interrupting him.

This was a bad idea.

I drag my gaze off him to turn back to the stairs, but a canvas against the wall near him makes me pause, then step forward instead of retreating. Even from here, it's breathtaking.

I'm drawn in by the soul-deep need to see more, to experience the type of beauty he's put on that canvas.

Cautiously, I turn sideways so I can slip in between the doors. And my eyes immediately scan the vast room, my jaw dropping as I take in everything.

Hundreds of paintings lean in stacks along the walls—in some places five or six deep.

All in black and white and varying shades of gray.

Landscapes.

Portraits.

Abstract images.

Statements about life, about the world, about people and the emotions they never want to talk about.

All of it laid out on these canvases with such precision and talent.

The sheer beauty and artistry covering almost every inch of the brick walls make my knees tremble as I move deeper into what is obviously Cam's studio.

With the loud music filling the air and his attention focused on whatever lies on the painter's tarps at his feet, Camden doesn't notice my approach.

But my gaze shifts from the works along the walls to the man responsible for them.

He squats and dips the brush into a tray of black paint on the floor, then leans over and drags it across a massive blank canvas in front of him. His muscular shoulders and back bunch and roll with every precise stroke, and he doesn't take any time before he is pressing the bristles down again and again. He grasps another brush from a tray of white paint, moving it with determined slashes. Like he knows precisely what it should be and where each drop of pigment should go in order to create the image in his head.

The movements become more harsh, matching the beat of the music.

Almost aggressive.

He streaks black paint across the canvas with such determined focus and power that a shudder rolls through me as heat fills my cheeks.

I shouldn't be watching this.

This is his work.

This is his space.

His *release.*

And I've just invaded it, uninvited.

What we need to discuss can wait.

I can wait.

But as I start to turn away, to try to slip out before he sees me, my eye catches a painting along the wall to the far left, and I freeze mid-step, a gasp falling from my lips precisely as the song blaring from the speakers in the corners of the room ends.

Shit.

Cam's head jerks to the side, and he looks over his shoulder at me as I do the same, tearing my gaze from what stopped my retreat.

His eyes widen slightly.

But I can't keep looking at him.

Not when *that* painting is standing there.

From the corner of my eye, I see him look away from me, dropping his head, resting his forearms on his knees for a moment before he pushes to his full height and turns from the canvas on the floor to face me.

The brush dangles from his right hand, black paint dripping from it onto the tarp at his feet, but he doesn't say anything as the next song starts up, merely watches me as I slowly approach the painting that made me stop.

The one I've seen dozens of times—because it hung in the Oval Office under the previous administration and was shown on television constantly in the background.

A black and white image of a smiling little girl holding a heart-shaped balloon.

My gaze dips to the signature on the bottom right of the canvas.

Cush.

The name flashes through my head, along with dozens of newspaper articles and internet blogs about the mysterious street artist who no one has ever identified. Stunning images that just appear painted on the sides of buildings. Canvases that create bidding wars at auctions...

My breath catches, and I shake my head slightly, trying to get my thoughts to form into anything coherent as I turn back toward him. "I don't understand."

He clears his throat. "This is...what I do for a living."

"Drew and your mom said you worked at an art gallery."

The corner of his lips twitches slightly, and he rubs the back of his neck with his free hand, his cheeks pinkening as if my question somehow embarrassed him. "That's half true. I own one in London that only features *my* work."

Holy shit.

His work.

His work.

This is *his.*

Camden Usher is *CUSH.*

I open and close my mouth a few times as my mind

continues to spin. "How did I not know any of this? Why didn't they or you tell me?"

He releases a little sigh. "I asked them not to tell anyone, so I could maintain my anonymity. And as to the second part, why I didn't tell you..." His shoulders rise and fall. "I don't know. It just...didn't come up."

It didn't come up.

I gape at him.

It didn't come up that he's one of the most famous artists in the world and that his art goes for literally millions of dollars.

The paintings in this studio alone are worth a fortune.

And they deserve to be.

My gaze sweeps over the stacks lining every wall, each canvas filled with something hauntingly beautiful in black, white, and grays. Every piece monochromatic. "Why don't you ever paint in color?"

We have far more important things to talk about, like the reason I followed him here in the first place, but now that I know who he is, what he's been hiding from me, I can't stop the questions from rolling out.

Cam hedges slightly, averting his eyes back to the canvas on the floor before they cut up to meet mine again. "Because I can't see it."

"Can't see what?"

He shrugs. "Color."

My mind races, trying to follow what he's telling me. "But Drew wasn't color blind..."

"No." Cam shakes his head. "He wasn't. And I wasn't born this way, either. When we were four, we were playing in the yard, and I fell. My head hit a large decorative rock in the garden. It caused cerebral achromatopsia, which basically means my brain can't process color signals anymore."

Every moment I've spent with Cam, every conversation I ever had about him with Drew and their mother, all of it flickers through my head. Not once did either of them mention Cam suffering a brain injury that affected his life so deeply. "How did I not know about this?"

He lifts a shoulder and lets it fall, offering me a sad smile. "Because I'm not Drew. It's not something you should have known."

His answer makes me stagger back a step, pressing my hands over my chest at the sudden flash of pain there.

Cam never wanted me to know him.

It wasn't just that Drew didn't want to talk about him. He *couldn't.* Because if he did, he might have let something slip that could have led to me discovering who he was—and hiding his identity, keeping that anonymity was the most important thing to him.

My head spins as I continue to scan all the various pieces he's painted that now stand almost haphazardly in this studio.

So many of them.

Many that I recognize.

A few that are so stunning, so poignant that I have to pause and swipe a tear from my eye.

I move toward the small kitchen in the corner of the space where a large number of paintings are clustered against the wall, and Cam sucks in a sharp breath, barely audible over the music playing.

And my footsteps falter again.

What the...

At first, it's just the flash of color that draws me toward one particular stack of canvases.

Bright red in a sea of monochromaticity.

But as I draw closer, my confusion only grows along with the tightness in my chest.

What?

This isn't just another portrait.

It's *me*.

My face turned up slightly, lips parted in invitation.

Bright red lips against the black and white paint.

But my gaze zeroes in on the earring I'm wearing in it— the peony.

A gift from Drew that I got to wear *once* before I lost one of the pair.

How could Cam have painted this?

I stare at it for a minute.

Two.

Long enough that another song starts, this one instrumental but with the same low, throbbing bass that Cam seems to like.

There's no way Cam could have *ever* seen me wear those earrings or even have any idea I owned them. And I wasn't wearing bright-red lipstick when we kissed the other night. I wasn't wearing anything but tear stains down my cheeks.

This *isn't* me from a few days ago.

This is me from a very specific night...four years ago.

I slowly turn back to him, my body trembling, mind still racing to make sense of it all. His jaw tightens as do his knuckles around the paintbrush he still holds.

"How did you paint this? How did you know?" I swallow the lump in my throat, trying to regain control so I can sort through all these things that don't make any sense. "Unless you and Drew literally shared a memory, there's no *way* you would have seen that and been able to recreate it."

He presses his lips together and inhales through his

nose, long and deep, letting his eyes drift closed, like he too needs a moment to try to find some sort of calm and control.

My knees shake. "That was the night—"

His eyes fly open and meet mine, a swirling maelstrom of uncertainty overtaking the blue. "The night of my mom's birthday party."

I nod hesistantly, holding out my hands as panic wells in my chest. "You weren't even *there*. I hadn't even *met* you. How did you..."

How?

That moment.

That *specific* moment.

No one else knows about it.

Not even Marlo.

I never told *anyone* about what happened that night.

The moment that changed everything between his brother and me.

Cam stands stock still and watches me, like he's anticipating my response before he even says whatever it is he's about to unleash on me. Goosebumps break out over my skin as I wait, and finally, he takes a half-step closer. "I was there that night."

"What?"

His throat works hard as he rubs his free hand through his hair, pushing it off his forehead and tugging on the ends before it flops right back into place. "I hadn't seen Andrew or our mom in almost a year, and I thought it would be a nice surprise. I checked into a hotel because I didn't want them to know I was in town, and I took a cab to the house. I wanted to sneak in through the back door and surprise them, but..."

I suck in a sharp breath.

He doesn't have to say the rest.

All the pieces are finally clicking into place.

Tears pool in my eyes. "But I was sitting out by the pool…"

A vivid memory of that night slams into me so hard that it's like I'm still sitting there.

The smell of the chlorine.

The slight summer breeze.

The side gate squeaking as *Drew* walked through it and closed it behind him.

The way his gaze drifted over me with so much heat. "That was *you*?"

21

IVY

FOUR YEARS AGO

Nancy's peal of laughter blends with the upbeat, lively music and voices of the sixty-plus people crammed into her home, filling my ears with the joyful sounds of a full-on rager. When Drew warned me that his mom's birthday parties were all-out, I definitely underestimated it, but she has reason to celebrate every single day she's on this planet after surviving cancer almost two decades ago.

And I'm glad Drew invited me.

Gave me this glimpse into his life and family.

Though, for the first time meeting his mom, this is a little...overwhelming.

Not to mention claustrophobic.

After three hours of revelry, my ears are ringing from the cacophony, and I need to get off my feet for a few minutes. Find somewhere quiet where I can get some fresh air, which is in short supply in the Usher house tonight.

I scan the living room, check the kitchen, and even wander down the hallway toward the bedrooms, searching for Drew to let him know I'm going to step outside, but I can't find him anywhere.

He's been running around, touching base with all their family friends to ensure no one needs anything and is having a good time. Playing the host with his mom and falling so easily into the role of the caregiver for everyone.

Exactly what he does day in and day out at the hospital.

And once he's completed his residency, that's where he'll stay. Right in the middle of the hustle of the ER because he's meant for *this*. Taking care of people. It's what he was born to do.

His warm, generous heart and caring nature shine through in everything he does, and he would bend over backward to make sure his mom—and everyone else here— has an incredible night.

So, I won't interrupt him.

He'll find me *eventually.*

My heart does an embarrassing little flip-flop in my chest at the anticipation of that smile spreading across his face, the way he brightens every time he sees me.

It's only been a few weeks.

Less than a dozen dates.

But tonight seems different.

And not just because I met Nancy for the first time.

The way Drew looked at me when I opened the door tonight—like I had stolen his ability to breathe—made my body and cheeks heat. Then he gave me the earrings, and I think all the breath may have rushed from *my* lungs the moment I saw them.

My fingers travel up to touch them at my ears now— peonies. Because he *remembered* my favorite flower and went out of his way to find these for me so I'd have something special to wear to the party.

Marlo thinks everything he's done since the moment I met him is swoon-worthy.

Just wait 'til she hears about this...

With a smile pulling at my lips, I make my way out of the sliding back door in the kitchen that leads to the backyard. As soon as I step out, the smell of the chlorine from the pool hits me, along with the scent of fresh wisteria and lilacs that line the fence around the yard.

I close the door behind me, sealing in the bulk of the raucous noise, and take a long, deep breath, already feeling better getting out of that madhouse for a few minutes.

The water ripples slightly in the light summer breeze, and I stare down at the bottom of the pool as I make my way to the back corner of the yard where a bench sits under a large willow tree that drapes down so low it almost touches the lush, thick grass.

Nancy really has a beautiful yard.

Nonni and Mom would have approved.

I settle onto the long wood bench and release a contented sigh. The light swaying of the branches creates its own melody, soft and sweet, relaxing as the stars start to wink in the patches of visible night sky.

A creaking sound from my left draws my attention to the front of the fenced yard as a gate swings open. Drew steps through it, latching it behind him. He walks toward the sliding back door I used to come out here, completely oblivious to the fact that I'm tucked away in this unlit corner of the garden.

"Did you need a break from that, too?"

He freezes mid-step and turns toward my voice,

narrowing his eyes in the darkness. Even from here, I can feel the potency of his gaze. The way it rakes over me with each deliberate step he takes, like he's memorizing every inch of me.

In his jeans and long-sleeve black dress shirt, unbuttoned at the neck to expose a hint of his tanned skin, the soft light from the pool casting its glow over him, he looks sexy as hell.

Since the first time we met, he's always been breathtakingly beautiful, but tonight, there's something different about him. A wildness. An untamed edge that I haven't seen in him before.

Maybe it's being in this environment. His *home,* even though he doesn't actually *live* here anymore. Maybe he's just more comfortable here and can really let go in a way he hasn't on our previous dates because we've always been surrounded by people in restaurants, the movies, the arcade, even mini-golfing.

But tonight, he looks so effortlessly hot as he approaches that it makes me squirm on the bench.

Drew ducks to slip under the willow branches, his focus never leaving me as it roams over my hair that I left loose and flowing down to my shoulders and the black and white polka dot sundress that pushes my breasts up to create the perfect cleavage and falls only mid-thigh, especially when I sit like this. His eyes dip to my exposed legs and to the sparkly sandals on my feet, then come back up. "Is that what you're doing out here? Escaping?"

I grin at him. "Maybe. You weren't kidding about your mom's parties."

He smirks, and it is so devastatingly sexy and full of

promise that my heart picks up speed, beating rapidly against my ribcage with each step closer he comes.

One of his brows rises slowly. "You're out here all alone?"

I nod. "Yeah. I looked for you but couldn't find you to tell you I was slipping out for some fresh air."

He finally stops in front of me, close enough that I can see the searing heat blazing across his blue eyes. His lips part slightly as he examines me, and he draws in a long inhalation, his muscular chest rising against the crisp material of his shirt. "Have I told you how fucking beautiful you look tonight?"

My cheeks warm at the compliment, and I avert my gaze, adjusting the dress around my thighs, suddenly shy under his perusal. "Not like that."

He snorts an incredulous laugh, then closes the few steps between us and lowers himself onto the bench beside me, spreading his right arm across the back of it. One hand dangling loosely over my shoulder, the fingers of his other one slide under my chin and tip it up until my eyes meet his.

The forcefulness with which he holds my gaze and the desire searing through his, along with his firm grip on me, makes me shudder in anticipation.

"I should have told you that a thousand times because you look incredible. His tongue slowly slips out across his lips. "Good enough to eat."

Sweet mother of God...

Heat that was in my cheeks now flares between my legs.

Red hot.

Searing.

I press them together against the sudden throb ignited with those simple words that are clearly meant to hold a very sinful meaning.

And that I *never* expected out of Drew's mouth.

He has always been such a gentleman, so concerned about ensuring he isn't overstepping or rushing me into anything during our dates. The attraction has been there, though. This low, incessant buzz of energy that seems to have burst into flames in the last thirty seconds...

My tongue darts out, wetting my lips, and his gaze follows the movement. I try to dip my head to avoid his gaze, to prevent him from seeing what he's doing to me, but he keeps a steady grip on my chin, refusing to let me look away.

Dark brows draw low over his eyes. "Why does that embarrass you?"

Shit.

"Um..." I bite my lip and shake my head. "I'm not sure."

He dips his head closer until his warm breath floats over me along with something vaguely citrus that clings to his skin. "You need to learn to take a compliment. Especially when I'm the one giving them to you because I wouldn't say it if I didn't mean it."

Something clenches around my chest, tightening around my heart with his words and the absolute sincerity in them. He *meant* every single one.

"I know."

A tiny grin plays at his lips, filled with so much promise. "Good. Now"—he inclines his head toward the house— "would you like to go back into the party, or stay out here for a while?"

It's such a loaded question with his hands on me, with my body buzzing the way it is. But he's giving me a *choice*. And we both know what could happen if I answer *yes* to the latter.

I wasn't completely sure where things were going with Drew before tonight.

All our dates have been incredible, the instant connection between us growing stronger with every hour we spend together, but *this* side of him is awakening something in me.

A burning, throbbing need for this man to take things to the next level, to get impossibly close to him even out here.

Walking back into that party would break this spell he's cast over me.

It would sever this exquisite, pulsating hold Drew has on my body and heart.

And I don't want to risk never finding it again.

Not when I see now where it could lead.

I shake my head gently, his grip on my chin keeping my eyes locked with his every second. "Definitely not ready to go in yet."

His grin widens, a breath of relief rushing from deep in his chest, like he was afraid I would bolt instead of staying hypnotized by him. "Me. Fucking. Either." He dips his head closer until his lips are a mere hairsbreadth from mine. "I just can't get over how fucking beautiful you look tonight."

I shiver slightly, though it isn't from the light breeze shifting the willow limbs around us. This moment feels frozen in time. As if we're in our own little world, completely separated from the one outside this bench, this shared breath.

The heat radiating from his body draws me closer, and he dips his head fully and captures my mouth in a soul-searing kiss that steals any other thoughts and my ability to think about anything but *it* and *him*.

A moan vibrates in my chest, and his tongue skims across the seam of my lips, demanding entry. I open for him willingly, shifting more toward him on the bench as his free hand comes to rest on my exposed thigh below the hem of my dress.

Sizzling need races through my blood from where our skin touches and centers straight at my core.

Throbbing.

Pulsating.

Burning.

I try to clench my legs together against that embarrassingly persistent ache, but he pulls away from the kiss and glances down to where his hand rests.

Oh, God, he felt that...

And now I want to crawl into a hole and die of embarrassment.

But a low groan rumbles in his throat, his fingers flexing into my flesh. "You are walking temptation, Ivy." He uses his hold on my chin to tilt my head slightly, examining me in a way that makes me feel utterly exposed. "Do you know that? What a walking sin you are?"

Fuck.

My thighs tighten before I can stop them, his fingers responding by digging deeper into my heated flesh.

I shake my head, struggling to find the breath to fill my lungs as he holds my gaze. "No."

His hand skims farther up my thigh, light callouses on his fingertips running along my skin and raising goosebumps in their wake. "I would love nothing more than to drop to my knees and make you come on my tongue right here, right now, so I can finally taste you..."

I shudder at his words, my clit throbbing even harder, my pussy embarrassingly wet without him even touching me.

Drew's gaze flicks to the back door of the house. "But I

don't know how long we have until company appears." He slides his hand down from my chin to wrap lightly around my throat, his thumb brushing across my thundering pulse. "And I don't want anyone seeing you like *that* but me."

Hell...

This side of Drew is something else.

Reckless.

Possessive.

Fucking hot.

I shiver again.

His brow furrows. "Are you cold?"

I shake my head because I am *anything* but cold.

My entire body feels like it's on *fire*.

Flames lick between my legs and up through me, a blaze that feels like it might burn me away completely if it isn't somehow doused.

The corner of his lips twitches into a devious grin. He tips his head and kisses the side of my mouth, across my cheek and to my ear, thumb still stroking the column of my neck. "How about I warm you up?"

Oh, God.

I squeeze my legs together, but all it does is press his hand tighter against my tense thigh, giving him confirmation of exactly what I want.

He chuckles low next to my ear, kissing me there, his hand grazing upward slowly until it reaches the soft, lacy thong I wore tonight. His fingers brush across the damp material, and I jerk in his hold.

"You tell me if you want me to stop, Ivy." His voice dips low, filled with so much tension that it matches my body perfectly. "I will...no matter how badly I want to see you come right now."

I slide my hand over his on my neck and shake my head. "No, I don't want you to stop."

He seems to hesitate—only for a few seconds—but it's there as he searches my face. But whatever thought or worry gave him pause evaporates just as quickly, and he tugs the already wet fabric to the side and slips his fingers along my slick core.

I gasp at his touch, my thighs tightening around his hand, and he issues another low groan of approval.

"Fucking hell, Ivy." He dips his lips against my ear, nipping at it lightly. "You're so fucking *wet*."

I nod, all my earlier embarrassment washing away with the brush of his skilled fingers. They move over my core gently, tentatively, an exploration of the slick folds that leaves me panting.

His mouth moves back to mine, and he uses his hand around my neck to tilt my head how he wants it. "I'm going to make you come, Ivy, and when your pussy clenches down around my fingers, I want you to know that I wish it was my cock, and that I will give you anything you want, anytime, anywhere. Always."

The promise rolls over me like waves on the shore, melting away the last of my inhibitions and any reservations or questions I had about this man.

I whimper and nod as his fingers slowly sink into me.

He catches my gasp with another soul-searing kiss, one that ignites every nerve-ending in my body and sends my head spinning. I clutch at the front of his shirt, pulling the crisp, black fabric between my fingers as his delve into me and his tongue probes along mine.

His thumb slips up over my clit, and I jerk in his hold, my dress barely covering what he's doing to me. If anyone were to walk out of the house right now, were to really search and look into this dark corner of the yard beneath the willow, they would see exactly what he's doing.

It should give me pause, yet somehow, the thought that we might be caught makes me even hotter, makes the warm rush of arousal even thicker, and I shift, spreading my thighs to give him better access.

He moans his approval, devouring my tongue and my lips like he's trying to steal each breath and memorize every piece of me. Even though we've spent the last few weeks exchanging heated goodnight kisses, a shared attraction that was on the edge of exploding, tonight is so different, so unexpected.

Drew is so *needy*, almost feral in the way he works me over.

Maybe it's the party, or the drinks he had. Maybe it's the fact that I'm in this dress. Or maybe it's the weeks that have built up to this. Because we both knew where it was heading, that we'd end up tangled up in each other.

It was only a matter of time.

I just didn't expect it to come to a head sitting on a bench in his mother's garden while a party raves inside.

His fingers curl into that perfect spot inside me as he continues to probe and drag them along my inner wall while his thumb spirals around my clit in loose circles that make blood rush in my ears and my limbs tingle.

I drag my mouth away, gasping, desperate for oxygen, for more friction, for more *everything*.

"Drew, please..."

I whimper in the most unattractive, despondent sound I think I've ever made, and his hand stills for a second, fingers embedded deep inside me. He searches my face, eyes raking over every inch of me and finally focusing on my parted lips. A storm rages in his eyes, swirling hot and dark, and he redoubles his effort, pumping into me harder, rolling his thumb faster until my orgasm starts to build.

Heat flaring.

Flames rippling.

Ecstasy stacking higher and higher and higher until my body is coiled so tightly and ready to fly that if I don't come soon, my heart may lose its ability to keep pumping in time with the throbbing between my legs.

He captures my mouth again and kisses me hard. Deep. The kind of kiss that's intended to *claim* me. And I want to let him.

I groan and tighten my grip on his shirt, my hips rolling against his hand as he continues to fuck me mindlessly with his fingers until I finally reach that pinnacle I've been racing toward.

My sharp cry slips from my lips, but he catches the sound, swallowing it as I jerk in his hold, my pussy pulsing and clenching around his fingers as he keeps rolling his thumb across my clit and dragging out my orgasm.

"Fuck, you're beautiful when you come, Ivy."

His ministrations continue, expertly playing over me until I finally collapse, sagging forward against him, dropping my forehead to his chest as I struggle to find my breath and thoughts through the fog overtaking my head.

Drew stills his hand between my legs, but he doesn't pull his fingers free.

He holds me like this for a few moments, his hand cupping my neck as my pussy flutters along his fingers with the final aftershocks of my release. My eyes flutter open to find his hard cock straining under front of his jeans. I stare down at it, clenching around him, wanting exactly what he said he did earlier.

For *him* to be inside me.

To feel that kind of fullness and passion.

He gently drags my face back with his hold on my neck and kisses me softly, almost reverently, as he draws his fingers from my pussy and adjusts my dress into place.

When he starts to pull back, I continue to clutch his shirt, not ready to lose his heat or the feeling of him pressed against me. But he doesn't go far, just enough to slip his hand up between us and slide his glistening fingers into his mouth.

"Fuck, Ivy." A growl of contentment fills his chest. "I knew you would taste incredible." He licks them clean, a vision of his tongue doing that to my thighs and between them making me clench again. "But I certainly never expected *this*."

I barely manage to breathe, let alone get a word out. "Expect w-what?"

"For you to be so open." His gaze holds mine. "So *giving*."

"But...I haven't done anything."

He nods slowly, brushing his thumb across my thrumming pulse. "You've given me the one thing I thought I would never have..."

I tilt my head, trying to figure out what he's talking about through the lingering haze of lust that seems to be fogging my brain. "I don't know what you mean."

He offers me an almost sad smile and kisses me one last time. "Take a second to collect yourself, and I'll meet you back inside. I have something I have to take care of."

No.

Don't go.

It's stupid to want him to stay.

We can't remain out on this bench forever.

Eventually, someone else will come out for fresh air or looking for us, and even if he doesn't still have his hand buried between my thighs, it would be far too obvious something untoward happened out here.

I reluctantly release my death grip on his shirt and nod. "Okay..."

He climbs to his feet, adjusting his hard cock in his jeans, then takes one last lingering look at me before he stalks away, out the way he came through the side gate.

22

IVY

NOW

My legs tremble, threatening to give out as the memory washes over me like a destructive tidal wave. The details are so crystal clear, even after all this time, that I can still *feel* his hand between my legs and the way my heart yearned for more from him even after he made me completely unravel in the most sinful way.

But I can't speak.

Can't move.

Can't even *begin* to process this vicious truth bomb that just detonated in my mind.

Cam watches me with trepidation hardening his gaze, his brows drawn low, shoulders tense. "You keep asking me what happened between me and Drew, why we had a falling out, why we weren't speaking to each other anymore. That night is *why*."

Blood rushes in my ears, drowning out the music playing in the studio, making my head spin. My heart slams violently against my rib cage, and I stumble backward and grip the edge of the kitchen counter to keep myself upright.

He takes a step toward me with his free hand out, as if he's going to grab me to keep me steady, but I flinch from his touch, stopping him in his tracks.

The floor tilts beneath my feet, wobbling as all the pieces fall into place, clicking together like some strange puzzle built on lust and lies. "Drew knew..."

He knew *something had happened in the garden that night...*
And he knew it had been Cam.

I let my gaze drift up to lock with his, even though he's blurry through the tears now filling my eyes and sliding down my cheeks.

Cam looks utterly dejected, his shoulders slumped, free hand fisting at his side. "Of course, he knew."

He knew.
He knew.
He knew.
Drew. Fucking. Knew.

That night changed everything for us.

For all intents and purposes, it was the *true* start of our relationship.

The weeks leading up to that had been getting to know each other. Feeling each other out. Figuring out if there was anything there beyond the initial attraction and playful flirtation.

But that night was the defining moment—the single second in time when I *knew* Drew was *it.*

And...

"Oh, God..." I slam my hand over my mouth to prevent a sob from slipping out, but even biting into my flesh doesn't completely stop it. Not when the truth wrenches it from somewhere deep in my soul.

And...it wasn't even *him.*

My head spins wildly, trying to make sense of any of this, and I release the counter and stagger over to the painting of me from that night.

If I had never seen this, if I had never questioned him about it, would Cam have ever told me the truth? Or would I have gone on thinking that one of the best nights of my life was with Drew?

Other canvases stand stacked, leaning against the wall behind it, and I reach out with a trembling hand and pull it back, exposing the next one.

Of me—sleeping on the couch in my living room.

I move to the next.

Of me—holding my mother's lily.

The next...

Of me—tears streaming down my face as I stare up with utter devastation in my eyes that he somehow managed to capture perfectly.

Each one a snapshot of time we've spent together.

They're all of me...

I frantically move another stack, tugging back a landscape propped at the front to find half a dozen more of me—each depicting a single moment from over the past several weeks.

Each drenched in my pain, reflecting precisely what I was feeling as if he weren't merely witnessing it but actually *experiencing* it right along with me, each and every time.

These are my *life*.

These are my *anguish*.

These are *his*.

Cam moves, his footsteps making the old floorboards creak, but the look I cut his way over my shoulder makes him freeze, hand tightening around the still-dripping brush in it.

"You are my muse. You have been since the first moment I saw you..." His Adam's apple bobs on his forced swallow, like he's fighting through something lodged there. "And I haven't been able to paint *anything* else since the night I came to your house..."

My hands tremble as I let the canvases fall back into place with a *thunk* that draws a cringe from him.

But I can't care about that.

Not when the reality of what happened keeps smacking me squarely in the face. "Drew knew..."

Cam nods.

"But you never went in..."

"No." He shakes his head. "I left because I had just kissed my brother's girlfriend and gotten her off"—his voice rumbles, heavy with the same kind of agony tearing me apart right now—"and I wanted to do it again. I wanted to do worse."

And I wanted him to.

I practically wept when he walked away, desperate to keep him there, my body aching to free his cock and allow him to slide home.

"You must have said something to him when you went back to the party, something that tipped him off, because Drew texted me shortly after I left, and it only said five words. 'I know what you did.'"

He KNEW.

Because I walked into that house on shaky legs, found him, and told him I couldn't wait to get home to finish what we started in the garden.

He. Fucking. Knew.

I choke on another sob, my hands fisting at my sides, seeking anything to cling to that might stop this spiraling feeling. Nails bite into my skin, but I don't care. I need the physical pain to cut through the agony threatening to shred me apart right now. "That night changed everything..."

Cam nods. "Drew and I never spoke again."

"What?"

That wasn't what I meant.

I was referring to my relationship with Drew, to the fact that he brought me home after the party and made love to me for the first time. We were inseparable after that. I didn't just give my body to him; I gave him my whole heart.

Cam locks his jaw, a muscle there ticcing. "I'm sure he wanted me to call, wanted me to apologize, wanted me to offer *some sort* of an explanation for the way I acted, but I couldn't do it. I couldn't give him one. Because I didn't regret it. I couldn't when"—his bare chest rises and falls sharply—"when it was the single greatest moment of my life."

No.

I wince, squeezing my eyes closed against the flood of turbulent emotions and voices in my head.

They scream and thrash.

They fight to make sense, to find what was real and what was a lie, but I can't tell anymore. All of it blends together into a swirl of black and white like the paint Cam places on the canvases.

Something clatters to the floor, and this time, when I hear Cam move closer, I don't have the power to retreat.

My entire body feels numb.

Useless.

On the verge of collapse.

Everything I thought I knew about my relationship with Drew was a lie.

All spawned from one night—that I didn't even have with *him*.

Cam stops in front of me and grips my chin, forcing my face up, and I let my eyes open, almost blinded by the intensity of what stares back. "Everything the two of you had was real, Ivy. You had over four years together. You had a life together. A *future* together."

His words barely register over the whooshing of blood in my ears.

I can't look away from his penetrating gaze, from the force of it and the way it locks me in place.

How did I not see it?

How did I miss it?

The differences between them...

The darkness that creeps into his blue eyes that Drew's never had...

The slightly more crooked smile...

The way this heat that blazes across Cam's gaze as he looks at me *burns* like a wild inferno, whereas when Drew looked at me, it smoldered.

"I-I should have known."

Cam shakes his head. "No. You shouldn't have. Drew and I often wore similar clothes without even planning it. And back then, I didn't look like *this*." He motions toward his face. "I always covered my tattoos for my mom's parties. We probably looked exactly the same that night to *everyone*. And I was a fucking selfish prick who took advantage of the situation."

"But *why*?" My lip trembles along with my body. "Did you really hate him that much that you had to—"

I can't even say the words.

Can't even bring myself to *think* them.

His brows draw low, his gaze confused now. "*Hate* him?" He shakes his head, and a humorless laugh slips from his mouth. "I didn't hate him, Ivy. I loved Drew more than anyone on this planet." He sucks in a long, slow breath as he searches my face, and then his thumb moves up and brushes over my lips. "Until the moment I walked into that yard and saw you."

My breath catches at the passion burning in his gaze, the absolute surety in it, even when I'm not sure about *anything* anymore.

"It was like time stood still, Ivy. Lightning struck. The earth shifted under my feet. All those clichés you always hear about in the movies and romance novels. All of it happened to me the instant I laid eyes on you that night. I saw you sitting there, and I just…" He shakes his head, tilting it as he stares at my lips. "I knew who you were instantly. I knew you thought I was him. I knew I was doing something wretched and wrong. But I couldn't walk away. I couldn't stop myself. I couldn't let you slip through my fingers."

Instead, I came on them…

I unraveled in his arms, under his touch and kiss.

I came *apart*.

"But I wasn't yours to *have*…"

He flinches, his eyes squeezing closed. "You think I don't fucking *know* that, Ivy?" His palm slides away from my face, and he steps back, shoving his hands through his hair. "I'm not a good person. I'm the guy who tries to steal his brother's girlfriend. And that night destroyed *everything*. My relationship with Drew, my relationship with my mother because I couldn't ever come home. All of it *gone* in a fucking instant because I saw you and had to have you. Because I wasn't strong enough to walk away. Because I wasn't a big enough man, or a good enough person to just tell you who the fuck I was and let Drew have you." He pounds his fist over his heart and opens his eyes, now wet with tears. "I had to take you, and it cost me my fucking *sanity*."

The cracking of his voice on that final word rips my chest open, as if his pain has become my own. But I don't understand what he's saying. I don't understand *any* of it.

"What do you mean?"

"Just because I knew it was wrong doesn't mean I regretted it. Not for a fucking second because I was fucking obsessed with you, Ivy. *Obsessed*. I followed your social media, stalked your posts about romantic dinners with Drew, watched you two fall even more in love through photos and words you said...and every minute of every day afterward, you were all I thought about. How your lips felt against mine, how your tongue tasted, how fucking wet you were, and mostly how, for the first time in my life that I could remember, it wasn't all black and white. For the first time that night, with my hand between your legs and your mouth on mine, I saw fucking *red*. An explosion of color. That vibrancy of *life* was pushed back into me, and it was all because of you." He shakes his head, as if he can't find the words to express what he's really trying to say. "Kissing you tasted like red, Ivy, and knowing that I couldn't have you...it *broke* me."

It *broke* him.

That word echoes in my head, along with the confessions he made to me over the past several weeks.

"Oh, God. Is that when you..."

I can't even get the question out because I know the answer.

He *told* me.

Explained it all when he tried to warn me away from him so many times.

His life crumbled, and he fell down that hole of addiction that took him so long to climb out of, that he still battles every day.

And it all started because of *me*.

Cam shoves his hands through his hair, shaking his head. "I'm not blaming you. None of this was your fault. It was *mine*. *My* weakness, *my* inability to cope with all the emotions exploding within me. The guilt over what I did to Drew. The shame of *not* feeling guilty and wanting to do it again. The *want* that I couldn't stop feeling for what wasn't *mine*. It was volatile, Ivy. *I* was. It was *my* selfishness that made me descend into that pit I dug for myself. All of it was *my* fault."

He destroyed his life.

He went down a path that left him this tortured, anguished person...

"No." I shake my head, the tears streaming down my cheeks as hot as the anger and shame burning through me. "It was mine. I should have known. I should have—"

Cam closes the distance between us in two steps and takes my face in his palms. "Stop saying that, and stop thinking that way. This is why I didn't tell you when I showed up at your house. Because I didn't want you questioning everything, didn't want you thinking that your entire relationship with Drew was a lie or that you could have, in any way, known in that garden. *One night* doesn't change what *four years* built. It doesn't." He presses his chest into mine and tightens his grip on my face, ensuring I'm holding his gaze. "But now you see why I warned you away, why I told you that I was toxic and bad for you, why what happened the other night when we got back from the shore never should have happened. And never should again."

Everything he says, every single agonizing word of it is true.

Cam is selfish.

He's unhinged.

He has no control over his life or his emotions.

He's exactly the type of guy women should avoid.

He's the opposite of Drew in every way.

Drew *never* would have done what Cam did that night.

He never would have lied to me—

But he did, didn't he?

Instead of telling me it wasn't him out in the garden that night, instead of coming clean and exposing what Cam had done, what I had allowed to happen, he simply maintained the lie.

He took that memory that I made with Cam and made me believe it was *ours*.

He lied to me as much as Cam did.

Why?

To spare me the shame of what I did?

To spare himself *that embarrassment?*

Or because he was afraid of losing me to his brother?

As I stand here now, staring at the man who slid into my damn heart, pretending to be someone else that night, everything I thought I knew crumbles away to ashes.

And all I want is to let myself float away the same way Drew did on that dark beach.

I squeeze my eyes closed, a sob tearing from my chest, cracking me open, splintering the last four years of my life into fragmented lies, unspoken truths, meaningless words and promises filled with deception and deceit.

"Ivy..." Cam shifts his hold on me, swiping at my tears with his calloused thumbs. "Please look at me."

It's the last thing I want to do.

Because I don't trust him.

But more importantly, I don't trust *myself* with him.

He waits.

Holding me steady.

And eventually, I force my eyes open to look into his again.

The sadness floating in them twists my stomach tightly. "All I've ever wanted since that moment was you, but I'll never be good enough for you. I've done horrible things, Ivy. Things..."—the tortured waver in his voice makes my knees give out, only his hand dropping from my face to wrap around my waist keeps me upright and pressed to him— "you need to stay out of my life. You need to stay far away from me. All I do is bring pain to people I love, and I won't keep doing that to you. I can't. Not after everything you've already suffered."

The past two months have been a living hell.

Moving through each second, each minute, each hour, each day with forced breaths, dragging steps, false smiles, and fake strength I never had.

Time passed, but I felt like I was standing still.

Stuck in quicksand sucking me down into the black abyss created by a world without Drew.

One where I was alone forever.

But as Cam gazes down at me, the warning written in his darkened-blue eyes, red flags waving violently like on the beach with a dangerous riptide, I can't help noticing the heat seeping into my body and the unwavering power of his hold.

He prevents me from completely collapsing the same

way he has every time I've needed him since he arrived in my life.

Every moment I've needed him—he's *been* there.

Offering me what I could never have found on my own.

Laughter.

Joy.

Strength.

Even when he was suffering just as badly.

That first night brought color back into his life.

And kissing him last week seemed to bring a spark back to mine.

For the first time in months, I felt alive, if only for a few moments. Even though it was wrong, even though I knew it was, it was somehow the only thing that felt right in a long time. That release was more than just sexual. It was an unleashing of everything that had kept me prone and stagnant. It was what I *needed*.

I don't know what to do with him.

I don't know what to do with myself.

I don't know what to do with *this*.

All I know is that walking away and heeding his warning when he did that for me isn't an option.

23

IVY

The mere thought of never seeing him again brutally rips the air from my lungs. Dread coils around my spine like a poisonous serpent and tightens. My knees threaten to buckle again.

And still, I *don't* understand it.

I have *every* reason to hate him for what he did—to Drew and to me.

Rationally, there is no other choice but to walk away and never look back. To flee with what's left of my heart, even if it is only scattered, fragile pieces that threaten to crush into nothing but dust under the weight of truths now bombarding me.

The longer I stare at him, the worse it all gets until my ribs feel like they're going to snap as I attempt to process everything he just told me and make sense of the riot of feelings warring inside me.

All this time...I had it wrong...

"It. Was. *You.*"

I just keep coming back to that fact. Reliving that

moment in time when my eyes met his across the yard. When I called him over to me on that bench with that simple question. When he sat down beside me. When his hand came up to my chin. When his lips met mine. When he stole my fucking soul. All on the same night that I *gave* myself to Drew.

Tears blur my vision, red hot with anger, disbelief, and a kind of soul-crushing confusion I've never felt before.

Cam softly brushes them away with trembling hands as soon as they hit my cheeks. "You should go, and don't come back, Ivy. I never should have..." He stops and swallows thickly, glancing away as his clenched jaw tics. "I would love to blame what I did on being high or drunk or some other way out of my right mind, but I wasn't that night. And I never should have touched you. Never should have allowed myself...that. And I *won't* do it again."

An unexplainable panic seizes me. "W-why not?"

The question slips out before I can stop it, before I can contemplate *why* I'm asking, why it matters when he's *right*.

His eyes widen slightly, confusion furrowing his brow. "Because it's *wrong*, Ivy. I'm not a good person, and every fucking thing I've done from that moment on has been *wrong*—"

Wrong.

Wrong.

Wrong.

One word that has come into my head so many times since that night we spread Drew's ashes, since Cam's touch lit me aflame and I wondered what the *hell* I was thinking, since I finally *felt* something again other than utter despair.

Only it wasn't the first time he had done that to me.

It wasn't the first time he had awoken something deep inside that blistered and seared me permanently.

Camden sees the world in black and white, and he's acting like that's what this convoluted situation is, too. But there are so many varying shades of gray.

Ones I *see* in his works.

They add depth and allow him to take something that would be flat and make it something vibrant and stunning.

Nothing is truly black and white.

Not on his canvases.

Not in our lives.

Not in this situation.

Just like there isn't simply right and wrong.

What we shared was something in between, something far harder to define—one of those varied shades of gray.

Staring into his tumultuous blue eyes that plead with me to listen to him, to walk away and never look back, all I see are those gaps between the black and white, the spaces between right and wrong.

All I feel is the lingering memory of that night, and I shake my head. "It didn't *feel* wrong."

My voice cracks on the final word, and his entire face falls as he recoils slightly, as if I've slapped him rather than admitted the uncomfortable truth that weighs heavily on my soul.

What felt wrong was that it *didn't* feel wrong. It felt *right*.

He shakes his head, his lips pressing together in a firm line. "You don't mean that."

"I do." I swallow through the emotion clogging my throat, willing it to stay down so I can say what needs to be said. "I don't understand it, Cam. I haven't since the moment you showed up at my house. Even though everything tells me it's wrong, every logical thought says you're right and I should run...the only times I haven't felt like I was alone, drifting in some dark, endless sea of despair in the last two months have been when I've been with you."

He flinches, his palm cradling my face so gently yet forcefully, like it too is stuck between the two polar opposites.

"You've been there for me, Cam. Given me your strength. Taken care of me when I couldn't take care of myself. You knew what I needed even before I did and made sure I had it, whether it was a story about Drew that brought me *joy* and laughter again, a great fucking sandwich, a push to finally put him to rest, or a release of everything I had let build up so staggeringly high that I was on the verge of total collapse under its weight. So"—I shake my head, willing the tears to stop falling, though I know they won't—"I don't know what to do with that. What to make of it or what it says about me now that I know the truth. But I do know I want more of *that*—of what you gave me the other night, even if it *is* wrong in someone else's mind because they can't understand this *thing* between us."

Not that I do, either.

I don't understand it at all.

Maybe I never will.

But my confession fills the air between us, mingling with the thumping bass of the music still playing. Buzzing in my ears and through my body as much as the heat from having Cam this close does.

We stand frozen as he searches my gaze, and I watch the war in his.

It seethes violently, that haunted part of him wrestling

with the half that cares so deeply, the one that wants to do the right thing even if it will cause him more pain.

Cam has warned me away from him more than once, and I should have listened to that undercurrent of fear in his words. But now, it's too late. I'm already hopelessly caught in his riptide, and I can't get out of it, even if I wanted to. Which I'm not confident I do.

I'm not sure about anything anymore...

Except the way it feels to swim in his gaze and have his rough hands on my skin and his leather and citrus scent invading each breath.

He tightens his grip on my cheeks, tilting my face up to his, and lowers his lips until they're just barely brushing mine. "If we do this, Ivy, if you let me touch you, if you let me get my hands on you like *that* again, it will not be slow or sweet. I spent four goddamn years wanting you, fantasizing about all the ways I would take you, of how it would feel to have your lips on mine again, your hands against my skin, your nails clawing at my back, and your hot, wet cunt wrapped around my cock, so if you really want this to happen, then it will be hard and fast. I've reached the limits of my control when it comes to you, and one simple word from those beautiful lips of yours will send me careening over that edge."

His new warning, tinged with a savage energy, licks over me, coursing through my veins, heating my blood, flaming to life that part of me I thought died with Drew; the part that wants, the part that feels anything other than absolute agony every moment of every day.

And I want that part to stay lit.

I want to *feel*.

So, I say the only thing I can. "Yes."

The word lives in the air between us, thickening it more and more each second that ticks past, and I wonder if he actually heard me say it. Then, as if he's made some decision that flicked a switch somewhere inside him, his eyes darken and his mouth crashes onto mine so quickly and so fiercely that I yelp against his lips and stagger back slightly.

But one of his strong arms wraps around me, pulling me up against him fully, and his hard cock strains between us, pressing deep into my belly as he devours my mouth, kissing and licking, probing and taking, like he can't get enough of it.

It isn't sweet.

It's borderline feral.

An animalistic tinge to his movements that tells me he's hovering on the edge of completely letting go of everything that restrains him.

And I want him to let go.

I *want* the recklessness I see in his eyes.

Crave all that passion and energy focused solely on me and *this*.

My core aches, the dull throb pulsing there relentlessly as my need for the man who kisses me so fiercely envelops my entire being. All thoughts of everything else, including all the reasons this is so bad, all the ways it's wrong, and all the secrets and lies that led to it, melt away in a single instant.

I wrap my arms around his neck, tunneling my fingers through his thick hair, and he groans, angling my face slightly so he can get a different position, utterly consuming me with everything he has and trying to take all that I am from me.

The bed on the other side of the studio seems so

goddamn far away all of a sudden, and he seems to have the same thought because instead of backing me up that direction, he turns and forces me to retreat three steps until my shoes bump up against the edge of the canvas he was just painting on.

I jerk and look down at it—the few strokes of black paint he swiped across it before I interrupted—then up at him. "What are you doing?"

Hand pressed into my lower back, keeping me pinned to his warm, hard body, Cam ignores my question and kisses my neck. I crane it to the side, giving him better access to work his way down, his lips raising goosebumps everywhere they touch as his fingers trail along the waistband of my jeans.

"You're the most beautiful thing I've ever seen, Ivy. That's why I've painted you too many times to even count." His words vibrate against my skin where his lips are pressed to it. "But now that I have you here like this, I get to really paint *you*."

What?

Paint...

Me?

It takes me a second to figure out what he's saying, my brain trying to process the words while it short-circuits under his touch, but when his hand slips into my pants and cups me between my legs, I jolt against him, my nails digging into the back of his neck.

I groan at the sensation of the heel of his palm rubbing across my clit, and he pushes harder, rolling it until my hips buck against him and his hard cock is pinned between us.

He tugs at the hem of my shirt with his free hand, and I allow him to pull it up and toss it unceremoniously to the floor. Hot, frantic lips move across my collarbone as he reaches behind me and unhooks my bra, exposing my breasts to the chilly air.

My nipples harden instantly under his assessment, and he issues a deep groan and drops his head, sucking one between his lips. I gasp at the sensation, my head falling back, eyes rolling up as his hand continues to move against me, the other wrapped around my hip again, holding me steady as his seeking mouth and tongue send jolts of pleasure straight between my legs.

They tremble violently, and he releases my nipple and moves to the other as he pulls his hand from my core long enough to undo my jeans.

I toe off my shoes, the bass lightly shaking the floorboards beneath my bare feet, and he growls his approval along my lips as he slowly lowers me onto the canvas.

My head lands in the sticky black and white paint, but he doesn't seem to care that we will ruin whatever vision he had for this piece.

He shifts back, dragging down my jeans and panties, exposing me to him fully for the first time. The forgotten fabric falls from his hands, his eyes never leaving my naked body spread out across the canvas.

Everywhere his gaze touches heats like a fucking napalm fire going off, moisture pooling between my thighs, that throb so incessant that it thumps in time with the bass from the stereo.

I squirm under the assessment.

The pure adoration in his gaze only grows as it moves from the top of my head over my chest, my stomach, and finally between my legs. His cock strains against his jeans, the hard length as intimidating as the man who looks ready to devour me.

Unable to bear the potency of it any longer, I allow my eyes to drift over him, taking in every inch of his exposed muscled chest and arms.

Those two snakes twist up his left arm—one light, one dark—and I can't help but to wonder what they signify.

And another tattoo sits on his ribcage, though I can't make it out from here.

My gaze drifts lower, over his rock-hard abs to that delicious trail that leads down to his unbuttoned fly.

The heat his perusal had ignited flares hotter, and I shift restlessly, pressing my thighs together, the urge to slide my hand down between them and give myself some relief so strong that my fingers actually twitch on the canvas.

Cam's sharp eyes catch the movement, the corner of his mouth curving as he drops to his knees and grasps my thighs. His fingers dig into them as he drags them up and over his shoulders, leaving me arched up with my hands splayed out wide across the paint.

"Fuck, Ivy..." It comes out more growl than spoken, an edge to his voice I've never heard before, like he's close to finally snapping the way he warned me he would—"I've been dying to taste you like this for four years."

It's the only warning I get before he plunges his face between my legs.

His thick tongue glides along my entire slit and up across my clit in a long, smooth motion that has me bow up even more, digging my heels into his shoulders and mashing my hair further into the wet paint.

My fingers slide through it as I scramble for purchase, for anything to cling to while his groan vibrates against my thighs and damp flesh, making me twitch and twist in his grip even more.

But Cam doesn't relent.

He doesn't give me an inch to direct him, just licks me again and again in long, luxurious strokes. Ravishing me like he can't get enough, as if this is his sole mission, to unleash *my* soul against his mouth.

And then his tongue plunges into me as deep as he can go.

"Fuck!"

My cry echoes across the studio, bouncing off the brick as my neck arches, eyes rolling back, my entire world centered on that scalding, throbbing spot between my legs. A low tingle starts in my core, my clit aching as he flicks his tongue across it rapidly.

Good God...

Cam utterly destroys me with his attention to that spot.

Intense.

Single-minded focus.

The same passion he directs onto his canvases now centered on my clit.

"You're going to come against my mouth, Ivy." *Lick.* "So I can taste every sweet drop of you." *Suck.* "So I can have it *all.*" *Lick.* "And then..." *Suck.* "I'm going to slide my cock into this slick cunt of yours and let you come on it, too."

Nip.

That fucking *nip...*

It makes me twist my thighs against his head, and I lift my hands to tunnel them into his hair. He groans his approval, muttering an unintelligible curse into my damp flesh. He redoubles his efforts, his tongue shifting between spearing into me and flicking across the apex of my thighs.

It's too much and not enough.

My skin sticks to the canvas as I try to shift, try to adjust my legs so I can keep him right on my clit, but his firm grip on my thighs prevents me from budging an inch.

I tighten my grip on his hair and tug, trying another tactic, but he pulls his head back so he can look up at me with a lust-soaked, hooded gaze.

He keeps eye contact as he plunges his tongue into me again, then flicks it up over my clit once. Twice. A third time.

Slowly.

Deliberately.

Proving that he's in control of this and will do whatever the fuck he wants to me, *how* he wants it, while I'm spread out like this.

And I want to let him.

Because he's demonstrated his expert skills where getting me off is concerned.

But if he doesn't do *something*. If he doesn't nudge me over that edge soon, I'm going to rip out his hair or tear a damn hole in this canvas.

As if sensing I'm reaching my breaking point in more ways than one, he shifts his hand off my thigh and plunges two fingers into me easily. The slick sound of them sinking in meets my low, throaty moan at finally having some part of him inside me.

It isn't what I really want.

Not what I really *need*.

But my pussy still clenches around them, clasping and trying to keep them inside as he pumps them in time with his flicking across my clit.

My breath hitches. My fingers twine in his hair. My thighs tense. All in anticipation of what is about to come. I hover over the precipice. Where I can see the promised land. The place where all my fears and worries, all the reasons I have to be confused and angry just don't exist.

It's so close I can *taste* it—it tastes like Cam.

Rich.

Citrusy.

And when he drags my clit between his lips and sucks it in a relentless rhythm that matches his thrusts, I finally topple over that edge.

Instead of floating on that vast, empty sea, I'm now spiraling on top of the wave as it crests and then crashes down onto the shore, so violent I arch up even more off the canvas as he continues to suck me down. He drags my orgasm on and on and on. With his fingers. With his mouth. Until I'm left panting and begging for him to stop, my whole body thrumming and over-sensitive in a way that only follows a mind-blowing release.

He slowly lifts his head and licks his lips, then allows my thighs to slide down until my legs are sprawled out on the canvas. Trembling. Twitching. Completely at his mercy.

Which seems like a very dangerous place to be.

The unimaginable heat blazing across his eyes burns hotter than any fire I've ever seen, what I imagine the surface of the sun looks like up close, and as his gaze travels over me, it feels like being swallowed up by it. Like it's branding my skin the same way the tattoos cover his.

Black and white paint streaks across his neck and in his hair—visual evidence of how completely out of control he made me with just his mouth and fingers.

He shoves his jeans down, freeing his hard cock.

My breath hitches again, watching it bob gently as he tugs off his pants and tosses them to the side.

"I haven't been with anyone in over a year, Ivy." His gaze turns hard. "Since before I went to rehab. And I've been tested and retested for everything under the sun and come back clear..." He takes his length in his hand and strokes it once, twice, a third time. "I need to feel your cunt without anything between us."

Fuck.

How awful is it that I hadn't even *thought* about that until this moment...

His dark brow furrows. "Can I do that, Ivy?" Still stroking his cock, he tilts his head, examining me on the canvas before he kneels back down between my legs and runs his free hand across one thigh, and then the other. "Can I fuck you bare and come deep inside you?"

Good fucking God...

There are things I should tell him about why I'm not worried about getting pregnant, but this isn't the time or place to have that discussion. Not when his words, his stare, his hard, ready body are poised over me and mine is trembling to take him.

Fluttering and clasping at nothing when all I want is to feel him *filling* me.

I release a little gasp at the sensation of his fingertips along my hypersensitive skin and nod.

A slow grin spreads across his face, and his gaze sweeps over me again. "I wish I were a more talented artist so I could capture how fucking perfect you look right now. A truly breathtaking masterpiece..."

Instantly, I tear my eyes from him to scan all the paintings surrounding us in the room, and I can't help but chuckle at the absurdity of his statement. "I think you've done a pretty good job."

Cam shakes his head and braces one hand to the side of my neck as he drags the head of his cock through my slick folds, making me shudder. "Not even fucking close, Ivy." His lips feather over mine. "Not." Another light brush. "Even." Another. "Fucking." A final one where he lets them linger before slowly pulling away. "Close."

He pushes into me in one hard, determined thrust.

Fuuuuck!

Air rushes from my lungs.

My head spins.

Heat licks across my body, centered between my legs where Cam has filled me so completely.

A low, guttural groan vibrates in Cam's chest pressed to mine, and my hips arch up to meet him, taking him even deeper, until he's buried all the way to the hilt.

"Fuck..."

His strangled curse rolls through me, echoing across the studio as he buries his face in my neck and digs his teeth into my collarbone. That sharp bite of pain coupled with the way his thick cock stretches me so completely makes my pussy flutter along it, and I clench down, digging my nails into the canvas under me. Another animalistic sound falls from his lips, and he nips at my still-stinging skin again, moving up my neck to my ear with hot presses of his lips and tiny licks of pain.

"If you keep doing that, this won't last very long, Ivy."

I loop my arms around him, desperate to cling to him, to keep him *right* here where I can feel *all* of him pressed against me. But he seems to have other ideas.

He pulls his head away, my arms falling to the canvas as he pushes my thighs open, throws my left leg over his shoulder, and shoves my right knee up, spreading me wide and allowing him to draw his hips back and plunge impossibly deep.

A startled gasp tumbles from my lips, my neck arching, my hips clutched in his tight grip as he sets an unyielding rhythm I know I won't survive.

There is nothing tentative about it.

No feeling me out.

No easing into our first time together.

Camden fucks like he paints, in long, sure strokes filled with an intensity, focus, and passion that explodes from somewhere deep in his soul. An all-consuming devotion and dedication to every movement. As if every drive of his cock into me has a purpose. Every retreat, another one. Like he meticulously planned out each detail of how he wanted to claim me and is now enacting his plan.

Just like he does with his paintings on these canvases...

He holds nothing back.

The man lives and breathes his art, and he's making it with his body tonight.

Creating his own masterpiece on this canvas by moving me exactly where he wants me, by taking me exactly as he wants, without reservation or any barriers.

All the lies are out in the open now.

The painful truths have all led to *this* moment.

Each stroke builds me higher, the head of his cock catching on the *exact* spot inside me like he knows exactly what angle to hit and how to bring me there quickly.

His hips pump wildly, his hands tightening around my thighs as he holds me spread wide, and then he angles his hips down and thrusts up, and I see stars flashing against my closed lids.

My already labored breaths seize in my chest, each

attempt to draw in air only getting harder and harder the harder he fucks me.

And this *is* pure, unadulterated *fucking*.

This is *consuming*.

This is *claiming*.

These are the things I never thought I needed so badly but now can't imagine living without...

My pussy ripples around him, my body primed and getting ready to explode.

He issues a rumbling groan of appreciation, dipping his head to capture my next gasp as he reaches a hand between us and twists my clit. "I can't wait to feel your pussy clamp on my cock as you come, Ivy—"

I do it as soon as the word leaves his mouth, and he bites off a curse and kisses me intensely, moving his fingers across my clit viciously as he plunges unfathomably deep and hard enough to rock me across the canvas.

My eyes drift closed, the world spinning around me, a violent rebellion of my body and heart until I can't contain it any longer.

I gasp and erupt.

Tears stream down my temples in a hot rush.

All the pain and agony I've felt over the last several months dissipates on a cloud of pure ecstasy as he continues to pump into me. His hips snap. His cock stretches me as my pussy ripples and clasps at his length, trying to keep it inside, trying to keep this bliss going forever.

His fingers move over my clit, helping to drag out my pleasure, the sparks of release tingling through every limb and bright flashes of light against my closed lids drawing a shudder through my body.

My lungs burn, and I finally realize I haven't breathed,

forcing myself to suck in a gasp of air as the orgasm threatens to pull me completely from the safety of his arms.

Cam pulls his hand from where our bodies connect and grips my chin, forcing my head toward him and consuming my mouth with a kiss that's all desperation and promise and tangle of tongues until he groans and comes hard, emptying himself inside me and pinning me to the canvas.

The faster my chest moves, trying to give my body the oxygen it lost, the more aware I become of his slick skin pressed to mine, his still-hard cock embedded in me along with his release.

And the more I *relish* it.

His scent fills every breath I manage to take, and I suck it down greedily, wanting more, needing it.

Camden Usher is fucking dangerous.

I knew it the moment I opened my door and saw him at my house.

I just never knew how much.

Until he stole my soul like this.

24

IVY

I hardly register it when Cam scoops me up off the canvas and carries me into his bathroom. Barely understand what's happening when he holds me up with one arm and cranks on the shower with the other, then presses languid kisses along my collarbone, my neck, my tear-stained cheeks, my lips while holding me steady.

My mind and body both float in that heady post-orgasm space where I can't care about anything, blissfully allowing Cam to take control just like I did out in the studio.

He tugs me under the spray, and the hot water starts to soak into my skin, washing away the paint that must be covering us by now. Everything in me sags, giving in to the exhaustion, relying on Cam to support me physically and emotionally because I am utterly spent in both respects.

Gentle hands scrub a loofah across my wet skin, and goosebumps erupt over every inch of my body, a little moan slipping through my lips.

Cam chuckles low, burying his face in my neck as he

continues to wipe away the evidence of what he just did to me. "Don't worry, Ivy. I'll get you to bed."

My thighs clench at his words, every part of me remembering what we did with a dull ache, and my legs tremble so badly they can hardly hold me up. Only his strong arm wrapped around my waist keeps me from falling over as he washes my body and hair with such care that more tears slip from my eyes that I pray he can't see under the spray.

This is the real Cam.

This is the one I saw that he tried so hard to hide.

He switches off the water, wraps me in a fluffy towel, and dries himself off carefully, with one hand on me to ensure I stay upright, then scoops me back into his arms effortlessly. I don't have the energy to do anything except snuggle against him, pressing my face to the damp skin at his neck, breathing in the vibrant citrus scent that always clings to him that must be from the soap he uses.

Considering how often he must wash his hands to cleanse away the paint, no wonder he always smells like it...

He pads across the studio and sets me down beside the bed, pulling the towel from around me so he can dry me fully, before he settles me onto the mattress and tugs the sheets up around me.

Instantly, sleep tugs at me. This warm, blissful place my mind is floating in starts to be encroached on by that welcome darkness that has been so hard to find for so long.

The lights in the studio shut off, and a few seconds later, the bed dips behind me.

Cam settles in at my back. His strong arm wraps around my stomach, and he tugs me up against him—all hard, lean muscle and heat as he presses his lips to the nape of my neck.

"Mmm..." I instinctually shift back even more, rubbing against him, my ass nestled to his crotch, needing the contact, wanting it, despite how drained I already feel.

His cock instantly hardens, and he nips at my collarbone, making me twitch. "I'm trying to be good here, Ivy. I'm trying to let you *sleep*."

I arch my neck and tilt my head toward him, then reach and run my hands through his damp hair. My nails score over his scalp, drawing a low groan from him and a shift of his hips that presses his hard cock between my ass cheeks in a way that reawakens the heat I thought had ebbed after what happened on that canvas. "You told me you weren't good..."

Cam's own words from earlier seem to hang between us for a moment before he issues a low, muttered curse and tilts my head back enough to kiss me. His tongue delves into my mouth, warring with mine, my body jolting alive again, and my already wrung-out clit throbbing, wanting more of what he gave me only a short time ago.

Why is it like this between us?

What sort of twisted game has fate been playing to lead me here? Into this man's arms and bed?

All the questions continue to race through my head as the heat builds with his searing kiss, and he slides his left hand from my stomach down between my legs to cup me gently. His lips flutter across mine. "Are you sure, Ivy?"

The promise is there.

He would stop if I said I didn't want this.

If I chose to drift off to sleep in his arms with his hard cock straining against me, he would gladly let me and hold me all night.

But that isn't what I want, despite the exhaustion I felt only moments ago.

Back in his arms like this...I want *more.*

I nod vehemently, pressing my lips to his hungrily. He tugs my left hip over his, spreading me wide so he can delve his fingers between my legs, my body starting to slicken there with my renewed arousal. Heat licks across my skin, every inch of me already aflame. He skims a finger through my folds, dragging the liquid up across my clit, and I groan, arching back even more.

"Fucking hell..." He mutters the words next to my ear, then reaches between us and adjusts his cock so it rests against me, my wetness coating him as he rubs it back and forth, and his fingers play with my most sensitive spot, drenching him even further.

A desperate little mewl slips from my parted lips.

It feels so fucking good that I don't want it to end.

But I also need more.

Faster.

He seems to sense my growing frustration and alters the angle of his hips so he can slide the head of his cock inside me. I gasp as he spreads me wide, then shoves up, fully impaling me.

I gasp at the sheer force of his entry, and he rolls, taking me with him onto his back so I'm draped across him. With his arms looped over mine, he pins me in place so he can brace his feet into the mattress and hold me hostage.

Completely at his mercy.

Again.

Only, instead of the almost manic pace of earlier, he thrusts up into me slowly. In long, steady strokes that make me feel every single inch of him in exquisite detail.

So unlike what just happened on the canvas.

That was rough and wild.

Fast and hard.

This is...almost reverent.

Every brush of his lips against my ear. Every breath fluttering across my skin. Every drive of his hips designed to worship me in a way that makes tears burn in my eyes again.

He releases my arms, and I reach back to tangle one hand in his hair as he nuzzles my cheek. My other hand drifts down to the mattress, clutching at the sheets, seeking a way to ground myself when he expertly tries to make me spin out of control with every move he makes.

The roll of his hips. That extra little thrust at the top that catches the head of his cock inside me. The sweep of his tongue and lips and scrape of teeth against my neck and shoulder.

Then he lifts my leg, dragging it up and back, giving himself a better angle and exposing me more as he thrusts up in that same rhythm I'm convinced is a slow form of torture.

I bite my lip to contain the whimper that tries to slip out, and Cam slides his hand across my stomach to the apex of my thighs.

"Tell me how you want it, Ivy. Like this?" He rolls his finger over my clit, and I jerk, clenching down around him. "Slow and steady?" His grin presses to my neck. "Or do you like it fast and hard, like before?"

The whimper falls out.

God, I like it all.

I want it all.

Tonight is truly the first time that I've felt alive. The other night, my world was collapsing around me, and what happened between us was tangled in grief, guilt, frustration, and regret.

But not now.

All of that is gone.

All that exists is the feel of his cock filling me, his calloused hands gliding across my skin, and his hot, frantic mouth all over me.

"Answer me, Ivy." He keeps pumping in that dangerously languid pace that's more like torture, thrusting up, languidly dragging his fingers across my clit, not giving me what I desperately need...

But God, it feels so good.

His teeth scrape along the column of my neck, his lips following with so much care that the tears finally slip free.

I can't breathe, let alone *speak,* to offer any sort of answer.

And he just keeps going, setting a completely unhurried pace, as if he has nothing else to do, nowhere else to be but right here.

Where I want to be.

I don't want him to move from this exact spot.

Something about being spread out across him like this, feeling every move of his chest, his tightening and flexing abs, his rolling pelvis, his tense legs braced to give him leverage against my own as he works me up, heightens *everything.*

My skin feels too hot.

Too tight.

Every brush of his fingers across my clit too intense.

The drag of his cock inside my cunt too damn *good.*

But it never crests.

A languid build that doesn't seem to lead *anywhere* but my extended purgatory.

"Cam, please." My plea comes out as a whimper, the kind of noise that I never like making, that makes me sound so needy, so desperate.

But I am.

For him.

For more.

He takes mercy on me and plants his feet, driving up into me harder, faster, but still completely in control, an artist with his canvas, every stroke deliberately placed, all the tension and harsh lines of his body coiled beneath and around mine. And when he finally takes my clit between his fingers and pinches, twisting it, I come on a strangled cry that echoes off the exposed brick and steel beams of the ceiling.

His own gasp joins the sound as my pussy clenches around him and unleashes something he had managed to restrain until this moment.

Cam's hips piston harder.

His body tenses as he chases his own release with hammering drives up into me until he finally finds it, lips and teeth clamping down into my collarbone as he comes underneath me.

He drags my head to the side until he can get to my mouth, kissing me in the same rhythm with his tongue as he just did with his cock.

Advance and retreat.

Long and slow as we both try to catch our breath and come down from the high we just experienced.

Finally, I sag fully against him, and he rolls me back onto my side, coming with me, his cock still embedded inside of me. His arms tighten, his body twitching as he nuzzles me, gently dragging his fingers down my arm.

Minutes tick by in comfortable silence, only our heavy breathing filling the air until his chest finally stops heaving against my shoulders.

He kisses my cheek and pulls out, slipping away with a groan.

I roll over to watch him as he climbs from the bed, his semi-hard cock glistening with our releases. He stalks across the studio, buck naked, completely, unabashedly nude, tattoos coming alive as he moves. "Cam? What are you doing?"

He grabs a blank canvas and moves toward the paints lined up along the floor near the one we spent the evening on earlier. "I have to paint you."

"What?" I push up onto my elbow, my head spinning, still foggy from exhaustion and the pleasure still making my body twitch. "Camden, no."

The look he tosses over his shoulder at me shuts me up immediately.

He wasn't asking.

His eyes blaze with the same absolute focus I saw when I first arrived and watched him start painting. This is his muse speaking to him, telling him what to create. And apparently, it's me.

Almost frantically, he gets what he needs on his palette and brings it over toward the bed, along with the blank canvas and several brushes.

He pauses, stares down at me, and under his assessment, I fall back, allowing my head to hit the pillow.

"Just like that. Don't move."

With one leg up, my pussy, still dripping with his release, is fully exposed, as is the rest of me. The corners of his lips curl as he takes me in by the pale moonlight shining in from the row of windows, and he casually moves back a few feet, sets the canvas on the floor, then squats, still fully nude, and starts painting.

Every movement of his hand makes the corded muscles of his forearm and biceps bunch. He uses broad strokes of blacks and whites, then creates three different shades of gray, slicing the bristles across the canvas so fast that I can barely follow it.

His eyes narrow on me. "Don't move."

"I'm not."

The corners of his lips twitch. "You are. You're trying to peek."

"Well, it is me..."

He chuckles low, the sound doing something to me that I don't want to admit as he keeps painting, his gaze flicking between the canvas and me.

Minutes tick by, the time melting away easily, the longer I watch him work.

Because he's a fucking masterpiece himself.

The way he moves, how easily he creates something so beautiful with seemingly so little effort...

By the time he rests back on his heels and examines the painting, my eyes are drooping, the emotional and physical events of the evening taking their toll.

I don't even know when he finishes, just that I feel the bed dip and his body align to mine. He drapes his arm across me and tugs me against him, fluttering his lips to my cheek and then my ear.

"Fucking stunning, Ivy. A true masterpiece."

It's the last thing I hear before the world starts to darken at the edges, and I finally allow myself to drift off, blissful in the arms of the man whose warning I undoubtedly should have heeded.

25

IVY

I push my breakfast around with my fork—bacon, eggs, and toast that should smell delicious but instead makes acid climb my throat. And I barely even see the food on the plate.

My eyes won't focus.

My mind only able to concentrate on one thing.

And it sure as hell isn't eating.

The same questions I somehow managed to lock away last night, long enough to give in to my merciless attraction to Cam, are screaming in my head now. An incessant spiral of guilt, shame, and disbelief over everything that has happened—that I've *allowed* to happen—has left me dizzy and unsettled.

My stomach roils violently, and my eyes burn with tears I've been fighting all morning. Since I woke in Cam's arms and fell back into *him* so easily and completely, let him take command of my body again, and again, and *again*, until we finally came up for air—and breakfast.

Which he *insisted* I needed.

Given the...exertion of the last twelve hours, he's probably right.

Every muscle is sore in the best way possible. The aches remind me of how utterly Camden consumed me—enough that I was able to forget. Or at least, pretend to for a glorious period of time that eventually had to come to an end.

And it did end.

The moment we stepped out of his building and he lit up that cigarette.

Watching him take that long drag and blow out the smoke was like flipping a switch in my head, reminding me of that first time he warned me away and all the reasons he was right that I was not privy to.

All the deception.

Not just on his part, either.

And that's what hurts the most.

Drew's lies—the ones I built our life together on...

"Ivy?" Cam's voice draws me out of the haze of disbelief, anger, and self-loathing, and I glance up at him across from me in the booth at the diner down the street from his studio. As he watches me, his eyes still hold that same edge of uncertainty that they did when we climbed onto his bike this morning, but they also swim with steely determination. "You need to *stop*."

I clear the lump from my throat. "Stop what?"

He raises a dark brow at me, his hand tightening around his mug of shitty coffee sitting next to his empty plate. Because apparently he had absolutely no problem eating this morning, but I can't seem to bring myself to take more than a few bites, my stomach churning, acid billowing up, along with all the emotions that want to choke me.

And somehow, Cam seems to see *all* of it through the

wall of forced smiles, nods, and idle chit-chat I've tried to maintain.

This man knows me, while so much of him is such a mystery that he doesn't seem inclined to want to share with me.

But he clearly has something to say now as he shifts forward slightly, resting his elbows on the Formica tabletop. "You need to stop second-guessing your entire relationship with Drew."

I recoil slightly at being so blatantly called out when I haven't said a *word* about Drew or *anything* Cam revealed since we ruined that canvas last night. "That's not what I'm doing..."

That brow of his stays up in accusation and disbelief. "Isn't it?"

He holds my gaze, the sharpness of the blue in his like piercing ice straight through my soul. It shreds me, so easily getting down to the core of everything that's been billowing inside of me since I learned the truth.

All the emotions that want to smother me and bring me back to that horrible place I was in before Cam appeared in my life.

I finally let my fork clatter to the plate, giving up the pretense of actually eating when he clearly knows I'm not. "I just don't..." Dropping my face into my palms, I rest my elbows on the table and release a long sigh. "I just don't know how I'm supposed to... I don't know"—pulling my head back, I throw my hands up with a frustrated noise in my throat—"*process* any of this."

Last night and this morning were...a beautiful distraction I let myself drift away in so I wouldn't have to deal with the *hard* things. The questions and feelings that I knew would end up making me like this—a quivering mess.

I let myself give in to this attraction to Cam, submitted to whatever this magnetic pull is that keeps bringing me back to him—apparently from the first fucking second we met.

But now, in the bright light of day, sitting across from him, knowing the truth, my whole life looks different.

Every single word that was spoken. Every shared kiss and touch. *Every*thing that happened over the last four years with Drew seems like it was a lie, like it was something else entirely than the life I thought I had lived.

So much of what made my relationship with Drew so special, what I *loved* so much about it and him, was that he was always so *open*. So *honest* with his emotions. And he had the ability to pry out what was bothering someone so they could talk about it and move past those things that held them back.

And now, even *that* feels like a lie.

When he was keeping something so *big* from me...

Cam reaches out and grasps my hand, squeezing it gently, and that simple touch sends a little thrill racing through me as every inch of my body remembers that touch.

The way he worshipped me last night.

Not just with his hands.

But with his mouth.

His cock.

Every fiber of my being still buzzes from it.

A relentless, pulsating thrum that seems to rush in my blood and heat me from my core outward to every limb.

Yet all of it, everything we shared, is now tangled up in the lie that started that night. The lie Drew maintained for so long so he could pretend like it hadn't happened.

Cam brushes his thumb across my knuckles, and I watch his lazy, comforting strokes. "Just because it was me that night doesn't change anything that happened between you and Drew after it."

I jerk my head up to look at him. "How can you say that?" My mouth opens and closes a few times as I try to make sense of any of it, but the longer I attempt to find reason in the lies, the harder it becomes to rein in my emotions. "Of course it changes things."

It changes *everything*.

Each day we spent together. Each night in bed. Each and every one of them was built on that lie that he perpetuated.

I pull my hand out from under his and shove it back through my hair, unable to concentrate on *anything* rational when he's touching me, even so innocently. "He *knew*, Cam." A little mirthless laugh floats from my lips. "He fucking *knew* that something had happened between us out in your mother's yard, and he never told me. He never came clean and told me it was you. He never told me the *truth*." I scan the diner around us to ensure no one is at the tables close by and dip my head closer to him. "We *slept* together that night."

Cam flinches slightly at my confession but does his best to try to hide it.

"It was our first time together and..." I squeeze my eyes closed, trying to stop myself from spiraling the way I want to into all the questions, all the lies he must have told. "I mean, was that all because he was trying to...one-up whatever happened between the two of us?" That thought seizes my chest. My breaths come in hard, short pants, my vision blurring. "Was...any of it even fucking real or just some game he had to win with you?"

Pure panic clutches at me.

Threatening to make me lose control of myself in this very public place.

"Stop." Cam's command comes low, deep, filled with the absolute potency to end my spiraling with that simple word. His hard eyes bore into mine, holding me captive, preventing me from looking away. "Nothing that happened between you and Drew was a lie. None of it. When I walked into the yard that night, I already knew all about you. I had already seen all his pictures from your first several dates. He had sent me your goddamn social media links so I could check you out because he was already falling in love with you. He told me that he knew you were the girl he was going to marry after he met you the first time, remember?"

I nod.

Cam *had* told me that the last time I melted down about the secrets Drew was keeping, and I believed him then.

But that was before.

Now, I know the truth about the start of our relationship, and it makes everything after it seem so tainted.

"He was obsessed with you from day fucking one, Ivy, and all he ever wanted was to be with you. So, none of it was a lie. None of it."

"But—"

His eyes sharpen even more, leaving no room to argue with him further. "No buts, Ivy. *I* was the selfish fucking prick. Anything Drew did after that point wasn't about my betrayal or some game; it was about how he *always* felt about *you*. And I *need* you to understand and believe that."

The way he emphasizes the word *need*. The forcefulness of his stare and voice. The wall of emotions that appears to be bottled up behind his gaze and ready to unleash, all send goosebumps skittering over my skin.

My chest tightens, my lungs threatening to stop as I try to swallow through the sob that wants to slip out and embarrass me in front of all the customers in the diner.

Several people already cast furtive glances at us, and I'm sure I look a mess after what we did last night—and this morning.

And I *am* a mess.

Far more than what I must appear like on the outside.

Tears blur my vision, then slide hot down my cheeks. "He lied to me about so many things..."

Cam presses his lips together tightly. "Only because I forced him to."

I shake my head. "You never forced him to do anything. He could have told me that night. He could have told me *any* time. He could have explained it to me when I asked him what happened between the two of you, why you had your falling out. He could have said, 'Because he fucking kissed you and fingered you in our mom's backyard.'"

Cam flinches slightly, but now that I've started, I'm not sure I can bite back the anger from bursting out.

"He could have told me. He had *four years* to tell me. *You* could have told me."

At least he has the decency to look contrite, running a hand through his hair, messing it up even more. But he doesn't offer any explanation for their silence on the topic.

The mystery of Camden Usher was so enticing, something to unravel and explore, but now I'm just frustrated with his inability to come clean, even when we're already airing out his dirty laundry.

I fist my hands on the table. "Didn't he ever *want* to?"

That kind of secret would have crushed me.

I couldn't have kept something like that from the man I loved.

"Of course he did, Ivy." Cam slowly shifts, scrubbing his hands over his face. "He wanted to come clean with you from the beginning."

But he didn't.

Drew left me in the dark about something so important —not only to *me* but to *us*. To his *family*. That night changed everything for *everyone* he loved, and its ripple effect continues today. Nancy still doesn't understand what happened between her sons or why Cam won't come home to her, and it all stems from that *one* moment in time.

And in my heart, the fact that Drew kept it from me is just as bad as what Cam did.

"Then why *didn't* he?"

I try to keep the anger out of my voice, but apparently, I fail because Cam winces.

He fingers his mug again, drumming his nails along the side of the chipped ceramic. "He didn't tell you because I made him believe that he would lose you if he did."

"*What?*"

Cam stares at his coffee, which must be cold by now, unable to look at me, his jaw clenched. "I told you I was a prick, Ivy. I was so wrapped up in what happened between us that I didn't think about the consequences for you, for him. And when he sent me that text, I told you I didn't apologize, but..." He releases a troubled sigh, finally looking up at me with regret in his gaze. "I replied and told him that the connection we had was so instantaneous and real that he would never have with you what I did in those twenty minutes we sat there together."

I gape at him, unable to reconcile something so vicious with the man who has been so giving and kind to me.

"I was a different person back then, Ivy, and I'm not proud of what I did or what I said to him." He rubs his palm across his stubbled cheek. "He probably believed it. Probably thought that he didn't stand a chance against me because he always thought I had such an easier time than he did with women. That's why he didn't come clean with you. It's why he cut me off. Not only because I did the unforgivable but because he would never risk losing you by telling you the truth."

Fuck.

I squeeze my eyes closed and run my hands through my hair, dropping my forehead to the table.

Several minutes pass by with just the noises of the diner —clinking silverware and plates, laughter, voices, orders being called out—floating through the air.

Cam gives me time. He gives me space. He lets me process everything in my own way, even when I don't doubt he has more to say.

When I finally lift my head again, he's watching me cautiously. "Do you think he ever would have told me?"

He offers a shrug. "I don't know."

"After he died, I knew he had been lying to me about stuff." I shake my head. "But this?" I release a little laugh that doesn't hold any humor. "Never crossed my mind."

"I don't want you to keep questioning your life with him." His voice cracks, and he swallows down the emotion. "I told you the other day he never would have cheated on you, and I mean it. The whole love-at-first-sight thing doesn't happen very often, but it did for him."

Cam looks at me with so much unbridled passion in his gaze that my breath hitches.

And me.

He doesn't say those words, and if he did, I'm not sure what I would do with them right now, but they're still *there* in the way the blue seems to ripple and heat the longer he stares at me.

"He never would have done anything to lose you, Ivy, even if that meant lying to you. You may not agree with it, you may be pissed at him for it, but he had a reason. And it was because he loved you from day fucking one."

The vehemence in his statement helps shatter some of the anger I've let build up over what Drew kept from me. Because somehow, somewhere deep down, I do believe what Cam says.

I saw it in the way Drew looked at me, felt the way he touched me, experienced the way he made love to me, and just *loved* me every day.

I saw it.

I felt it.

But I also felt what I did with Cam that night—that electricity, that spark, that undeniable draw that allowed me to throw inhibition to the wind and let him do such decadent things to me right out in the open.

And that *thing* I felt is what convinced me that Drew was the right man for me.

Would that have even happened if Cam hadn't been there?

If he hadn't come along?

If he hadn't touched me like that?

I suck in a long, slow breath and release it, trying to force myself off that path of thought, because if I go down it, I'm not sure how I would get back.

"Please, don't ruin your memories of your life with Drew because of something stupid I did. Just don't."

"I'm trying really hard not to, Cam, but—"

"I know." He nods, sympathy wetting his gaze. "And I'm sorry for that. For ruining what you had with the truth. I never would have told you but..." He swallows hard, looking down at his coffee rather than at me. "But you deserved to know, especially after the other night."

When we said goodbye to Drew...

And reawakened something that maybe should have stayed dead...

But even as I think that, my body buzzes with memories of the way he held me when we returned from the shore and let me cry, how he touched me and sent me flying because it was what I needed in that moment, even if it was wrong, the way he fell apart with me after and let down his guard.

"Why didn't you tell me then?"

He works his tense jaw, the conversation clearly getting under Cam's skin. "Because you were already breaking after going to the shore. There was just no way I could do that to you. But I wasn't about to let what happened that night ever happen again...until you showed up last night and you discovered the truth, until you knew what you were doing. For both of us."

"What was I doing?"

The corners of his lips curl into a sad smile. "Opening the floodgate..."

Opening the floodgate...

It's definitely a very good description of what happened both that night and in the last twelve hours.

Because Cam is a force of nature.

Dangerous. Brutal. Destructive. But also staggeringly beautiful in a dark way that threatens to consume me.

And I don't know how to stop him from doing just that.

Or even if I *want* to stop it from happening.

"Promise me you'll stop letting yourself get wrapped up in your head, Ivy."

The plea in his voice, the strain of so deeply caring and not wanting to see me suffer, proves that he isn't the horrible person he believes himself to be. His goal right now isn't staking a claim on me, nor rubbing in the fact that he "had" me first. He's worried about my memories of Drew and how he will stay with me for eternity. His focus is on ensuring I never forget that love.

Something I am desperately trying to do...

I've spent months wallowing in my grief over losing Drew, so allowing any other emotion seems like such a *relief.* And holding on to the anger at few for lying to me for so long rather than that pain is so much easier.

Cam told one lie. A really fucking big one. But Drew told years' worth.

And that's something I'm going to have to get past if I ever want to be able to concentrate on all that we *did* have that *was* real.

"I'll try..."

"Good." Cam glances out at the street through the massive window to our left. "It's your day off, right?"

I nod. "Yeah."

"I want to take you somewhere today." His cheeks pinken with an almost embarrassed blush that I have never seen from him. "I want to show you something."

"Okay..."

He pulls my hand into his, the warmth seeping into my

skin, grounding me while it simultaneously sets my heart racing. "I want you to know me, really know me, and that's hard for me to do with anyone. But you deserve it, Ivy." His grip tightens. "You deserve so much more than I can give you..."

The pain lacing his words twists like a knife in my chest, and I squeeze his hand, pulling it closer to me. "Don't talk like that."

Cam's lips tilt into a crooked half-smile that doesn't reach his eyes. "But it's true."

It may be.

And Cam may be fucked up in ways I can't even begin to comprehend.

But I don't think there's any way that I can look at Cam and not see his many dimensions.

Like his paintings, there isn't just black and white.

There are a thousand shades of gray in his art and in Camden Usher.

26

IVY

The vast hall surrounds us.

Towering ceiling.

Highly polished floors traversed by thousands over the years to see the art lining the walls.

Masterpieces going back hundreds of years.

Some so stunning, they make me stop in my tracks—which I suppose is the intent the artist had in the first place.

A group of kids here on a school field trip dashes past, giggling as the teacher chases them and whispers at them to slow down and be quiet, and Cam tightens his grip on my hand, tugging me forward and leading me confidently around the Philadelphia Museum of Art.

Just like he was with his brushes in hand, Cam seems to know exactly where he wants to go, weaving through the maze of hallways and galleries as if he's memorized them.

I scan the works on the walls as we pass, trying not to get too distracted by them when Cam clearly has something specific he wants to show me. But that's hard, given my newfound respect for the art world that suddenly developed

in the last twenty-four hours. "I haven't been here in probably twenty years."

Cam grins, giving my hand a light squeeze. "That doesn't
surprise me."

Raising a brow, I allow him to move me through another
gallery, past several groups on tours who stand intently
listening as the guide talks about various pieces of priceless
art. "Why is that?"

He shrugs. "It's kind of one of those 'you go once, you see
it, and you're done with it' kind of thing for most people."

Sadness laces his words, and he doesn't have to explain
why that thought is so depressing for him.

This man's life revolves around expressing himself
through his art.

Paint and canvas—or a bare wall in a city somewhere
around the world—are his entire focus.

To think people don't appreciate it—despite the noto-
riety he's gained with his works—has to hit squarely in
the gut.

"But not you?"

Cam shakes his head, the corner of his lips twitching
slightly. "I still vividly remember the first time I came here. I
was six and on a first-grade class field trip." He stops walking
and pulls me to the side, out of the way of the flow of
patrons, and points across from us to a Monet. "I saw *that*,
and my heart just *stopped*."

"Really?"

But looking at it, I can see *why*.

The loose brushwork, fleeting moments of light and
color, all combine to create a stunning landscape that
somehow screams to be looked at, even with the muted
palette and soft touch.

He gives me a moment to examine every detail of the painting, and the longer I stare at it, the more my eyes start to burn with unshed tears.

When was the last time I stopped *and looked at something just because it was beautiful?*

Day in, day out, I'm surrounded by life—flowers, plants, endless greenery—and I spend my entire career putting together bouquets and arrangements to celebrate the love people have for each other, but at some point, I stopped *seeing* it.

And I know exactly when that happened.

It was the moment I got that call from Nancy.

The second I knew Drew was gone, so was my ability to appreciate anything beautiful anymore.

Cam wraps his arms around me from behind, resting his chin on my shoulder, his lips feathering over my ear. "I knew that's what I wanted to do—create things that were that beautiful. I didn't know what a soul was at that point, but I understood what looking at it did to me"—he presses his hand over my heart, which picks up its beat under the warm press of his palm—"*here.*"

A single tear falls from my eye, and he leans in and kisses it away so gently that I practically collapse back into his hold.

I don't know how long we stand, looking at this single painting.

Minutes...

An hour...

People stream past us.

More school groups.

Couples with their hands clutched or arms linked.

And still, I can't look away.

The longer I examine it, the more I see those little details and expert precision that make it so breathtakingly spellbinding.

Cam finally squeezes me, breaking the spell, and I glance back at him.

"Is that what you wanted to show me?"

He shakes his head and drags his lips over mine so softly it makes my knees quiver. "No. Come on."

When I climbed onto the back of his bike, he was very cryptic about why he was bringing me here, and even now, he seems tense, like whatever his reason, he isn't quite sure he wants to expose it to me.

Given everything he's revealed since I showed up at his studio last night, thinking about what that could be has left my stomach churning even more than it did earlier at the diner.

Cam takes my hand in his again and leads me around a few more corners until we pause in front of a massive canvas that drags my eyes up and up and then across its vast size. "*This* is what I wanted you to see."

It takes me a few seconds to truly take in what's hanging in front of us, the macabre scene tightening my gut the longer I stare at it. "What *is* this?"

A naked man sprawled out...

Chained to a rock...

With a hawk yanking what appears to be intestines from a cut in his side...

Cam stands behind me, wrapping his arms around my waist. "Prometheus."

"The titan?"

He nods, pressing his cheek to mine. "This is *Prometheus Bound* by Peter Paul Rubens and Frans Snyders. It depicts the torture Zeus inflicted on him after he gifted man with fire and the arts."

I slip from his hold to move closer, examining every facet of the breathtakingly disturbing piece.

Despite the violent imagery, there's something so beautiful about it that I can't tear my eyes away.

Cam shifts to my side, staring up at it. "It's my favorite painting."

"Here?"

He shakes his head. "Anywhere. I've been to the Louvre more times than I can count, and to just about every other fine art museum in the world over the last fifteen years, but I still come back here, to this one, to this painting, for the feeling I have right now."

I glance over at him, the way his eyes rake over the image with so much fascination, reverence, and appreciation. "Which is what?"

It's what I've been wondering all day, ever since I woke in his bed and his arms...

At breakfast, he pushed me to face the questions that were plaguing me, spent an hour trying to get me to accept that the life I thought I knew with Drew was *real*.

But he must be feeling something, too.

About me.

About what happened.

About the future that seems so uncertain and complicated.

But he said he wanted to show me something about *him*.

This is it.

Cam gives me a sad smile and returns his attention to the painting. "I guess I feel like I understand him, his pain, how he suffers. Even more so now than I did when I first fell in love with it."

His enigmatic words move through me like a tsunami rolling across my heart. I can feel the agony in them, but I don't understand it. Can't understand the enigmatic man standing beside me. Because he won't let me in, not really.

He keeps so many things locked away, so many secrets that I know he hasn't told me. Things that go far beyond what he revealed about that night four years ago, and I want to know them.

I want to know him.

I want to understand what makes him tick.

What made him so different from his brother.

Why he turned in on himself when their father died, while Drew sought out others for comfort and became that comfort for other people—including me.

I want to know why Cam always looks so haunted.

But I'm afraid to ask, afraid I'll send him running if I probe too hard.

Deep down, I'm afraid of him and what his answers might hold.

I ask anyway. "Why?"

He stares at the painting for a while, long enough that I don't think he's going to answer, but he finally does, never tearing his eyes from the gruesome display. "He thought he was doing the right thing..."

"Who did?"

"Prometheus." He tilts his head slightly, taking it in at a different angle, even though I have no doubt he has every single brushstroke memorized. "A lot of people consider him kind of a god of unforeseen consequences. It's something that, the older I get, the easier it becomes to recognize in my own life."

Unforeseen consequences...

"Like what happened with us."

It isn't a question.

He slowly turns to face me, his eyes hooded, that darkness overtaking them as he examines me. "One example in a long line and many years of them, Ivy. It isn't just about you and how badly I fucked things up."

I open my mouth to ask him what else it's about then, but the clicking of heels and a gasp cut through the noise around us.

"Camden?"

The woman's voice floats over us, and my back stiffens as we both turn toward her.

Cam's eyes widen slightly at the stunning woman standing to our left, red hair floating down over her shoulders, tight black dress hugging every curve of her body, and bright-green eyes locked squarely on him.

"It is you!" She rushes forward and throws her arms around him, giving him a hug that says they are definitely well acquainted.

He returns the embrace, pulling away from her slightly to look her up and down. "What are you doing in Philly?"

She smiles brightly at him. "I work here now."

His brows rise. "Seriously?"

Her head bobs enthusiastically. "I got the job almost four months ago. I've been meaning to call you this whole time since I knew you had moved back a while ago, but I got distracted. You know..." She waves a hand toward the gallery. "It's a large collection to keep track of."

She laughs lightly and places a hand on his shoulder, so casually and intimately that my stomach roils.

I retreat a step, and my movement shifts Camden's gaze from her to me.

"Oh, umm...Ivy, this is Roxy." He rubs at the back of his neck, a strange look on his face that I can't quite place. "We went to art school together in London."

Roxy smiles at me, her eyes sliding over me in assessment, and she holds out her hand. "Nice to meet you."

I accept it and shake. "You too."

She quickly turns to Camden. "But now that I've seen you and you know that I'm in town, we have to get together for dinner and catch up."

He nods. "Absolutely."

Her smile falters slightly, her brow furrowing as she looks him over. "I've been worried about you. I called the gallery a few times, and your cell, but never heard back."

His gaze cuts to me quickly before it returns to her, and he forces a smile I can tell isn't real. "Yeah. Sorry about that. Things have just been...difficult."

She frowns. "I heard about your brother. I'm so sorry. If there's anything I can do..."

"I appreciate it." He reaches up and places his hands on her shoulders, then leans in and kisses her on the cheek. "I'll call you. Same number?"

Roxy nods, then motions over her shoulder. "I need to get going, but I better hear from you."

She darts away and disappears around the corner, leaving me awkwardly standing beside Cam with my heart in my throat and my stomach threatening to make the few bites of breakfast I managed to eat come back up.

Cam turns back to me—agonizingly slowly—running his hands through his hair as his uncertain gaze meets mine.

"Art school together, huh?"

I don't mean it to come out so accusatory.

Or to sound so damn laced with jealousy.

But that's exactly what happens.

I've suddenly become *that* person who turns green with it the moment another woman who clearly has a past with the man I'm—

I don't even know *what* we are, but this heat spreading through my body isn't a pleasant, warm glow. It's the kind of uneasy feeling I only ever got before with Drew when I saw the way women flocked to him.

He clears his throat and approaches me, stopping within touching distance but not moving to do it—maybe because he senses my current mood. "We were friends."

I raise a brow. "Friends?"

He nods.

"That looked like more than just friends."

Cam releases a labored sigh, his shoulders slumping beneath his leather jacket. "I wasn't very careful with my actions when I was using. Before I went to rehab. We were friends. *Just* friends," he clarifies, "but things went further than they should have, even though I thought we were on the same page and knew what it was. I think she wanted more." He shakes his head. "No, I *knew* she did. Crossing that line with her is something that wouldn't have happened if I'd been thinking clearly. I'm not a thoughtless person, Ivy, despite what some of my recent actions might suggest, but..."
—he sighs again and glances toward where she went around the corner—"I definitely fucked up where she was concerned, and I owe her an explanation. And an apology."

His confession blasts away any green tinge of jealousy and replaces it with embarrassment for the way I acted.

My cheeks heat, and I dip my head, unable to look at him. "Part of the whole making amends thing?"

He lifts my chin, forcing me to meet his gaze as he nods. "Something like that."

"Is that...why you came to my house?"

His brow furrows. "What do you mean?"

"That night, when you came back to town. Is that why? Because you were making amends?"

Cam watches me for a second, as if he's unsure how to answer or how I'll respond to it, before he shakes his head. Those warring emotions that always seem to battle in his eyes continue their melee. "No. That wasn't why I came."

"Then why did you?"

He clenches his jaw, a muscle there ticcing as he considers me. "I had to make sure you were okay. To check up on you..."

"So, you came all the way from London to do that? You couldn't have just asked your mother? You couldn't have called?"

All those things would have been *much* easier, especially since he apparently has no intention of letting Nancy know he's here anytime in the near future.

But Cam shakes his head, his hold on my chin tightening. "No. I had to see you myself. And warn you."

"That you were back in town?"

He nods.

None of it makes any sense.

The way he looks at me...

These overwhelming feelings that seem to bubble up inside me with a simple touch from him...

All the secrets and lies that have been told to me by Drew and him have left me unable to grasp what's real without questioning it.

And having to stare into Cam's eyes doesn't help matters.

I pull free from his hold, turn, and look at Prometheus again.

At the agony he's suffering.

His clenched fists.

The eagle's talon digging into his eye, tearing into his flesh.

This is how Camden sees himself—a victim of unintended consequences.

And my heart shatters for him because of that.

Because he's proven to me time and time again since he's been back how caring he is, how kind, always looking out for me, taking care of me even when I don't want to let anyone.

Yet, it's right there in the blood spilling from Prometheus —the unintended consequences.

Cam sitting down on that bench with me that night, not correcting me when I thought he was Drew, led to their relationship being destroyed, even as it helped build mine with his brother based on a lie.

A tear starts to blur my vision, and I quickly blink it away, refusing to cry again for a man who still holds so many secrets.

I can see them in his eyes, hiding in those shadows that always consumes them.

He may have come clean about a lot of things, but there are some he keeps locked down deep. Truths he refuses to tell because he's terrified of the consequences.

Something tells me I'll never know—not those hidden truths and not the man standing beside me.

Not truly.

He and Drew both had secrets, but Camden's are undoubtedly far worse if this painting is any reflection of them.

27

IVY

The moment I open the front door, Marlo pushes through it, carrying a grocery bag in one hand and raising a bottle of wine in the other. "I brought wine, chocolate, and cheese. This sounded urgent."

I roll my eyes as she moves straight toward the kitchen with her haul. My hand tightens on the knob, and though I have every intent to close the door, my eyes lock on the street —the *empty* street.

It's only been a few hours since we parted ways so he could go to his meeting, and I came home alone, but I'm twitchy.

Restless.

Unable to stop waiting for the rumble of his motorcycle's engine that will announce his presence.

Get your shit together...

I force myself to tear my eyes off the street, close the door, and follow Marlo into the kitchen, where she's already pulled out a box of crackers, three different types of cheese, and a container of truffles.

Standing at the end of the counter, I drum my fingers on it, drawing Marlo's sharp gaze.

She spreads her hands wide over what she brought. "All the essentials."

Any night before Drew died, I would have been thrilled with her bringing our typical snacks and settling in for a night of crappy TV or a cheesy movie, but tonight, the tension I've been holding in my body, along with everything I have to tell her, makes the thought of eating anything twist my stomach.

Still, I force a smile.

She tugs open the drawer under her and pulls out the wine opener, twisting it into the pinot noir as she glances at me. "Now, *spill*. You were very mysterious on the phone."

For a reason.

A very good one.

With thick, almost black hair...

Blue eyes the color of the Caribbean that darken to an almost navy...

Calloused hands that can create such beauty and pleasure...

A beautiful mind so tortured by his guilt...

And a heart strained under the weight of secrets...

I chew on my bottom lip as Marlo struggles with the cork. Her brow furrows in frustration, her teeth clenched as she tugs on it. Rolling my eyes, I snatch it from her, pop it off, and hand it back to her.

"Thanks"—she narrows her gaze on me—"but you still haven't answered my question. All you said was, 'We need to talk. Come after work.' So here I am. After work." She spreads her hands again. "Prepared to listen."

"And not judge."

Her brows fly up. "*Okay*...and not judge."

She says it tentatively, like she isn't sure she should be making that agreement, but even if she can't commit to keeping her judgment out of this conversation, I can't *not* tell her.

Not when she's the only person I really trust to give it to me straight.

Yet, I already dread her possible response.

Because deep down, I know all of this is...

Really.

Really.

Fucked up.

Marlo pulls out two wineglasses, then snags the cutting board from beneath her and a knife and sets all the cheese and truffles on it before ushering me toward the living room and the couch.

"Take the wine and the glasses and go. I've got the snacks."

I do what she asks, a strange icy tingle rippling across my skin and turning my stomach again as I set everything on the table and settle into the corner of the couch.

It's just nerves.

And guilt.

And all the other things that have been filling my head all day.

But when Marlo settles next to me and watches me expectantly, I suddenly feel like I'm a criminal suspect in an interrogation room with a skilled detective who will stop at nothing to get to whatever I'm trying to hide.

I thought this would be easier.

That as soon as I saw her, everything that I've learned

and that happened would come pouring out of me like a tidal wave.

Instead, my throat feels tight.

Like something is clamped around it, making it hard to breathe and impossible to speak.

Marlo sighs and leans forward, pours the wine into our glasses, and shoves one into my hand. "Drink. Then spill."

Shit.

I take a sip of the sharp, tannin-heavy wine and clutch the glass in my hands so tightly I'm afraid I'll snap the delicate stem. "So, you told me to go talk to Cam yesterday..."

She nods. "Yeah..." Her brows rise. "Did you find him?"

Normally, she would have been *all* over me last night, texting and calling for updates after she basically encouraged me to stalk the man again. Only sheer luck and her own romantic distraction prevented her from doing just that.

I bite my lip, glancing down at the red liquid I should be enjoying.

Kissing you tasted like red.

Cam's words ring in my ears, igniting that scorching heat throughout my body that keeps coming every time I remember last night.

I clear my throat. "Yep. We...talked."

Then fucked like wild animals and fell asleep with his cock still buried inside me...

"And?" She motions to me expectantly. "Don't leave me hanging, girl."

Cam would never do that—leave me hanging.

While he certainly seemed to enjoy dragging out my pleasure to torturous lengths, he was also crazed in his focus on ensuring I came hard—and often.

My pussy clenches, heat rushing between my legs at the

memories, and I shift my position on the couch so I can try to alleviate the ache. "I don't even know where to start."

Marlo sips her wine and cuts off a piece of cheese to pop into her mouth. "At the beginning."

"I followed him after his meeting—"

"Well, aren't you becoming the perfect little stalker..."

I snort, burying my face in my free hand, cheeks heating with absolute mortification. "Please don't say that. It's embarrassing enough." Releasing a sigh, I look back up at her. "I don't need you making fun of me for it, especially when *you* are the one who encouraged me to do it."

"Okay, okay." She holds up a hand defensively, then snags a truffle and bites into it with a little groan, chewing slowly. "God, these are good." She swallows. "So, you followed him and...?"

"And he went to his studio."

Her eyes widen, and she grins. "Ohhh."

Curiosity piqued, she leans closer, waiting for me to expand, but something stops me.

All those beautiful paintings flash through my head.

So filled with everything that Cam is—beauty, tension, darkness, light, *life*.

But he keeps his identity hidden for a reason.

He doesn't want the fame. He doesn't need accolades. He just wants to *paint*.

And revealing his secret feels like a betrayal of the trust he put in me by exposing everything he did last night.

I take another sip of wine, but it almost instantly sours in my stomach, so I set my glass on the coffee table and swipe my sweaty palms across my leggings.

Not only am I a shitty liar, I'm apparently also awful at keeping secrets—my own or other people's—because I don't know how I can explain everything without telling Marlo who he really is.

So much of Cam's identity is wrapped up in his art.

To understand *him* you have to understand *it.*

"I need you to promise me you're not going to tell *anyone* what I'm about to tell you."

Her blond brows draw low over her eyes. "Okay, now you're freaking me out..."

I shake my head. "It's nothing bad, just...something that has to stay private."

Marlo scoffs. "Who do you think I talk to you besides you?"

"Trina? Everyone else who works at the shop."

"Oh, pu-lease." She rolls her eyes. "I keep the good stuff to myself, and you know it. I'm fucking Fort Knox."

She's *far* from that, but I do trust Marlo more than anyone else in my life, so if anyone can keep this secret, it's her. Especially now that she knows how important it is for her to keep her lips sealed.

"You're not going to believe this but"—I lock gazes with her so I can watch her reaction—"he's Cush."

Her eyes widen, brows rising comically high. "That street artist who does all the murals on buildings and has his paintings auctioned for millions of dollars?"

I nod. "Camden Usher. C. Ush. *Cush.*"

Once I saw it, I don't know how it never clicked, why I never made the connection between his name and the one scrawled at the bottom of all the art I've seen from him on the internet over the years.

Maybe because Nancy and Drew so casually brushed off talk of his art as if he were barely scraping by in London, working at some small gallery, selling other artists' works instead of his own without anyone knowing.

"Ho. Ly. Shit." Marlo's jaw drops. "Drew knew, didn't he?"

I nod, my stomach continuing to knot with yet another thing he kept hidden from me over the years. "Yes."

"But he never told you?"

"Cam asked Nancy and Drew not to tell anyone."

She gapes. "Why would he keep that a secret?"

I shake my head. "I don't know, but it isn't one to me anymore because I walked into his studio while he was painting and saw dozens of them lined up along the walls."

"Oh, my God." She takes a gulp of her wine like she needs it to fortify herself for the rest of the conversation. "What did he say?"

I clear my throat, imagining the way he looked in those jeans and nothing else, bent over the canvas, applying such smooth strokes with the hands he then used on me.

"Holy shit, you're blushing."

"What?" I glance up. "Uhh, it's the wine."

Marlo purses her lips. "You've literally had two sips. What happened?"

Shit.

Too much.

Far too much.

I run my hand over my face but can't look up at her when I make the confession. "I saw a painting of me."

"The man painted you?"

"He did." I draw a deep breath and force myself not to hide. "And it was from *that* night."

Her eyes narrow on me. "What night?"

"Remember Nancy's birthday party? The first time Drew and I...you know?"

"Oh. You mean when you finally fucked?"

I cringe. "Jesus, Marlo, do you have to say it like that?"

She barks out a laugh and takes a sip of her wine. "How else am I supposed to say it? That's what happened, isn't it?"

"Sort of..."

Her body stiffens. "What do you mean, 'sort of?'"

This is where it's going to hurt because this means exposing the great lie—the one Cam and Drew *both* kept from me for so long.

"Well, I discovered why Drew and Cam stopped talking..."

She keeps watching me, waiting for me to continue.

"Because earlier in the night, I left the party to get some fresh air out in the garden." I squirm, shifting to tuck my feet under me. "And Drew eventually joined me, and things got... very inappropriate for public."

Marlo's jaw drops and stays open. "Did you *fuck* Drew in his mother's garden during her damn birthday party?"

I shake my head. "No...I let who I *thought* was Drew kiss me senseless and get me off on his hand in his mother's garden during her damn birthday party."

"Oh. My. Fucking. God." Marlo shifts forward and sets her wineglass on the coffee table, like she doesn't trust herself to hold it anymore. "It wasn't Drew?"

"No." I shake my head, running my hands through my hair. "That was Cam that night out in the garden. He came to surprise his mom and Drew at the party. They didn't even know he was in the country, and he was going to slip in through the back door and surprise them. Only, he got interrupted on his way in." I press my hand against my chest. "By *me*."

"Holy shit. And he just *pretended* to be Drew so he could hook up with you?"

Her outrage matches what I felt when I discovered the truth last night.

And how I *should* still feel about the situation.

But it's so much more complicated than that.

The fact that he lied, that he pretended to be Drew and didn't correct me when I made that assumption doesn't bother me as much as the aftermath does.

I was a very willing participant in what happened on that bench, and I don't have any way of knowing how things would have been different if he had sat next to me and introduced himself.

Would there still have been that spark?

Would attraction still have sizzled red hot between us?

Would I have slipped under his spell and completely forgotten that I came to the party with his brother and given into it?

I want to believe the answer is *no* to every single one of those questions.

I want to believe that I am too good a person and far too loyal to have ever acted that way when I had already started developing feelings for Drew at that point.

I want to believe I would have shaken his hand, chatted for a few minutes, then gone inside with him to help surprise Drew and Nancy.

But deep down, I'm not that confident.

A dark little voice that sounds like the one Cam used as he pounded into me last night whispers that I wouldn't have cared about all the reasons it was wrong, that I would have kept going, that Drew's fear of losing me to his brother was very valid.

Nausea roils my stomach, and I gulp in air, trying to

prevent myself from throwing up the more that little voice talks to me.

The more it insists the reason I'm not more angry with Cam about what he did was because of how fucking much I *liked* it and *him* that I'm willing to forgive something so utterly unforgivable.

"Ivy?"

I jerk my gaze back to hers.

"I just want to make sure I'm following all of this. So, you hooked up with Camden and then that night, went home and slept with Drew..."

Hell.

Why is it so much worse when someone else says it?

It isn't as if that fact hasn't been slamming around in my mind since last night, hasn't blown holes in those beautiful memories and turned them into something completely different—ones that will torment me.

Nodding, I squeeze my eyes together. "That pretty much sums it up."

"Hmmm." The scrape of Marlo snagging her wine from the table fills my ears, and I can feel her watching me, my skin flushing under the assessment. "So, what did you do after he told you? Did you smack him?"

My lids snap open, and I glare at her. "No, I did not resort to physical violence."

She snorts. "I probably would have."

Of that, I have absolutely zero doubt.

Marlo has always been the stronger of us. She stood her ground, refused to back down to anyone, even in school when we were still finding out who we would be as people, she knew she wasn't the type to allow anyone to dampen her light, step on her toes, or do anything to hurt anyone she cared about.

She defended everyone in our circle with a vicious ferocity I could never find.

Maybe because Nonni and Mom were true pacifists and believed in free love, beauty, and that nature had the answer for everything.

If only it were that simple...

While I'd give anything to have them here, to feel their warm, comforting hugs again during a time when I need them the most, Marlo's presence brings a tough-love, smack-in-the-face reality check that I so often need.

And he probably did deserve to be smacked for what he did.

"He warned me to stay away from him, that it had been a selfish and shitty decision on his part, that he understood if I couldn't forgive him for it, but..."

But I'm weak.

The last several months have beaten me down, crushed what little strength I had before Drew died, and left me on a downward spiral to something incredibly scary. And I faced it alone.

Marlo, Trina, even Nancy being around, checking on me, trying to help, couldn't break through the wall of anguish that had covered me so completely.

Yet, Cam broke through it.

Our shared grief and love for Drew allowed it to crumble, and when I did, he was there to hold me and keep me steady.

I don't think Marlo could *ever* understand that, even if I tried to voice it.

Apparently, my inability to finish my sentence says it for me.

"Oh, girl." Marlo's eyes widen. "You stayed."

The disbelief and disappointment hang heavy in the air between us, and I nod, biting my lip again, trying to figure out how to justify what I'm feeling in any way that won't make me sound like the horrible person it seems like I'm becoming.

"I just...couldn't walk away from him, Marlo. The other night, after we spread the ashes, him holding me, being with him like that, all of it felt right. Normal."

She purses her lips, considering her words. "Because he looks exactly like Drew, not because he's Camden."

I wince at her statement.

Partially because I suspect it might still be true somewhere I don't want to acknowledge, but also because I know there's a part of me that understands it isn't true at all.

"No." I shake my head. "When he first got here, all I could see when I looked at him was Drew, but I don't anymore. I see *Cam*. For who *he* is. For *what* he is."

"Which is what, Ivy?" Her brows rise. "The guy who lied to you? The guy who pretended to be his brother to get in your pants?"

I scowl at her.

"Isn't that what happened?"

"I mean, yes, but also...I don't think so."

"What do you mean?"

I finally can't sit still anymore, and push up from the couch, pacing in the living room. "The way he talked about that night, the way he explained it to me, it was almost like he was drawn to me and he couldn't walk away. And I understand that because that's how I felt with Drew, and that's how

I felt in that garden with Cam, too." Pausing, I close my eyes and envision that night again. The scent of the pool and lilacs. The way the summer breeze blew over me so gently. And then he *appeared*. "I knew I shouldn't have let that happen out in the garden. Good God, you *know* that's so not me. But it was like I couldn't help myself. The way he looked at me, the way he kissed me, the way he touched me. It just melted the rest of the world away."

Marlo studies me for a moment, her lips twisting. "And it still does that?"

There's the ultimate question, the one that's been rattling around inside my head since the moment he made his confession.

Given the way we spent hours wrapped up in each other, not thinking about anything else, and simply *feeling*, it would be impossible to say otherwise.

I nod. "I don't know why, if it's some big cosmic fucking joke, but being with Cam? It gives me something I never thought I'd have again."

"What's that, Ivy?"

"*Life.*"

She settles back as if I've slapped her, her brow furrowing. "Really?"

"There's just something about him, his energy, the way he lives his life so unapologetically and on his own terms, yet he cares so deeply for other people. The beauty he can create with a flick of a hand. He makes me"—I smile because I don't know how else to describe it—"happy in a way I didn't think was possible after Drew died."

Marlo considers me for a few moments. "Does he, though? Because all I've seen since he's been in your life is you confused and anguished and constantly second-guessing your decisions and what you're feeling. You were never like that with Drew. With Drew, it was all-in."

"I know." I shove my hands through my hair. "But Drew was always so easy to be like that with. He was so open with everything, with how he was feeling, with what he wanted out of life and from me. It was effortless to do that with him. Cam isn't like that, and that mystery, that reticence and haunted look in his eyes somehow draws me to him."

"You can't fix him, hon." She raises a concerned brow. "You know that, right?"

Anger flashes hot through my blood, and I clench my fists, glaring at her. "That's not what I'm trying to do."

"Aren't you?" She lets that question settle for a second before she continues. "Cam's messed up. He said it himself; he *warned* you. The man was addicted to every drug on the planet, abused all of them, and he's only been clean for a year. He ruined his relationship with his twin brother, the closest person to him in his life, by finger-fucking you in the goddamn garden of his mother's house on her birthday, pretending to be him. And you're honestly going to tell me that this is the man you want to be with? That, what, two months after Drew's death, you're ready for all of *that*?"

Fuck.

Tough love hurts.

I squeeze my eyes closed and shake my head. "No. I'm just saying..." Frustration taking over, I throw up my hands and walk away toward the front windows to stare out at the street again. "I just keep waiting for him to show up. My heart beats faster knowing he will. I don't know what to do with that, Marlo. I don't know what I'm *supposed* to do with it. Do I ignore it? Pretend it doesn't exist. Go back to sitting on that couch or lying in my empty bed every night, sobbing and miserable and wishing I could join Drew wherever he is?"

Because that's what my life had become.

I was drowning in my despair the night Cam appeared on my doorstep, the closest I've ever been to doing something unimaginable that couldn't be taken back.

His arrival saved me, even if it brought a deluge of other problems and questions with it.

Marlo releases a heavy sigh, and I hear the clink of her glass as she sets it on the table and her feet padding over to me. She wraps her arms around me from behind and gives me a squeeze. "I'm sorry. You know I'm only trying to get you to actually see what's happening, right? I don't want you falling down some rabbit hole, chasing after some fantasy that doesn't exist. He's not Drew."

My bottom lip trembles. "I know."

"He's never going to be Drew."

I choke on a sob. "I know. And I don't want him to be."

Because it was *Cam* who dragged me from that dark abyss.

It was *Cam* who brought me back to life again.

She releases me in order to step up next to me, and I turn to face her.

Green eyes filled with concern search mine. "Did you sleep with him?" I don't even have to answer her because she gives me a tight smile. "Okay, so, we've already gone that far. What's the plan?"

"What do you mean?"

She sweeps an arm toward the window. "I mean, he's here in Philadelphia, right? But he still hasn't told his mother."

I cringe. "No."

"And you two are sneaking around..."

"We're not sneaking around. We went to the art museum today."

Her brows rise. "Really?"

"Yeah." I release a sigh. "And ran into, I guess, an ex-friends-with-benefits of his so that was awkward."

She cringes. "Yikes."

That same green monster rears its head, the vision of Roxy and how casual and intimate she was with him making me have to swallow back wine-tinged bile.

But I can't be that person.

"Look, he had a life. Just like I did." *With his* brother. "A past, one he isn't proud of. Who am I to judge him?"

"You're his brother's fiancée."

"A fact I don't need to be reminded of, Marlo." I don't mean to snap at her, but she recoils slightly at my tone. "I don't know what's going to happen. I don't know if it's possible for me to sort out all the feelings I have for Cam, but I know that right now, I *need* this feeling because the alternative is me pulling back those covers, climbing into that bed, and staying there indefinitely. And I don't want to do that anymore." Tears stream down my face, and I shake my head. "I can't."

She grabs my hands and squeezes. "Okay. Just...be careful, Ivy. He warned you away for a reason."

"I know."

And there are a thousand reasons it shouldn't happen again.

Why I shouldn't want him to pull up his motorcycle on that street and come walking through that door tonight.

But not a single one seems to matter.

28

IVY

By the time the sound of Camden's motorcycle engine rumbles through the front window, I've paced enough that my bare feet ache, and I still don't have any answers. Still don't have any clarity regarding any of the things I talked to Marlo about until I was hoarse and my eyes red and swollen from the tears. And I still don't know how to feel about the man who pulled up outside.

Each minute I've waited, wondering if he was actually going to appear, was one also spent considering the ramifications of what we did last night.

The potential fallout with Nancy has left me trembling, wondering if it's really all worth it if it risks losing her place in my life.

I peek out the window into the night.

Cam sits on his bike at the curb, staring at the house, a lit cigarette dangling from his mouth, but he's still poised, as if he's ready to pull away at any moment. The nearest street-light casts a glow on one side of his face, the rest of him covered in shadow, a place where he seems more at home, anyway.

He remains still, other than lifting his hand to his mouth to take another hit from the cigarette.

I smoke so I don't put worse things in my body.

My heart sinks into my stomach.

Cam just came from a meeting, from a place where he's supposed to find support through his recovery, but he seems agitated tonight, his stillness belying the tension in his shoulders.

What's he doing out there?

Maybe he's having second thoughts, too.

Maybe all the things said last night can't counteract all the reasons this is such a terrible idea.

Maybe it's a sign that I should let this go, that I should let him drive away and never look back.

That would certainly make things easier for both of us and alleviate any worries about what *this* might do, not only to us but to the people we love. But like he said this morning, we've opened the floodgates.

All these conflicting emotions will continue to crash over us like waves on that beach where we stood and said goodbye to Drew. There is no putting that back behind a protective wall designed to stem the flow. There is no pretending we aren't both drowning in this.

I'm desperate to come up for air, to take a full breath again without feeling that vise around my chest that doesn't want me to, but I don't know if that's even possible anymore.

For Cam or for me...

My feet move toward the door, and I pull it open, stepping onto the porch as I flip on the bulb he replaced, which casts light out into the front yard.

His eyes meet mine from the street, and he takes a long drag off the cigarette, the smoke flowing out of his slightly parted lips in a slow trickle.

I walk toward him, the concrete cool under my bare feet, the crickets already chirping and filling the warm summer evening air with their song, but he remains silent. Watching me, gaze raking over me with an piercing focus that makes me shiver under his assessment. "What are you doing out here?"

"Thinking."

He brings the cigarette to his mouth again, inhaling deeply as he continues to hold my gaze on my approach. I stop in front of him on the curb, finally putting me at a height advantage since I met him, and he finally tears his eyes from mine to turn his head slightly and blow the smoke away from me.

I wrap my arms around myself, rubbing at the goosebumps that don't have anything to do with it being chilly because the warm, humid summer night couldn't be more perfect. "What are you thinking about?"

It's probably a dangerous question to ask.

One I'm not entirely sure I want the answer to, given how tense and troubled he looks.

But it's out there now, just filling the space between us.

"Everything."

He doesn't really have to expand.

That one word is enough for me to understand exactly why he looks absolutely wrecked because it's the same thing I've been struggling with all day. Yet somehow, knowing that we even share this torment over the situation makes it easier to want to ignore it all.

I step down onto the street, not even caring how dirty my

feet are getting, so that I can be closer to him. Needing to be. And that rich scent of his leather jacket mixed with citrus and a hint of smoke floats on the breeze ruffling his hair. "Are you coming in?"

His gaze flicks up over my shoulder to the house, and he stares at it for a minute before his stormy eyes return to mine. "I can't, Ivy."

My stomach tenses. "Why not?"

Despite my best attempt to keep the disappointment and hurt out of my voice, the hurt still leeches into my question.

Cam reaches out with his free hand and pulls mine into his. "Because we both know what'll happen if I come in there with you, and I can't..." He squeezes his eyes closed and shakes his head. "That's my brother's house, my brother's bed, and you are my brother's fiancée. I'm not a good man, Ivy. I've made a lot of really bad mistakes in my life and done a lot of things I'm not proud of, but *that*...I can't do."

His confession makes all the little pieces of my shattered heart drive into my ribcage, the pain so deep and so real that it makes me suck in a sharp breath.

It isn't about him not wanting me, not wanting this; it's about his loyalty to his brother and respect for what Drew and I shared in that house, and for some reason, that only makes me want him more.

He trembles and opens his eyes, revealing the depth of pain and conflict brewing in them. When he brings the cigarette to his mouth this time, it's with a shaking hand, and he takes a long drag from it before tossing the remaining butt onto the street and crushing it with his boot.

Smoke curls from his lips as he watches me with so much trepidation.

I take a half-step forward until my knees brush against

his bike, and I can lean into him, our entwined hands pinned between us. "That's *my* house, *my* bed, and I don't belong to anyone anymore."

As painful as those words are to say, actually *hearing* them soothes some of the guilt over what happened on that couch the other night.

At least, for me.

Cam's gaze softens, a sadness sweeping through it like a storm blowing across the sky on a summer night. "You don't mean that." He uses his other hand to grip my chin and tilt it up toward him. "You still belong to Drew in your heart, and you always will. And that's okay. That's the way it should be. The way it was *meant* to be."

A tear trickles from my eye before I can stop it, because he's right.

Drew was my future for so long.

The only thing I wanted.

And the sole path I could see myself going on in this life was with him at my side as my partner, as my other half.

But he was ripped away from me so violently in a way I still don't understand.

Almost as if fate had other ideas and was playing some cruel, twisted game with all of us, starting with that very first night Cam showed up and kissed me.

I press my forehead against his and draw in a long, slow breath as I try to sort through the riot of feelings thundering inside me. "You're right. A part of me will always belong to Drew. A huge part." I drag my head back and meet his gaze again, seeing the pain there. *Feeling* it. "But it doesn't mean I don't have room for you, too."

"Fuck..." The word tumbles from his lips on an exhale, and he grips my chin harder, holding me there, our lips a mere hairsbreadth from each other, sharing the same air, the same oxygen. "I shouldn't want you like this."

Agony sears through me, making my legs tremble, and I clutch his jacket tightly, fighting the pain that wants to take over and rule in this moment. "I shouldn't want you. It doesn't change the fact that it's true."

My confession makes him shiver, and it's the warning I get before he crashes his lips to mine in that same all-consuming way he did last night that has my entire body heating in one split second. He drags me up against him as much as he can while he still straddles his bike, my legs on either side of his thick thigh that now presses into my throbbing core.

Clinging to him tighter, I allow him to devour my mouth with a ferocity that makes my knees wobble. His hands tunnel into my hair, holding me in place so he can kiss me senseless out here in the street instead of inside, where we belong.

Where he is so reluctant to go.

And something clicks inside my head, a fear that rears up and lashes out at me, stronger than my grip on him.

Oh, God...

I tear my lips from his, an agitated pant slipping out as I search his face.

Was that a goodbye kiss?

There was something about it, something in the almost manic way he moved his mouth over mine that suggested I'll never see him again.

"Please, come inside, Cam." I drop my forehead to his again. "Please..."

I hate that I'm begging.

I hate that I have to.

And I despise how desperate I sound, but I *have* been desperate for the last two months. Desperate to find anything, any way to escape the pain of what my life had become once I lost Drew. And now that it's finally here, in my reach, I don't want to lose it for any reason.

Not because of guilt or misconceived loyalty or because of what I think other people will say when they find out.

I just want this, like I had last night.

The two of us entwined in each other and nothing else.

His warm breath flutters over me, and he feathers his lips across mine, his whole body trembling. "Okay."

I slowly step back, releasing my grip on him and allowing him to swing his leg off the bike. As soon as he does, he tugs me against him, staring down at me as he cups my cheeks between his rough palms.

"You really are the worst kind of temptation, Ivy."

Coming from a man who understands addiction so well, I don't know if that's a compliment, an insult, or a warning. Maybe all three. But he still dips his head and kisses me deeply, that same explosive, whole claiming he did that first night on that bench when I apparently gave myself to him even though I didn't know it.

I groan and fist my hands in his jacket again, and he reaches down and scoops me up, lifting me easily to wrap my legs around his waist. He stalks back to the house, throws open the door, and steps inside, kicking it closed behind him.

The sharp slam jerks me away from his mouth for a split second, but then his lips are skimming up my neck, over my cheek, at my ear, where he nips in a way that sends a shudder of anticipation through me. I shift my hips, aligning my core with his hardened cock encased in his jeans.

A gravelly moan falls from his lips, hot breath fluttering the hair on my temple. "I've been thinking about you all day." He kisses down my neck to my collarbone, pulling my T-shirt away to give himself better access to the skin there. "The whole time I was at my meeting, all I could think about was coming here, doing this, touching you, tasting you again. I still can't believe I can."

I whimper at his words, at the frenetic desire lacing them, and tunnel my hands through his hair, tugging his head back so he looks at me. He pauses next to the kitchen, and I catch him glancing over my shoulder, down the hallway toward the bedroom, but instead, he turns and sets me on the edge of the counter, spreading my thighs wide and settling between them.

"I need you now, Ivy." He tugs my bottom lip between his teeth, biting down sharply. "Like this."

Cam rocks his hard length against my core, and flashes of pleasure course through me, making my hands tighten in his hair. He groans in response to my tug, grinding into me even harder.

And suddenly we're moving too slowly.

There are too many clothes.

Too much time that has passed since he first crushed his mouth to mine outside.

My pussy throbs, already wet and wanting, rolling against him, seeking that delicious friction.

His hands come up to cradle my head, keeping me upright as he leans into me, bowing me backward slightly. The glint in his eyes now isn't trepidation or confusion. It isn't a warning that he's about to walk away. It's a promise that makes me whimper. "I will fuck you on every surface of this house but one, do you understand me?"

I nod even as my heart aches for the reason he feels that way, and his mouth crushes to mine again, hot and heavy and desperate, stealing away any other thought and sending me spinning. Away from rational thought. Away from all common sense. Away from all reason.

How can reason exist where Camden Usher does?

He destroyed me last night, shattered me into a million pieces, only to rebuild me and do it all over again.

He will again now.

And I'm going to let him.

29

IVY

Everything Cam does is with fervent intent and unbridled determination.

Every brush of his hand across my skin. Each kiss perfectly placed to elicit those little shivers through my body and mewls that fall from my lips whenever he touches me *just* right.

The man knows what he's doing, and *good God*, when all his passion and attention focuses on me, it would be impossible not to be entrapped in his snare.

His fingers brush along the waistband of my leggings as he kisses me, urging me to lift my hips so he can peel them down and toss them behind him. I clutch at his jacket, not wanting him to pull away, not wanting to end the kiss, but he chuckles against my lips, low and dark, the sound making my clit throb where it's currently pinned to his hard cock.

"I'm more than willing to fuck you like this, Ivy, but I will say, I enjoy it far more when I get to see *all* of you."

The lust thickening his words ushers a little thrill

through me, and I know he isn't just saying them to stroke my ego.

He *wants* to see me.

All of me.

The good.

The bad.

The ugly.

The things I want to keep hidden.

I watched the man paint me last night, spend hours on my form, highlighting every curve, every dimple, every scar, every line of my body so perfectly it almost looked like a photograph by the time it was completed. Seeing the final result this morning made me believe those people who say God speaks through the hands of artists—because Cam made me see God and captured the aftermath with such utter precision and clarity it could only come from a divine hand.

He brushes his thumb across my trembling bottom lip. "What are you thinking about?"

I shake my head, trying to clear the haze of my desire surging through me. "What?"

"Your cheeks just got *very* pink, and your thighs tightened around me."

Shit.

It wasn't soley my mind wandering to those carnal memories. My body remembers it all with vivid clarity and wants more.

So much more.

"I was thinking about you painting me last night..."

His eyes flare wide, the heat in them blazing even hotter. "Did you like that?" He slips his thumb into my mouth, and there's something so erotic about tasting his skin this way that I moan around it. "Lying there naked with my cum dripping out of you while I painted every inch of your beautiful body?"

He cups me between my legs possessively, a low growl rumbling in his chest against mine as a moan slips from my lips around his thumb.

There's no way he can't feel how soaked I am already, how slick and ready my cunt is for him.

And I can't deny it.

Something about watching him paint me, completely nude, so intensely focused on the canvas and my body...

A slow grin pulls at his lips, making him even more handsome, even more feral looking. Like some sort of animal was just unleashed when he realized what watching him paint me does to my body, even now. "You *did* like it, didn't you, Ivy?"

I nod, a breathy, "Yes," slipping from my parted lips.

He grinds the meaty part of his palm against my clit, ghosting his lips across mine, teasing me in both places. "I loved it. Seeing you in my bed, knowing I was just inside you, how fucking beautiful and pink you were after I made you come."

I tremble again, unable to stop myself from rolling my hips along his length and hand, so desperate for the friction now that it's embarrassing.

"Would you like me to do that again, Ivy?" Another brush of his lips and a crush of his hand. "Twist you up into different positions and paint you so you can see how fucking stunning you are?"

"Oh, God."

I drop my forehead against his shoulder, and he grins into my neck, his tongue snaking over my thrumming pulse.

"That can be arranged, Ivy. All you had to do was ask."

Fuck.

I thought losing Drew was going to kill me, too, but Cam has become my sweetest agony.

This man...he will be what truly destroys me.

His fingers delve through my slick core, easily drenching my clit in my arousal, and my hips twist at the contact, jerking in his hold. He groans as he devours me, his tongue lashing against mine, his hips grinding forward, his body seeking the same thing mine is—that connection we found last night. The utter desperation and need that completely wash away everything else—all our reservations, all our worries, all our *sins.*

The longer we kiss, the harder he grinds his hand and cock against me, the more delerious I become, scoring my nails over his skin, clinging to him with a kind of frenzied, burning, soul-deep desire that feels like it might consume me in its flames.

When Cam tears his head back and steps away, both of us panting, struggling to find our breath, I brace my hands on the counter and watch him shuck off his jacket and let it fall to the floor. Then he reaches between his shoulders and pulls off his shirt in one smooth motion that leaves his upper body exposed in the kitchen light.

Every deep groove and valley of hard-earned muscle, his tattoos practically alive as they dance across the sun-kissed skin. The snakes coil and writhe over thickly corded forearms as he reaches for his waistband.

"I wish I could paint you."

He freezes, his head cocking to the side. "Why can't you?"

I bark out a laugh that has him grinning. "Because I don't have an artistic bone in my body."

His fingers pop the button and gradually drag down the zipper, releasing his hard cock before he shoves his jeans the rest of the way down, tugs them off, and tosses them haphazardly behind him.

My mouth goes dry as he takes himself in one hand and strokes it, then steps forward, sliding his free one along the hem of my shirt, dragging his fingers back and forth gently, teasing my sensitive skin and leaving goosebumps across it.

He dips his head to mine, fluttering a kiss across my lips. "I beg to differ."

The head of his cock glides through my wetness, and I grin at him as he slowly pushes inside me.

My eyes roll back, my head dropping as he fills me—inch by glorious inch.

"Fuck..."

The word tumbles from my lips on a sob he catches in his mouth, and he uses his hands to push my shirt up and over my breasts, then tears away long enough to get me fully naked.

When his lips find mine again, it isn't the needy, desperate, frantic kisses he's given me before. It's torturously slow, as is the way he draws back his hips and sinks into me again, grinding against my clit when he reaches the hilt. His tongue drags along mine at the same tempo as his languid hips.

In.

Out.

Advance.

Retreat.

Over and over.

The head of his cock stroking that wonderful spot deep inside me that draws out a whimper and sends heat spiraling through me.

I shift to wrap my arms around his neck, clinging to him, and his hand comes to rest at my shoulders to hold me steady as he thrusts into me with such slow, determined strokes.

Feeling him like this, every glorious fucking inch, so unhurried yet decadent in a way that steals my breath with each thrust, overwhelms my senses to the point of tears.

One slips down my cheek, and he catches it with his tongue, dragging it across the damp skin. "I don't like to see you cry, Ivy." He stills his hips, and I whimper. "Tell me what's wrong."

Nothing and everything at the same time.

Shaking my head, I squeeze my eyes closed, willing the tears away because *God*, I don't want him to stop. I might die if he does. I need this, him, so badly. He's a beautiful distraction from everything else that's so wrong.

"Look at me, Ivy."

I force my eyes open to meet his. The blue shimmers tonight with so many emotions that it's impossible to separate them, and he captures my cheek in his palm, brushing his thumb across my lips.

"Tell me."

"N-nothing is wrong, I just..." I shudder under him, my pussy clamping down on his cock. "You feel so good. This. Being with you does..."

His gaze softens, and he dips his head to kiss away another tear before moving to my mouth again so I can taste the salty drop on his tongue. He resumes his languid, leisurely pace, building me up so *fucking* slowly that my entire body trembles violently, my hips bowing to meet his as he pumps into me.

Just a bit more.

Just a little more.

So fucking close.

The simmering heat wants to spark. It wants to combust. That explosion of pleasure is right there, barely out of reach.

Then he draws back, slipping from inside me, and I gasp, reaching for him, but he drops to his knees, dragging me to the edge of the counter, and buries his face between my legs before I can object further.

His tongue replaces his cock.

Probing into me.

Dragging over my clit.

Gliding through the wetness seeping from my cunt for him.

His low growl of satisfaction vibrates against my skin. "Fucking hell. I could stay with my face between your thighs for eternity, Ivy."

In this moment, that sounds really fucking good, like a magical plan I can *completely* get behind one hundred percent.

I brace myself on one hand so I can watch him as I bury the other in his hair, holding him in place, directing him where I want him. But this man doesn't need any direction, doesn't want any. He reaches up and grabs my wrist, pinning it onto the counter as he drags his head back.

His lips glisten, and he *very* deliberately flicks his tongue across my clit as he holds my gaze, making me twitch. "Trust me to give you what you need, Ivy."

Bloody hell...

I groan, so desperate for it now that the tears start to leak out again. But I *do* trust him. With this. With my life. Even with what's left of my heart. Even if I shouldn't.

He slips a finger inside me, curling it up and dragging it

along the walls of my pussy. Then another, pumping into me in that glorious spot that makes me see stars. I whimper as my body trembles, starving for release, and he watches with hooded, hungry eyes, eating at me like a starved man.

Heat blooms from my core as his tongue rapidly laps at my clit, but just as I'm about to come, he pulls away, stands, and slams his cock into me, driving me backward on the counter. His arm comes up behind me to catch me before I fall completely, his mouth ravaging mine as he drives into me ruthlessly.

My head starts to spin, that slow smolder igniting into a raging inferno where we're connected that spreads out through every limb and fiber of my being until I finally burst.

Tears stream down my face as the orgasm rips through me.

My body convulses against his as he holds me tightly and pumps into me harshly, driving me through the orgasm and keeping it going.

Only just as it starts to ebb, his hand slips between us and finds my clit. I gasp at the contact on my overly sensitive spot, but he rolls his thumb across it rapidly, keeping the orgasm going *impossibly* long until he finally stills deep inside me and releases on a strangled groan.

"Fucking hell, Ivy…"

He buries his face in my neck, both of us panting, our sweat-slick bodies pressed to each other as we labor to calm our racing hearts and find our normal breaths.

Each minute that passes, I fall further into him, allowing him to hold me even closer, absorbing all his strength and passion and anything else he's willing to give me, because without it, I'd be lost again.

And I'm terrified this was a goodbye as much as I thought that kiss outside might have been.

My skin starts to cool and pebble with goosebumps in the chilly air, and he finally lifts his head and meets my gaze again, emotions wrestling with each other to take control.

He didn't want to come in here, didn't want to be in this house with me like this, but this is my home, where I belong, where I'm going to stay, and I need to have this man in it.

So much so that it terrifies me.

"Please don't leave." My impassioned plea makes his brow furrow, and he squeezes his eyes closed, dropping his forehead to mine as he takes a long, deep breath.

"I can't..." He shakes his head, still keeping it pressed to mine. "I can't stay, Ivy. Not here. I'm sorry."

The plea in his voice for me to drop it, for me to let him go, makes my eyes burn with a different type of tears than before, and I bite my lip to try to hide how badly it trembles right now, to bite back the words I want to say.

That this is my house, and though I may have shared it with Drew and made memories and plans with him here, he's gone. Something the man still buried inside me forced me to admit to myself, forced me to see. He's the one who made me let go of the unhealthy death grip I had on Drew's memory, and yet *he* can't.

And I don't know if I'll ever be able to make him.

30

IVY

J ust like the first time I showed up at the studio uninvited, unease crawls up my spine and tightens around it, making my hand shake where it grasps the massive metal door.

It grinds along the old track as I tug it open.

The piercing sound makes me wince.

Tonight, there isn't any music playing to absorb the noise.

Absolute deathly silence clings to the studio, making it feel lifeless, like stepping into a tomb instead of the vibrant life that pulsated in it two nights ago.

Goosebumps spread across my skin.

The familiar scent of fresh paint fills the air, and a blank canvas lies on a tarp on the floor in his work area. Brushes and trays of black and white acrylic sit beside it, ready to be used—all completely untouched.

Almost like he got interrupted before he could even begin...

Considering he promised to stop by after his meeting

tonight, I wouldn't have expected him to come to the studio at all, but given how shaken he seems after his meetings sometimes, maybe he needed to blow off some steam *this* way.

But I can't deny I'm worried about him.

Last night, he seemed so tormented by his guilt. As if being in my house, even with my assurances, was weighing far too heavily on him.

Which is why I made the drive across town again to check on him tonight, even when I probably should have given him some space to sort through his conflicting emotions.

I just can't seem to stay away.

Drawn like a moth to a flame.

And that's what Cam is—a dangerously beautiful inferno that burns brilliantly bright but will also consume all the oxygen and sear your soul.

Why else would I be here except that, for some reason, I like the exquisite pain. I crave it. It's so much easier to live with than the crushing agony of living alone without Drew.

"Camden?"

His name echoes off the high ceilings and metal beams as I take a second step in with my heart in my throat.

The soft clink of glass hitting the floor hard draws my attention to the far-left corner of the loft, near where the windows overlook the street.

Cam sits shirtless with his back to the brick wall, skin brushing against the rough material, knees up, bare feet planted on the floor, a bottle of whiskey dangling from his fingertips. A needle and a packet of something that makes my stomach turn sit a few feet away from him, next to his lighter and cigarettes.

All well within reach.

With his head dropped down, thick, dark hair tumbling across his face, I can't get a good look at his eyes.

But I don't need to see his face to understand the gravity of the situation.

Oh, shit...

My heart plummets into my churning stomach, my steps faltering. "Cam?"

Slowly, he lifts his head, and his red-rimmed eyes meet mine. Shadowy circles sit under them, tear stains running down his cheeks.

Bile threatens to gag me, and I force it down, trying to process what's happening without losing my shit. Because that's what *he* looks like at the moment, as if his entire world has imploded with him inside it, crushing him under the cataclysmic weight.

He doesn't say a word, just lifts the bottle to his lips and takes a long pull from it. Watching the amber liquid disappear slashes at my heart like a knife, flaying away parts of it as I watch him drink away his hard-won sobriety.

My eyes shift to the drugs on the floor near him, but I can't tell from here if he actually *used* them yet.

Fuck.

I move in cautiously, keeping my gaze locked on him, afraid that if I look away, he's going to drown in that bottle or pick up the needle and do something very stupid.

"Cam, what's wrong?"

Something drove him to *this*.

After over a year of not touching drugs or consuming any alcohol, I can smell it now, that sweet and spicy scent mixing with that of the paint and desperation clinging to him.

And it is desperation I'm seeing.

He looks utterly *destroyed*.

This isn't the same man who left my house last night with a sexy grin on his face and promises to see me tonight after his meeting.

This is someone completely different.

This is the Cam he warned me about.

One corner of his mouth twitches slightly, but there's absolutely no humor in the half-smile he gives me. And he doesn't answer my question, just uses his free hand to motion absently to a small, partially crushed box open on the floor in front of him that I can't see into from my position barely inside the door.

I narrow my eyes on it as I approach. "What is that?"

He swallows another gulp of his liquor and watches me warily. "It came in the mail. Apparently, the reroute from my place in London took a while because it got lost along the way somewhere, stuck in some facility. They finally delivered it today..."

The unsteady waver in his voice makes my chest tighten even more.

What the fuck could it be?

I finally make it over to the box, and this close to Cam, I can see just how awful he really looks. Not only do tears streak down his cheeks, but his bottom lip trembles as he raises the bottle to it again, red, hooded eyes glossy and unfocused.

He's drunk...

"Cam..." I lower myself to my knees in front of the box and pull out the only thing inside it—an old GI Joe action figure. Turning it over in my hand, I glance back up at him. "I don't understand."

He motions toward it with the bottle. "It was my father's."

I stiffen, the seemingly innocuous item in my hand suddenly taking on a whole new importance. "Where did it come from?"

That sad tilt returns to his lips, and he drags the bottle back to his mouth and takes a long sip from it, his Adam's apple bobbing as he swallows while staring at the doll. Then his gaze finally lifts to meet mine again. "Who do you think?"

My breath catches, and I flip the front panels on the box down to check the return address.

Drew's handwriting.

Our address.

Addressed to Camden Usher at his place in London, with one of those stupid little stickers stuck to it saying, "We Care," and explaining that the package got lost and was damaged.

One side of the box is smashed in, but the toy appears unharmed—old, well-loved, but intact.

"Drew sent this to you?"

He nods and takes another sip. "It's what I was looking for in those boxes in his office..."

I watch him gulp from the half-full bottle, my concern for him mixing with the complete confusion over what's happening. "But...it wasn't there because he had already sent it to you?"

Cam swipes the back of his hand over his mouth. "Yeah. Look at the postmark."

With a trembling hand, I flip the top flap on the box again, examining the other corner. It takes a moment for the date to register. "It was mailed the same day as our wedding invitations..."

Which I only know because I sent them six months to the *day* of our wedding.

Cam nods slowly. "Yep."

I shake my head. "I never knew he sent this. I took care of everything with the invitations—"

His brows rise, his shoulders tensing against the brick. "*You* sent them?"

I nod. "Yeah."

A humorless laugh, heavy with the liquor already affecting him, slips from his lips. "Did he know you sent one to *me*?"

My back immediately stiffens, a vise tightening around my chest. I chew on my bottom lip and try to gauge how to answer it without upsetting him.

What does he want me to say?

What answer will stop whatever is happening right now from escalating?

Cam is clearly walking a tightrope and seems perilously close to falling from it—if he hasn't already. Considering how much he already drank from that bottle, one foot is definitely off.

He watches me carefully, waiting for my response, his chest not moving as if he's holding his breath.

It may not be the right thing to do in this situation, but I tell him the truth. "No, he didn't." I brace myself for a reaction from him, but he sits motionless, blurry eyes locked on me. "I thought maybe if you got the invitation, if it looked like he was reaching out to you, you'd come. You guys would reconnect..."

And now I realize how naïve that was because I didn't understand what had forced the rift between them in the first place.

"Fuck." Cam drops his head back against the brick and releases a sardonic laugh, scrubbing his hand over his stubbled cheek as he stares at the ceiling. "I thought he sent it to me and was gloating"—he tilts his head, his eyes meeting mine—"about marrying you. I thought it was a 'fuck you' from him rubbing it in that he *won*."

"Jesus, Cam..."

His confession twists the knife in my heart, driving it in even deeper.

He gives me a little half-smile again and takes a sip. The lower the level of bourbon drops in that bottle, the harder it is for me not to walk right over there and snatch it from his hands. But the way he's shaking, I don't want to do anything that might make things worse, that might push him off that thin wire currently tethering him to whatever reality might still exist for him to stand on.

"I don't understand the GI Joe, Cam. Why would he send this to you? Why are you so—"

He holds up his hand to stop me, the sadness seeping into his gaze so heavy I physically feel it in my gut. "It's a peace offering. It *was* one." One of his shoulders rises and falls, but the motion is strained, as if any movement is too much for him right now. "My best guess is that when you two were going over the guest list and you were handling all the invitations, he had the same idea you did, to reach out to me. But *this*"—he motions toward the box the toy came in—"was his way of doing it..."

With an action figure?

The alcohol must be messing with Cam because he isn't making any sense. I stare at the doll, trying to grasp what he's telling me, but Drew never mentioned a GI Joe.

He never told me he reached out to Cam.

None of it.

Just more secrets he kept.

Cam lets his eyes drift closed, still resting his head on the brick. "When our dad died, everything we had of his became that much more valuable to us. And he had only *one* of those. And Drew was the oldest, so it was *his*, no matter how much Mom told him to share it and that it was *both* of ours."

Of course, she did.

Nancy never would have drawn lines in the sand with something like this that clearly meant so much to the boys.

"Drew didn't let you have it?"

He shakes his head, taking another sip without looking at me. "I stole it from his hiding spot a couple of times to play with it, but it always resulted in a fight Mom had to break up."

My heart aches for her and for them. The boys were clinging to something that belonged to their hero, and at that age, the thought that keeping the other from it would be so hurtful never would have occurred to them.

It was an impossibly sad situation, and this doll clearly still meant a lot to *both* of them since it was the thing that brought Cam to my house in the first place.

I swallow past the lump in my throat, examining the doll in my hand—the scratches and small imperfections that show how much it was loved. "But he sent it to you..."

The tears burn in my eyes as Cam angles his gaze toward me and nods before gulping down another drink.

"He did."

"Was there a note?"

He shakes his head. "There didn't need to be. He knew I would know what it meant, that it was time for me to come home. He didn't say anything about the wedding or you. I imagine he thought I'd call or maybe just show up."

A peace offering.

It's exactly something Drew would have done.

Cam put him in an impossible situation with what he did the night of that party, and no matter how mad I am at both of them for lying to me about it, I can see how hard it would have been for Drew to send this. To take that first step toward clearing the air and maybe forgiveness.

But that was the kind of person he was.

I never knew Drew to hold a grudge or bad feelings toward anyone, which is what always made the situation with Cam so confusing and out of character for him.

The fact that Drew reached out to Cam without telling me, at the same time I was reaching out to him, trying to get him to come to the wedding and maybe resolve whatever their issues were drives the already embedded knife so deeply that it steals my breath on a choked sob.

Tears slide down my cheeks as I stare down at the doll, adjusting the uniform coat before I look up at Cam. "I'm so sorry this didn't get to you before he died."

He nods. "Me, too. It might've..." Cam swallows painfully and clenches his eyes shut, wincing as if he's in physical pain. "It might've changed everything." When his eyes open, the depth of agony there is so great that I can see how he got lost in it, what drove him to where he is right now. His lips tremble, his hand holding the bottle shaking. "I'm so sorry."

I resist the urge to close the distance between us, too afraid I'll do or say the wrong thing and make the situation a thousand times worse. "Cam, nothing that happened is your fault."

A sharp, sardonic laugh floats from his lips, and he drops his head back against the brick hard, banging it intentionally in a way that must be so painful it makes me wince. "Yes, it is. All of it."

My stomach clenches, my hands tightening around the doll. "I don't understand what you're saying, Cam."

Those haunted eyes find mine, watery with his tears. "I have two things I have to tell you." A sad smile tilts his lips. "One will make you hate me; the other...will make you despise me."

The surety with which he says those words makes me set down the doll so I can go to him. "I could *never* hate you, let alone *despise* you, Cam."

He holds up his hand, stopping me from getting to my feet, and shakes his head, a sob tearing from his chest. "You don't know what I've done."

What he's done?

All the confessions he's made over the past few days race through my head, and while there are certainly things that he should seek absolution for, Cam hasn't done anything unforgivable. At least, not in my mind.

Maybe that's all he needs to hear to stop this spiral.

"There's nothing you ever could have done that I can't forgive, Cam."

He offers me another sad smile that I feel through every fiber of my being. It's the kind someone gives when they're saying goodbye, when they think they'll never see someone again. "I've been in love with you since the moment I first laid eyes on you..."

Love...

It's the first time he's said that word, and if we weren't

sitting here like *this,* I might have a very seriously hard time figuring out how to respond to his declaration. But given what he just said—that I would *hate* him for it—I can't waste a second answering.

"Why would I hate you for that?"

"Because"—he heaves in a breath, tears falling down his cheeks again—"it makes the second thing seem... calculated."

Calculated?

It's such an odd choice of words, and I can't think of a single thing that Cam could have ever done that would have been calculated where his feelings for me are concerned— unless he lied completely about *why* he approached me that night and let things go that far.

Was it intentional?

Did he do it to get back at Drew for something or set out to fuck up our relationship?

My stomach turns, and I have to swallow back acid that threatens to come out as I stare at the completely broken man in front of me. The one I don't recognize at *all* as the one I've come to know and care so much about.

"Cam, you're scaring me..."

The booze. The drugs. His vague statements and this confession...

None of it is making any sense.

Cam's gaze hardens, the blue shifting to an icy cold that sends a chill over me. "You should be scared, Ivy. Because I'm the reason Drew is dead. I killed him."

Cam and Ivy's heartrending story continues in *My Sweetest Obsession*. Dive into Cam's POV and feel the anguish of the final book in The Sweetest Lie Duet - available at all retailers:

www.books2read.com/MySweetestObsession

ABOUT THE AUTHOR

Gwyn McNamee is an attorney, writer, wife, and mother (to one human baby and two fur babies). Originally from the Midwest, Gwyn relocated to her husband's home town of Las Vegas in 2015 and is enjoying her respite from the cold and snow. Gwyn has been writing down her crazy stories and ideas for years and finally decided to share them with the world. She loves to write stories with a bit of suspense and action mingled with romance and heat.

When she isn't either writing or voraciously devouring any books she can get her hands on, Gwyn is busy adding to her tattoo collection, golfing, and stirring up trouble with her perfect mix of sweetness and sarcasm (usually while wearing heels).

Gwyn loves to hear from her readers. Here is where you can find her:

Website: http://www.gwynmcnamee.com/

Shop: http://www.gwynmcnameeshop.com/

Facebook:https://www.facebook.com/AuthorGwynMcNamee/

FB Reader Group: https://www.facebook.com/groups/1667380963540655/

Newsletter: www.gwynmcnamee.com/newsletter

Instagram: https://www.instagram.com/gwynmcnamee

Bookbub: https://www.bookbub.com/authors/gwynmcnamee

Tiktok: https://www.tiktok.com/@authorgwynmcnamee